He offered
She dared to

"I don't want to touch you."

The words hit me like a slap, but before I could respond, he went on.

"No one feels like you do, so every brush of your skin is a cruel reminder of what I've lost. I can barely stand the sight of you because you're more beautiful than I've allowed myself to remember, and when I cut that wire off Maximus and smelled you all over him, I wanted to kill him more than I've ever wanted to kill anyone in my life."

His voice thickened. "Now sit down and take my hand, Leila. The pilots are waiting for my command to leave."

Slow tears continued to trickle down my cheeks, but for a different reason this time.

"You care."

His hand tightened around mine. Currents sparked into him as though they'd missed him, too. I met his gaze and something else flared between us, not tangible like the electricity coursing from my flesh into his, but just as real.

. . . and Jeaniene Frost's Bestselling

Night Huntress Novels

"Cat and Bones are combustible together."
Charlaine Harris

" . . . a passionate and tantalizing tale, filled with dark sensuality and fast-paced action . . . irresistible . . . a smoldering hero to die for . . . unforgettable!"
Kresley Cole

" . . . witty dialogue, a strong heroine, a delicious hero, and enough action to make a reader forget to sleep."
Melissa Marr

"Put Jeaniene Frost on your must-read list!"
Lara Adrian

By Jeaniene Frost

JEANIENE FROST

TWICE TEMPTED

A NIGHT PRINCE NOVEL

AVON

An Imprint of HarperCollinsPublishers

AVON BOOKS
An Imprint of HarperCollins*Publishers*
10 East 53rd Street
New York, New York 10022-5299

Copyright © 2013 by Jeaniene Frost
Excerpt from *Up From the Grave* copyright © 2014 by Jeaniene Frost
ISBN 978-0-06-207610-6
www.avonromance.com

First Avon Books mass market printing: April 2013

Avon Trademark Reg. U.S. Pat. Off. and in Other Countries, Marca Registrada, Hecho en U.S.A.
HarperCollins® is a registered trademark of HarperCollins Publishers.

Printed in the U.S.A.

10 9 8 7 6 5 4 3 2 1

To Tage, Kimberly, Candace, and Carol,
for all that you do and for
the great ladies that you are.

-bis

Acknowledgments

Before anyone else, I must thank God. Apart from Your grace, Jesus, I have nothing. Additional thanks go to the usual suspects: my wonderful editor, Erika Tsang, and all of the other great people at Avon Books; my hardworking agent, Nancy Yost; my marvelous husband, Matthew; my loving family; my supportive friends; and last, but not at all least, the fabulous readers of the Night Prince series. I couldn't do this without you!

Prologue

This wasn't the first time I'd woken up as a captive. It wasn't even the second. I so needed to reevaluate my life choices.

From past experience, I knew not to snap my eyes open or alter my breathing. Instead, I took inventory while pretending I was still unconscious. Headache, no surprise, but other than that I felt okay. My arms were tied behind my back. The thickness around my hands was gloves, tightness around my ankles, restraints. Uncomfortable gag in my mouth, self-explanatory.

Once I was done taking stock of my physical condition, I moved on to my surroundings. The pitch and roll beneath me had to be waves, which meant I was on a boat. Some of my captors were topside, from the voices, but one of them was in the room with me. He didn't say a word, but after years of living with a vampire, I'd become adept at picking up the barely perceptible sounds they made.

So when I opened my eyes, my gaze landed unerringly on the black-haired vampire across the room. The only surprise he showed was to blink.

"Didn't expect you to be up already," he drawled.

I glanced down at my gag and back at him, raising a brow.

He translated the silent message. "Do I need to tell you that screaming is useless?"

I rolled my eyes. What was this, amateur day? He smiled before rising from the opposite berth. "I thought not."

During the short time it took him to cross the room and remove my gag, I gleaned as much about him as possible, too. The vampire looked to be around my age, but with his scar-free skin, short haircut, clean-shaven face, and average build, I judged him to be less than a hundred in undead years. Vamps older than that tended to have more wear and tear on their skin and they usually scorned modern hairstyles. But the most telling aspect was his gaze. Really old vampires had a certain . . . weight in their stares, as if the passing centuries had left a tangible heaviness. My nameless captor didn't have that, and if I was lucky, neither did anyone else on this boat.

Young vampires were easier to kill.

"Water," I said once the gag was removed. Between that and the aftereffects from being drugged, my mouth was so dry that my tongue felt like a wadded-up sock.

The vampire disappeared and then returned

with a can of Coke. I gulped at it when the vampire held it to my lips, which meant that I let out an extended burp when I stopped swallowing. If that burp happened to be aimed in my captor's face, well, it wasn't my fault. I was tied up.

"Charming," he said dryly.

"I lost my concern for social niceties when you shot my friend up with liquid silver," I replied in an even tone. "Speaking of, I want to see him."

The vampire's mouth quirked. "You're not in a position to make demands, but yes, he's still alive."

"You don't want to take me to him, fine," I said, thinking fast. "I assume you know I pick up psychic impressions from touch, so take these gloves off and let me touch you. Then I'll know if you're telling the truth."

The vampire chuckled, a brighter green swarming in the peat-moss color of his eyes. "Touch me? Don't you mean use that deadly electrical whip you can manifest to cut me in half?"

I stiffened. How did he know about that? Most of the people who'd seen me wield that power were dead.

"That's why these rubber gloves are duct-taped onto you," he went on, unperturbed. "Just in case."

"What's your name again?" I asked, glad I sounded casual.

Those wide lips stretched further. "Call me Hannibal."

I smiled back. "Okay, Hannibal, what do you

want me to do? Use my abilities to find one of your
enemies? Tell you if someone is betraying you? Or
read the past from an object?"

Hannibal laughed, and though it was more Dr.
Evil caliber than chilling, it was still foreboding
enough to creep me out.

"I don't want you to do anything, little bird. I'm
merely the delivery boy. I don't even know who I'm
delivering you to. All I know is you're worth three
times as much alive, but if you try anything, dead
is still a good payday for me."

Hannibal gave me a cheery wave before leaving the room. I said nothing, trying to think of a
way out of my predicament. I was *not* going to let
myself be delivered to some unknown baddie. I'd
find a way out of this if it killed me.

Chapter 1

Four weeks earlier

 I stood under a waterfall of flames. Vermilion and gold spilled over me, twining through my hair, separating into rivulets along my body before sliding between my fingers to fall at my feet. The flames were so dense that I couldn't see through them, reducing my world to a glowing arena of sunset-colored hues. Being engulfed this way should have killed me, but I was unharmed. I wasn't even afraid. A strange sense of longing filled me instead. I kept trying to catch one of the flames but I never succeeded. Fire might cover me from head to toe, yet it still managed to evade my grasp.

"Leila," a voice called, too faintly for me to discern who it was. "Leave before it's too late."

Logic urged me to do what the nameless person said, but I didn't want to. The flames didn't seem to want me to go, either. They kept gliding over me, caressing instead of burning my flesh. *See?* I thought in defiance. They wouldn't hurt me.

"Leila," that voice said again, more emphatically. "*Leave.*"

"No," I replied, and tried to clasp the fire to me again. As usual, those brightly lit bands slipped from my hands, but this time, their lustrous color darkened. When they landed at my feet, they looked like ribbons made of tar. Then the waterfall above me abruptly dissipated, leaving me naked and shivering in the sudden, overwhelming blackness.

Fear turned my insides to ice. The voice was right. Something bad was about to happen . . .

I didn't have time to run before fire lit up the darkness again. It didn't spill gently over me like it had before, but crashed into me from all sides. Pain ravaged me as the flames attacked me with all their devastating power, charring and burning every inch they touched.

"Why?" I cried, betrayal second only to the agony I felt.

"I warned you," that unknown voice replied, safe outside of the wall of fire. "You didn't listen."

Then I didn't hear anything but my own screams as the fire pitilessly continued to annihilate me.

"*No!*"

In my head the word was howled in anguish; in reality, it left my lips in a whisper. It was enough to wake me up, though, and I jerked away in horror until I realized I was covered in sheets, not flames. The only fire was safely contained in the hearth on the other side of the room.

It took several deep breaths to shake off the aftereffects of the nightmare. After a minute, my heart quit thudding and settled into a more normal rhythm. With a stab of dismay, I saw that the bed was empty. Now I wouldn't have to admit I'd had the same nightmare again, but I didn't like that more and more frequently, I went to sleep alone and woke up that way, too.

If I were superstitious, I'd worry that the recurring dream was an omen, but when I got warnings about the future, they didn't come as vague metaphors in my sleep. They *used* to come as merciless reenactments where I had a full sensory experience of whatever was going to happen, but I hadn't had one of those in weeks. I'd long wished that I didn't pull impressions—and images of worst sins—through a single touch, but now that I needed the ability, it was on vacation.

That thought chased me out from under the covers. I swung my legs over the side of the mattress and stepped off the raised dais that made the large, curtained bed look even more impressive. Then I went straight to the fireplace and knelt in front of it. Most of the flames had died down during the night, but the collapsed logs still smoldered. I pushed the grate aside, held my hand over a log for a second, and then plunged it straight into the crumbling wood.

The stab of pain made me gasp with relief until I realized it only came from one finger. The rest of my hand felt fine despite being immersed up to the wrist in the hotly glowing embers. I waited another few moments to be sure and then pulled it out. Aside from a splinter jutting from my index finger and a decade-old scar, my hand was unmarred, not a hair singed on it.

Damn. Six weeks later, and it *still* hadn't worn off yet.

Some women caught venereal diseases from their boyfriends. That was mild in comparison to what mine had given me—an immunity to fire that inexplicably also blocked my ability to psychically discern information through touch. Of course, I shouldn't be too surprised. Dating the unofficial Prince of Darkness was bound to have consequences.

I yanked the splinter out, sucking on my finger despite being one of the few people in this mansion who *didn't* like the taste of blood. Then I fumbled around until I found a large male shirt, the fabric soft as cashmere. It probably cost more than what I used to earn in a month working the carnival circuit, but it had been thrown on the floor with expectant indifference. I never saw anyone clean this room, but I also never saw it dirty. The servants must wait like ninjas for me to leave so they could render this place spotless again.

They wouldn't have to wait long. I had to pee, and despite the splendor of my boyfriend's bedroom, his bathroom lacked a toilet. Being a centuries-old vampire, *he* didn't need one.

I put on the discarded shirt. It was long enough

that it covered my tank top and panties, though I'd never run into anyone on my way from his room to the one that was officially mine. The lounge that bridged the two bedrooms wasn't used by anyone else. Its privacy and elegance made for a more dignified walk of shame, at least.

Once I was back in my room—a lighter-hued, smaller version of the midnight-green and mahogany magnificence I'd just left—I went straight into the bathroom.

"Lights on," I said, adding, "dim," when the instant blaze of brightness made me squint.

Soft amber illuminated the creamy marble, highlighting its gold and celery-green veins. A glass shower the size of a compact car also lit up, as did the vanity counter. I'd been awed when I first saw all the fancy fixtures. Now I muttered under my breath as I hurried to the discreetly screened corner.

"Fifty-yard sprint every morning because he won't add a toilet to his bathroom. It's not like he doesn't spend more each night on the dinner he never eats."

Part of me knew my griping was to mask my uneasiness about the increasingly empty bed, but my bladder twisted as if in agreement. After I'd dealt with it, I got in the shower, careful to only touch things with my left hand. Although the currents radiating from me were muted at the moment, there was no need to fry the pipes by accidentally sending a dose of voltage through them.

After I showered and dressed, I descended four

flights of stairs to the main level. At the bottom of the staircase, a hallway with soaring ceilings, stone pillars, antique shields, and ornate frescos spread out in front of me. Only the indoor garden kept it from looking like Bill Gates's Gothic Getaway.

At the end of that hallway was my frequently absentee boyfriend, Vlad. Yes, *that* Vlad, but few people made the mistake of calling him Dracula. His dark hair was the same color as the stubble that shadowed his jaw in something thicker than a five o'clock shadow. Winged eyebrows framed eyes that were a blend of copper and emerald, and sleek material draped over a body hardened from decades of battle when he was human. As usual, only his hands and face were bare. The rest of him was covered by boots, black pants, and a smoky gray shirt buttoned up to the neck. Unlike most well-built men, Vlad didn't flash a lot of skin, but those custom-tailored clothes flaunted his taut body as effectively as running shorts and a sleeveless muscle shirt.

My appreciation was cut short when I saw that he had a coat draped over his arm. He hadn't just slipped in and out of bed while I was asleep; he was also leaving without a word.

Again.

Ever have a moment where you know exactly what you shouldn't do . . . and you do it anyway? I didn't need my missing psychic abilities to know that snapping "Where are *you* going?" while striding down the hall was the wrong way to handle this, but that's what I did.

Vlad had been talking to his second-in-command, Maximus, a blond vampire who looked like an avenging Viking come to life. At my question, two gazes settled on me, one gray and carefully neutral, the other coppery green and sardonic. I tensed, wishing I could take the question back. When had I turned into one of those annoying, clingy girlfriends?

Right after the main reason Vlad became interested in you vanished, my inner insidious voice mocked. *You think it's coincidence that he began acting distant right after you lost your ability to psychically spy on his enemies?*

At once, I began to sing KC and the Sunshine Band's "That's the Way" in my head. Vlad wasn't just an extremely powerful vampire whose history inspired the world's most famous story about the undead. He could also read humans' minds. Most of the time.

His lips curled. "One of these days, you'll at least take requests on your method of keeping me out of your head."

If I didn't know him, I would've missed the irony that tinged his tone, heightening his subtle accent and adding an edge to his cultured voice. I doubted he'd ever forgive the vampire who taught me how to block him from my thoughts.

"Some people consider that song a classic,"

I replied, berating myself for what he would've heard before I stopped him.

"Proving again that the world doesn't lack for fools."

"And you didn't answer my question," I countered.

Vlad put on his coat, that slight smile never leaving his face. "That wasn't an accident."

My hand tingled as the currents within me surged to it. Thanks to an incident with a downed power line, my entire body gave off electricity, but my right hand was the main conduit. If I didn't lock down my temper, it might start sparking.

"Next time you want to brush me off, do what modern men do." My voice was rougher than sandpaper. "Be vague and say you're running errands. Sounds more polite that way."

That coppery gaze changed to glowing emerald, visible proof of his inhuman status. "I am not a modern man."

Of course not, but would it kill him to be a *little* less complex, infuriating, and enigmatic? At least some of the time?

Maximus slid a glance my way before returning his attention to Vlad. "Everything will be ready upon your return," he stated, then bowed and left.

What's that supposed to mean? hovered on the tip of my tongue, but I wouldn't get an answer. That didn't mean I was letting this slide. I was done wondering what his increasing absences spelled out for our relationship. If my being psychically neutered meant his feelings for me had changed, he needed to tell me. I paused in my mental singing long enough to think, *When you get back, we're having a talk*.

This time, his smile was wide enough to show his teeth. His fangs weren't out, but his grin still managed to carry shades of both lover and predator.

"I look forward to it."

Then the spot where he stood was empty. Only the massive front doors closing indicated where he'd vanished through. Vampires couldn't dematerialize, but some Master vampires could move so fast it appeared that way.

I sighed. In the past couple months, dating Vlad had proved to be as passionate and tumultuous as the movies portrayed. I only hoped Hollywood wasn't also right about the fate of every woman who fell in love with the infamous Dark Prince.

The thought was depressing, but I wasn't going to sit around brooding. Instead, I'd engage in the most time-tested and venerable of feminine distraction techniques.

I sprinted upstairs to my sister's room. "Wake up, Gretchen!" I called through the door. "We're going shopping."

Chapter 2

"This is the only thing that hasn't sucked so far about Romania," my sister stated as she unloaded a stack of clothes in front of the cashier.

I closed my eyes, not knowing who to apologize to first: the cashier for Gretchen's remark about her country, or Maximus, who now had to add more bags to the half dozen he already carried. This is what happened when you gave my sister someone else's credit card. Vlad had a standing rule that any purchases for his guests went on his card.

He might reconsider that when he got the bill. My attempts to encourage thriftiness hadn't worked, either. They'd only annoyed Gretchen to the point that she quit trying things on before she purchased them.

"I'm tired. We should go back," I said, changing tactics.

Gretchen's blue gaze narrowed. "No way. I've been cooped up in your boyfriend's castle for *weeks* even though his vamp enemy has to be dead or Marty and Dad wouldn't have gotten to leave."

I didn't point out that our father and my best friend, Marty, were less prone to recklessness. The odds were slim, but if Vlad's nemesis Szilagyi *had* survived, then Gretchen was safer here. She couldn't keep a low profile if her life depended on it, as she'd proved. I glanced at the cashier, forced a smile, and used Gretchen's sleeve to tug her toward me.

"No talking about you-know-what in public," I hissed.

"Why?" she shot back at the same volume. "Half the people in this town know about vampires since Vlad *owns* it and he uses some of them as blood snacks. As for the rest, Maximus can mesmerize them into forgetting what they didn't already know."

My eyes bugged as I glanced at the cashier. She held up a hand to the blond vampire and said something in Romanian.

"Don't worry, she's loyal to Vlad," he summarized for me. Then his stormy gray gaze landed on Gretchen. "You need to show more discretion or the next person I mesmerize will be you."

"You wouldn't," she huffed.

Maximus straightened to his full six feet, six inches, as if his thickly muscled frame wasn't impressive enough. "I've done far worse to protect my prince."

•

I still wanted to thump Gretchen, but no one—even a friend like Maximus—got away with scaring my little sister.

"She gets it," I said coolly. "And if she doesn't, *I'll* be the one who deals with her."

Maximus glanced at Gretchen, gave a barely perceptible shake of his head, and then bent low to me.

"As you wish."

My cheeks warmed. Since I was Vlad's girlfriend, the vampires in his line bowed to me as they did to him, much to my dismay. "Please stop, I hate that."

He straightened, the barest grin tugging at his mouth. "Yes, I remember."

When his gaze met mine, for a split second, I saw the man who'd pounced on the chance to date me when I first arrived at Vlad's as a reluctant refugee. Then that familiar veil dropped over Maximus's eyes, and my politely formal bodyguard was back.

"You have another hour, if you wish to continue shopping. Then we need to return to the house."

"Why?" I asked, beating Gretchen to it.

"Because you need to be ready for Vlad's dinner guests. You don't want to be late to dine."

Gretchen was faster this time. "Dinner guests? Who? Why weren't we told before?"

"*You* weren't told because your attendance is optional," Maximus answered. Then he smiled faintly at me. "I waited to tell you because you seemed to have enough on your mind."

Embarrassment and resignation mingled inside me. Did everyone know Vlad and I were having problems? *Of course they did*, I answered my own question. With the hearing abilities of the undead, they probably also knew that Vlad and I hadn't had sex in a week because I'd had my period.

I sighed. "Looks like I need to buy something after all." I hadn't yet despite visiting several stores, not wanting to add to the crushing bill Gretchen had run up.

Something I couldn't name flickered across Maximus's face. "It's not necessary. Vlad has your dress waiting in your room."

First leaving without telling me where he was going. Then unexpected dinner guests, and now a dress picked out for me. My eyes narrowed. What was he up to?

"You're not going to even give me a hint about what's going on, are you?" I asked Maximus.

His smile was a little too tight. "As I said, I've done far worse to protect my prince."

One look at the dress told me that dinner wouldn't consist of Vlad catching up with some old buddies who'd dropped by. It was a black velvet sheath that had a small train in the back and a low neckline in front that looked like it was encrusted with tiny black jewels. Black heels and similarly encrusted elbow-length black gloves—lined with current-repelling rubber, of course—completed the seductively extravagant ensemble. I tried it on, not surprised that it fit like it had been sewn with my exact measurements in mind. It even managed to give me cleavage—a rare achievement with my small breasts.

It was the nicest dress I'd ever worn, but I'd exchange it and every other expensive gift Vlad had given me to close the growing gap between us. I stroked the soft fabric, wishing my abilities were back so I'd know if this was his way of making amends for his recent coolness, or simply ensuring that I looked good enough to be on his arm tonight. Either was a possibility with Vlad.

That was why I had to confront him later, no matter the outcome. The last thing I wanted to do was primp, but this was clearly a formal occasion. When I was done, my straight black hair hung in thick curls and my makeup was subtle, aside from dark crimson lipstick that contrasted great with the black dress and my winter-pale skin. All those years in carnival show business made me deft at sprucing myself up. It also made me an expert at concealing the scar that ran from my temple down to my fingers. A glossy black wave hung over that part of my face, with more draped on my right shoulder. I'd pulled the gloves up so only a few inches of skin on my upper arm showed evidence of the accident that had given me my unusual abilities.

Abilities Vlad had stunted when he coated me in his flame-repelling aura to protect me from the explosion Szilagyi detonated. Vlad's enemy thought he was taking me down with him, but I'd survived the inferno. Figures my survival had come at a price. Fate didn't let anyone off easily.

I shook my head to clear the past from it. Then, feeling anything but festive, I headed for the main floor.

Vlad was waiting at the bottom of the staircase. His black tuxedo should've been too severe with its lack of accent color, but instead, he looked like a sensual version of the Angel of Death. I couldn't stop my shiver as his gaze swept over me. Emerald briefly shone from his eyes, and when he took my hand, I felt his heat even through my gloves. Normal vampires felt room temperature, but not Vlad. The pyrokinesis that made him so feared among his kind also made him warmer than most humans when his abilities, temper, or desire flared to life.

"You look ravishing."

His low growl let me know which emotion heated him now, and once again I shivered. My feelings for him might be rife with doubt, but my body wasn't conflicted. I'd moved closer before I realized it, my nipples puckering as soon as his chest brushed mine. Then something lower in me clenched as his mouth grazed my neck, that thick stubble deliciously chafing my skin.

He inhaled, air landing like the softest of kisses on my pulse when he let it out. Then his hands closed over my shoulders, their heat wonderfully potent. A flick of his fingers pushed my hair aside, exposing my neck. I gasped as his mouth lowered and two hard, sharp fangs pressed against my skin. The dark rapture of his bite was second only to making love to him, and I'd missed partaking of both recently. Without thought, I gripped his head closer, almost shuddering in anticipation.

He muttered something unintelligible and drew away, his gaze still lit up with emerald.

"Not now. Our guests are waiting."

I don't care! was my first thought, followed immediately by *What is wrong with me?* Yes, people were waiting for us, not to mention several guards lurked in this hallway. Even if none of the above were true, I had serious issues to work out with Vlad. Assuaging my libido should be the last thing on my to-do list.

"Right," I said, dropping my hands and stepping away. I didn't look at him as I brushed my hair back over my shoulder, covering as much of the zigzagging scar as I could. I wasn't ashamed, but the inevitable pitying glances from people who saw it for the first time got old.

"Leila."

The way he said my name made me jerk my head up. Vlad's eyes had changed back to burnished mahogany, the only green in them now the natural ring that encircled his irises.

"Don't hide for anyone," he stated, pushing my hair off my shoulder. "Only fools pity survivors their scars and you should never kowtow to fools."

Then he held out his hand, his own faded battle

wounds crisscrossing his flesh like tiny pale stripes. "Come."

I took his hand, forcing back the emotion that constricted my heart with invisible bands. Then I began reciting songs in my head, masking the most dangerous thought before it reached him.

That's one of the reasons I love you. You bend for no one.

Unfortunately, that same trait might also tear us apart.

Chapter 3

 As it turned out, I recognized some of our guests, though a lot of new faces were also present. Maximus sat at the dining table next to Shrapnel, Vlad's bald, beefy third-in-command. Next to him was Mencheres, the long-haired Egyptian vampire Vlad described as his honorary sire, a title I still didn't fully understand. The slender blonde next to Mencheres was his wife, Kira. Gretchen was there, too, seated farthest from the head and looking miffed about it. Everyone rose when Vlad and I entered, which made the whole scenario odder. I hadn't been late, so why was everybody at the table already? Weren't the host and hostess supposed to greet guests *before* they took their seats, not arrive last and have everyone stand at attention before them?

Vampires, I decided for the umpteenth time, had the weirdest way of doing things.

Vlad led me to my usual spot at the head of the table, which caused a few slanted glances among the guests that I didn't recognize. Once there, I stood at the empty chair to his right, uncertain. Did I sit now, or wait for a signal?

"I am glad that you have come," Vlad stated, the size of the room not diminishing the strong tenor of his voice. "I know some of you traveled a great distance to be here."

I expected more, maybe a thank-you to those faraway guests, but then he lowered himself into his chair. Before Vlad, I'd never guessed that the simple act of sitting could look regal and intimidating, yet he pulled it off every time.

Everybody else took their seats, so I did, too, wishing I'd been given an *Undead Etiquette for Dummies* manual. From the too-fluid way they moved, none of his guests were human. I was used to being around vamps in a casual setting—or a violent one—but this was my first formal event. *If I screw anything up, it's on you*, I thought to Vlad while affixing a pleasant smile on my face.

His mouth twitched, the only indication that he heard me. Then he gestured to his left.

"Leila, you already know Maximus, Shrapnel, Mencheres, and Kira, but let me introduce the rest of our guests."

I kept that pleasant smile throughout a list of names I hoped I wasn't expected to remember, because all twenty-eight seats at the huge table were filled. When I'd first seen the dining room with its wall of fireplaces, three-story ceiling, and gargantuan chandelier, I'd thought it was a dazzling waste of space since only me and Vlad ate here. Now its size and splendor came in handy. We would've needed another table if he'd invited more friends, and judging from the women's jewels and the men's resplendent tuxedos, those present were used to luxury.

I wasn't. Neither was Gretchen, who looked as ill at ease as I felt. Our father had been a career military man, so we'd grown up in modest sur-roundings that frequently varied depending on his change of duty stations. When I struck out on my own at eighteen, I'd scrounged for jobs that didn't involve technology or touching people—and all decent-paying jobs required one or the other. If I hadn't met Marty and joined his traveling carnival act, I might have ended up on the streets.

I certainly wouldn't have wound up at Vlad's, smiling at strangers through a sea of crystal glasses that servants filled with a dark red liquid too thick to be wine. Those same servants then brought out enough food to feed everyone twice over despite Gretchen and I being the only humans. Nerves had stolen my appetite but I dug in with feigned gusto, wondering when Vlad would reveal the true pur-pose behind this occasion. He didn't invite over two dozen people to his house merely to show off. Vlad was many things, but pretentious wasn't one of them.

The bombshell behind this event dropped during dessert. I'd just helped myself to a spoonful of bourbon butterscotch crème brûlée when Vlad stood and all chatter stopped.

"Thank you all for coming," he said in the sudden silence. "As you are either friends or honored members of my line, I wanted each of you to witness my actions now."

Then he moved behind my chair, resting his hand on my shoulder. I resisted the urge to twist around so I could see him. *What's going on?* I thought nervously.

He ignored the question. "Most of you know that Leila has been my lover for the past few months. In addition, she also risked her life to save my people and demonstrated unwavering loyalty even during torture. Because of her great value to me, I now offer her an eternal bond, if she accepts."

Then he leaned down, breath warm on my neck as he whispered his next words. "You've wondered if I felt differently about you since your abilities diminished. Let this serve as your answer."

I caught a glimpse of his scarred hand before he placed a small velvet box in front of me. My heart started to pound while my mind overloaded with shock and joy. At the far end of the table, I heard Gretchen gasp. Out of all possible reasons behind the surprise fancy dinner, I hadn't expected *this*. Things had indeed changed between us, in the best way possible.

"Vlad, I . . ."

Coherent thought and words might have failed me, but my motor skills didn't. With hands trembling from joy, I slowly opened the ebony box.

Gretchen rocketed out of her chair to come

toward me. At some point, happy tears must've sprung to my eyes because the box's content was blurry. Still, I could make out a ring. An avalanche of happiness swept over me. It wasn't until now that I realized how much I loved Vlad and how fervently I'd hoped that he loved me, too. I blinked to see the ring more clearly . . . and then my elation became tempered with confusion.

Maximus caught Gretchen's arm before she reached me, but she was still close enough to get a look inside the box.

"You cheapskate, that's not a diamond!" she announced with her usual tactlessness. "What kind of engagement ring is that?"

I'd wondered at his choice, too, since I recognized the ring as a replica of the heirloom that had been passed down from Vlad's father to him. No matter, I'd cherish any engagement ring he gave me. Besides, maybe proposing with a replica was a Dracul family tradition—

"It's not an engagement ring," Vlad replied crisply to Gretchen. "It's the symbol of membership in my line. All the vampires I've made carry one."

At those words, my ecstatic jumble of thoughts crystallized into one heartrending realization: *He's not proposing. He's only offering to make you a vampire!*

Vlad straightened and his hand left my shoulder. He'd heard that. With how it had roared across my mind, he'd have to be telepathically deaf to have missed it.

I knew I should sing something to keep him from hearing anything else, but I couldn't think up a single verse. My pride screamed at me to act as though I hadn't misunderstood, yet all I could do was clutch that box while my previous joy turned to ashes. Nothing had changed except Vlad thought my humanity needed an upgrade, and he'd decided to inform me of that with a roomful of vampires as witnesses.

I glanced up. Our guests' gazes skipped away with pitying quickness while their uncomfortable shifting told me Vlad wasn't alone in figuring out my misinterpretation. If I hadn't felt as though my heart had been ripped out and flambéed in front of me, I would have been mortified.

Gretchen's voice broke the loaded silence. "You want Leila to become a vampire? That is so creepy!"

"Maximus," Vlad bit out.

The brawny vampire had Gretchen hoisted up with his hand over her mouth before I could blink. Normally, such handling of my sister would've incensed me. At the moment, I was trying too hard to pull myself together to respond.

"Leila," Vlad began.

"Don't."

The word snapped out with all the force of my shattered hopes. I got up, almost overturning my chair, but it was either get out of here *now* or burst into tears, and I still had enough pride not to do that in front of everyone.

"I need some air," I muttered.

And some razors to finish the job you started when you were sixteen, my hated inner voice supplied.

I ignored that, blasting the first song that came to mind to hide my thoughts. It turned out to be "Taps."

Figures.

Then I left as fast as my new high heels could carry me.

Chapter 4

 I went straight to the small, rubber-lined room in the basement level that Vlad had set up for me. Once inside, I yanked off my right glove. As soon as I did, electricity spat out of my hand in sizzling strands as the emotions I tried to control manifested in miniature energy bolts. I gathered those currents into a single pulsating rope and then whipped it toward the stone statue in the room.

Its head came off, bouncing onto the base it was welded to. Another snap of currents and the statue lost an arm. Then the other arm. Then everything above the waist, yet my seething hurt, disappointment, and humiliation didn't lessen. Instead, I felt like I could go nuclear at any moment.

I didn't stop lashing the statue until it lay in dozens of ragged pieces. Before Vlad, I'd only worked to suppress my power, much as I'd done with the loneliness that came from my inability to touch anyone without harming them.

Vlad had changed all that. He taught me to turn

my abilities into an asset and awakened feelings in me I'd never thought to experience. He was more than my first lover. He was also my first love, yet I'd let myself fall too deeply. Despite all the warnings, I'd dared to hope that one day, he might feel the same way about me. This is where that hope had led me: to a basement, taking out my crushed dreams on an inanimate object.

I looked at the remains of the statue and felt a grim sort of kinship. Like me, it used to be solid and whole. Now, also like me, it was so shredded from destructive emotions that neither of us would be the same.

"Damn you," I whispered, and didn't know if it was directed at me, or the vampire I'd foolishly fallen in love with.

My gorgeous dress was now damp from my exertions, but I didn't care. I wasn't going back to dinner. Everyone had figured out the reason why I left so they'd understand my continued absence. If they didn't, screw 'em. I was done being the evening's entertainment.

Worn out, I climbed up the multiple flights of stairs to my room, glad I didn't pass anyone along the way. With luck, Vlad would be up late with his guests and I wouldn't see him until tomorrow. It would give me some much-needed solitude.

That's why I groaned when I saw that my bedroom wasn't empty. Vlad stood by the settee, hands clasped behind him, that cursed jewelry box thankfully out of sight. A rake of his gaze took in my sweaty, disheveled appearance.

"Feeling better now?" he asked with his usual bluntness.

Not even close. Just seeing him shattered the fragile control my electrical workout had given me.

"I'm glorious," I said curtly. "In fact, aside from intending to get blackout drunk, I've never felt better."

An emotion I couldn't name flickered across his face. Then his expression became impassive again.

"I regret how tonight turned out. I should have discussed my offer with you in private, but I never expected you to misinterpret it in such a way."

I don't know what I'd wanted to hear after this fiasco, but whatever it was, he'd missed it by a mile. His ironclad self-control was also salt on the wound. I was barely holding myself together, and he'd never looked more cool and collected. Anger joined all my other roiling emotions.

"The dress, the fancy dinner, all your flattering words, then the jewelry box." I ticked the items off on my fingers. "Really, what was I supposed to think?"

His snort cut me to the bone. "Anything but that. You and I have been together mere months. Do you know how insignificant that is to someone my age?"

A fresh wave of hurt made my tone scalding. "Yes, you're almost six hundred years old, but in *today's* world, when you say things like 'eternal bond' before giving your girlfriend a ring-sized box, there's usually only one kind of ring in it!"

"For centuries, every vampire I've made has been given a replica of my ring because it's proof of membership in my line. That's useful if my people are captured by allies. Or enemies."

I believed him, but it did nothing for the acid continually being poured over my emotions.

"You don't get it," I said sharply. "We haven't been together long by my standards, either, but your scorn at the *thought* of marriage shows how differently we value this relationship. That's the real problem, and I can't ignore it anymore."

His mouth tightened and flames erupted in the fireplace as that shell cracked and his temper flared. I didn't care. I was the one who'd been emotionally filleted in public and now again in private.

"I do value our relationship. I've never shared my private bedchamber with anyone except you—"

"Yet you can't be bothered to install a toilet," I interrupted. "It's like you keep showing me 'This far, no farther' every chance you get."

Now his gaze blazed pure emerald, all traces of copper gone. "I offered a different solution to that issue tonight."

Turning me into a vampire would indeed negate my need for a toilet. It would also ensure that I spent the rest of an unnaturally long life loving a man who never wanted me any closer than arm's length. Vlad was known for his mercilessness, but

I didn't think he realized what a cruel fate he'd be sentencing me to if I accepted his offer.

Part of that was my fault. I'd let the emotional standoff between us go on too long because I didn't want to lose him. Problem was, I never really had him, as tonight had forced me to acknowledge. Despite my heart feeling like it split apart within me, I met his gaze without flinching.

"It didn't occur to you that I'd see the ring as a proposal because you have no intention of ever offering me a real commitment. I was okay with that once. I'm not anymore."

"You don't understand."

His tone was flat even as the flames nearby shot higher.

"Divorce doesn't exist for vampires. With how people can change over time, few of my kind choose to marry. Feelings may fade, but a vampire union never will."

Then his warm, strong hands cupped my face.

"I *am* offering you a real commitment—a place in my life forever. Even if our relationship ended, our tie to each other never would. Let me make you a vampire, Leila, and watch decades slide by like days while you're by my side."

I wanted to say yes. The word trembled on my lips, but I forced it back with a ragged, indrawn breath. He wasn't offering me anything different, only a longer version of what I already had. The fact that I'd be willing to shed my humanity like an old suit was proof enough that I'd do anything for Vlad, yet he still kept his heart deliberately out of reach.

I couldn't live like that, as a human *or* a vampire. If it hurt this much now, how would it feel after decades of loving a man who regarded me as little more than a pleasant bedmate?

"I'll say yes on one condition."

He caressed my face. "And what is that?"

I didn't blink. "You can read my mind so you should already know. *I love you, Vlad*, so more than blood ties or the chance to live forever, I want you to say you love me, too."

His hands dropped to clench into fists at his side. "We talked about this—"

"I remember," I cut him off. "The first night we slept together, you told me you'd give me passion, honesty, and monogamy, but not love because you're incapable of it. I believed that then, but I call bullshit now. You remember the last thing Szilagyi said before he detonated that explosion?"

From the granite set of his jaw, he did, but he wasn't going to volunteer it. I continued on.

"Szilagyi said he was going to kill me along with him because *that would hurt you*. Even your worst enemy could see I was more than a mistress to you, but you refuse to offer me anything else. Until you do, I can't—"

My voice broke, and despite my resolve, two tears slipped past my lashes. I dashed them away, forcing myself to speak through a throat closed painfully tight from emotion.

"I can't be with you," I summarized. "It hurts too much to be close to you, but continually pushed away."

His expression changed to disbelief. "You're leaving me?"

From his tone, the idea was more shocking than hurtful. Another sledgehammer hit me in the chest, causing more tears to leak out that I couldn't suppress.

"What choice do I have? I know how this will end. With my abilities, I've relived it through countless other couples. I even watched my mother give everything to a man who kept rating her as second-best and I refuse to make that same mistake."

Despite knowing every word was true, I couldn't stop the spate of thoughts that ran across my mind.

Tell me you love me and I'll stay. Hell, tell me you'll be open to the IDEA of loving me and I'll stay. Tell me anything except to resign myself to always ranking a distant second to the coldness you keep wrapping around your heart.

He didn't say any of that. Instead, he said, "It's not safe. We excavated much of what's left of his mountain lair, yet we still didn't find Szilagyi's remains. If he managed to survive, he'll come after you."

That was his biggest concern? Not our relationship ending, but his enemy using me against him again? For a moment, I couldn't breathe from how savagely that tore at my heart. I thought I was braced to handle a rejection. I was so, so wrong.

"Szilagyi's dead," I managed hoarsely. "Even if he did survive, my abilities are gone. No finding people in the present or seeing into the future means he'd have no use for me."

Tell me that's not the only reason you want me to stay! burst across my thoughts with all of the vehemence of my last hope. Willpower alone kept me from saying it aloud.

Vlad only stared at me, his gaze changing from copper to emerald and back again while the fire raged on in the hearth. With every continued moment of silence, the tears I couldn't will away kept sliding down my cheeks.

Then, each movement slicing like razors across my emotions, he walked to the door. When he reached it, he paused for a moment, his hand hovering over the knob.

Don't do this! I wanted to scream. *I love you; can't you even try to let yourself love me, too?*

The fire flared so high that it breached the grate and licked up the wall, but still he didn't speak. When it reached the ceiling, I started toward it with an instinctive urge to douse the flames, but then they vanished in a whoosh that left nothing more than a trail of smoke.

By the time I turned around, Vlad was gone.

Chapter 5

 The car came to a stop inside the airplane hangar. I opened the door immediately, not wanting Maximus or Shrapnel to get it for me. About ten yards away, a gleaming, ivory-colored jet waited. Underneath my misery, I thought that it was a good thing I was traveling back to the States in Vlad's private plane. Even if my electricity issues magically disappeared, if I tried to fly commercial, my grim expression would guarantee that I got "randomly selected" for a pat-down.

A young, russet-haired man waited on the roll-away staircase next to the jet, but upon seeing me, he hurried down.

"Where are your bags, miss?" he asked in accented English.

"I don't have any."

"Yes she does," Maximus replied, getting out of the driver's seat. "They're in the trunk."

Only Gretchen's presence kept me from losing my temper. "I told you I didn't want any of that stuff. I came with the clothes on my back and that's how I intend to leave."

"You're taking them, Vlad's orders," Maximus said in a tone that made Redheaded Man hurry to the back of the limo. "What you do with them once you're home is up to you."

Vlad must not want any reminders of me cluttering up his house. He'd once told me that if I ever wanted out of this relationship, he'd let me go without argument. Had to give it to the man for keeping his word. Not only hadn't he argued, I hadn't seen him since the night he left my room. He didn't even say good-bye before Gretchen and I left for the airport.

No matter how hard I tried to tell myself that it was for the best, it hurt more than anything I'd ever endured.

"Fine," I said, forcing a smile for Gretchen's benefit.

My caustic sister had been uncharacteristically protective of me the past couple days. It reminded me of how close we'd been before the accident that claimed our mother's life and gave me my abilities. I kept telling her I was fine, so I couldn't ruin that by informing Maximus I'd sooner go naked than torture myself with memories by keeping the things Vlad had bought me.

Besides, he was right. I could throw them away later.

"Well . . . good-bye," I said when Maximus and

the other man finished transporting our bags from the trunk to the aircraft.

He smiled slightly. "Not yet. I'm traveling with you to ensure that you are delivered safely to Marty."

Delivered, like a package. Once again I bit my tongue to keep from losing it in front of my sister.

Gretchen snorted. "What about me? No one cares if I make it back to my apartment in one piece?"

Maximus nodded at the bald, mocha-skinned vampire who got out of the front of the limo.

"Shrapnel's taking care of you."

He grinned, showing his flawless white teeth. "We didn't think Marty would want to see me again."

Since Shrapnel once tortured Marty, probably not. Then again, Marty might not be overjoyed to see me, either. My best friend and carnival partner had warned me not to get involved with Vlad. Looked like I owed Marty an apology. I'd give it to him, too, probably while falling into his arms and sobbing. I hadn't let myself cry since the night Vlad walked out. With Marty, however, I could finally quit pretending that I wasn't devastated by the breakup. He'd always been there for me and I needed him now more than ever.

I cast one final look around, hating that part of me had hoped Vlad would show up, saying everything he'd refused to say before. Then I smiled at

Gretchen, wondering when I'd be able to do that without it feeling like a lie.

"All right, little sister. Let's get both of us home."

Eighteen hours later, Maximus and I arrived in Gibsonton, Florida, also known as Showtown, USA. The heat and humidity assaulted me as soon as I got out of the car. It was only May, but the temperature had to be near one hundred degrees. Maximus got out, too, looking at the homes lined up like splotches of dough on a bakery assembly line.

"Why do I smell elephant manure?"

"That's Betsy," I said, pointing at the gray modular house. "Her trainers keep a pen for her in their yard . . ."

My voice trailed off as I looked past the line of houses. I should've been able to see Marty's trailer since this was the shortest route into the RV park, but the spot where his 1982 Winnebago should be was empty.

"Oh no," I moaned.

Instantly Maximus was on alert, a silver knife appearing in his hand. "What's wrong?"

"Nothing that knife will help," I said, cursing to myself. "For once, Marty must've decided to get on the road early."

Both golden brows rose. "He's not here?"

"No."

I should've called, but Marty *never* started the season early. Plus, I'd wanted to tell him in person what happened.

Maximus put his knife away and pulled out a cell phone. "Call him. Find out where he is."

I gave him a jaded look. "You don't know Marty when he's on the road. He's doing great if he remembers to *bring* his phone, let alone charge it or answer it. But don't worry. I know another way to find out which carnival he'll be at."

After a quick stop to talk to some of the other carnies, Maximus and I got on the road again. At least Gretchen and Shrapnel had continued by air after dropping us off in Florida. If I thought I had a chance at convincing Maximus to let me catch a bus, I would've, but he wouldn't leave until he'd fulfilled his sire's instructions to the letter.

Several hours later, in a north Georgia carnival parking lot, I saw a Winnebago with our stage names of Mighty Marty and the Fantastic Frankie painted on the side.

"There," I said, pointing at the RV.

Maximus parked as close as he could get. At this predawn hour, everything was quiet in the employee section of the carnival. I got out, so tired I almost stumbled past the vehicles, tents, and cages along the way, yet I was also relieved. I was back to my old life where Marty and I traveled state to state performing our act. In a few months, if I was lucky, my time with Vlad might even feel like a strange, faraway dream and it wouldn't hurt so much. Propelled by that thought, I banged on the trailer door.

"Marty, open up! It's me."

The door opened so fast it bashed into me. I caught a glimpse of bushy black hair before Marty's quick grip saved me from toppling. Then I was enveloped in a fierce hug around the waist. I bent until I was even with Marty's four-foot height and hugged him back so hard that a current made him yelp.

"Sorry," I gasped.

He chuckled. "My fault. Forgot to brace for one of those."

Then Marty pulled back to get his first real look at me. He inhaled, and his mouth thinned into a single slit while green enveloped his chestnut-colored eyes.

"You smell awful, kid. What happened?"

I knew he wasn't talking about it being a day since I showered. Vampires could scent emotions and I was probably serving up a stink platter of brokenheartedness.

"What you warned me about," I responded with an unconvincing attempt at nonchalance. "Guess I'm one of those people who learn the hard way."

Marty sighed before giving me another hug, and then he patted my back when he let me go.

"No one's died of a broken heart yet, so you'll survive. Now come inside, you look like you're going to collapse."

I felt like it, too. Then Marty scowled, looking past me.

"What's *he* doing here?"

"How do you think she got here?" Maximus replied coolly. "Now help me with this luggage."

I was about to reiterate that I didn't want it when someone else appeared in the trailer behind Marty.

"Who's here?" a groggy feminine voice asked.

If the moonlight hadn't broken through the clouds at that moment, the darkness would've made me miss the sheepish look that skipped over Marty's face. In the next moment, I figured out why. A slender girl with long black hair blinked sleepily at us, and she couldn't have been more than twenty.

"Marty, you're a hundred and thirty-eight!" I exclaimed before realizing the hypocrisy behind that statement.

"It's not like that, we work together," the girl offered, smiling hesitatingly at me. "I'm the new Fantastic Frankie."

Chapter 6

 Maximus offered to drive me five states away to Gretchen's. Marty refused and said we'd figure this out. I didn't know how, but I wasn't about to involve Maximus any further. I gave him a hug and told him I'd be fine. That was getting a lot easier to say. Maybe soon, I'd even believe it.

Marty waited until Dawn—the new Fantastic Frankie's real name—went back to bed in my old room before offering his idea.

"I'll tell her she can finish this event, then she has to find another gig. Bill the Beetle Man could use an assistant—"

"You can't do that," I said, exhaustion making my voice sharp. "Being a carnie isn't most people's first *or* second career choices. Dawn's broke and desperate, isn't she?"

He nodded glumly. "Yeah, plus she's got a warrant on her. Petty theft, multiple counts. People seem to forget that eating isn't free. She could pull a small stretch if they catch her."

How like Marty to come to this girl's rescue by giving her a job, a place to live, and safety by green-eyeing any suspicious cops that came sniffing around. He'd done the same for me when I was Dawn's age and only a little more desperate. I couldn't take a young girl's best chance away from her, no matter my own crappy circumstances.

I smiled and hoped it didn't look like a grimace.

"See, you can't fire her. Don't worry about me. I, ah, have some jewelry I can sell that'll keep me flush for a year or so." Good thing Vlad had insisted that I leave with everything he'd given me. "In the meantime, I'll create my own solo act."

He reached across the fold-down table and grasped my hand. "You'll stay here until you've booked some slots for that act."

"No, really—"

"Don't argue," he cut me off, squeezing my hand. "You're not my daughter by blood but I love you as much as Vera, God rest her soul, so shut up and let's get you a place to sleep."

I laughed at that, blinking past tears that were caused by happiness for a change. "I love you, too, Marty, and I've always thought the couch was *really* comfortable."

She's pretty good, I thought a week later as I watched Dawn perform with Marty. Granted, he had added some of the more complicated flips and tumbles to his part of the routine, but Dawn had a good sense of showmanship that made up for her acrobatic weaknesses. By the time she landed on his shoulders at the end, I could almost pretend I'd been watching myself. We looked alike with our slender builds and long black hair. Aside from wanting to shield her from the law, no wonder Marty hadn't bothered to change Dawn's stage name from the one I'd used. I doubted any of the spectators who'd seen our act before realized that I'd been replaced with a younger, less-electrified model.

I'd gone to their show to prove that I was okay with how things had turned out. Dawn was a sweet girl who needed this break and I did have other options. Limited ones, true, but options nonetheless. Starting tonight, I was reclaiming my life. Cheering Marty and Dawn on was step one.

Step two was talking to Edgar. He might be nicknamed The Hammer for his fierce negotiating tactics, but he was more honest than your average pawnbroker. Despite Marty's assurances that I could stay as long as I wanted, the Winnebago really was too small for three people, even if one of us was a dwarf.

Most of the crowd left while Marty and Dawn took their encore bows. I waited in the uppermost section of the stands, wanting to avoid as much contact with spectators as I could. I wore specialized gloves, but even casual contact would feel like static electricity to anyone who touched me. That's why I had on long sleeves and long pants though it was eighty degrees in the tent. The hat, well. That and my hair were to hide my scar from nosy on-lookers.

When there was no one left in the upper stands except me and a strikingly attractive brunette, I rose. She did, too, still staring at the stage as if waiting for Marty and Dawn to reappear. They wouldn't. This had been their final show.

I was about to say that when the woman leapt off the top of the bleachers, landing with more grace than an Olympic medalist. That, more than the thirty-foot jump, told me she wasn't human. She must've realized she'd outed herself because she glared up at me and her eyes changed to glowing green.

"You saw nothing," she hissed.

I nodded, not bothering to tell her I already knew about her kind. Or that the vampire blood I had to drink every week to keep my inner electricity from killing me meant I was immune to mind control. She left and I continued down the bleachers at my humanly slow pace, making a mental note to tell Marty he'd had a vampire in the audience tonight.

From there, I headed to the employee parking lot. Edgar's trailer wasn't far from Marty's, but he wanted to do business at his place. Maybe he was worried that Marty would green-eye him into overpaying me for the jewels if Marty witnessed our transaction. Edgar *wasn't* immune to mind control and he, like a lot of the regular carnies, knew what Marty was.

I knocked before a gruff voice told me to come

in. Once I did, I blinked at the glare. Edgar had every interior lamp on, all the better to appraise what I had inside my purse.

"Frankie," he said, using the name most carnies knew me by.

I smiled wryly at the bony, white-haired man. "One of them."

Edgar waved at the dinette table. I sat opposite him and began to empty out the contents of the velvet pouch inside my purse. This was the first I'd dared to look at the jewels, and I silently willed myself to be unemotional.

It didn't work. Each piece had a memory that tore at my heart. *How warm Vlad's fingers felt when he slid the ruby and diamond cuff onto my wrist. The stunning aquamarine earrings he'd said matched the color of my eyes. His lips on my throat as he fastened the black diamond necklace around it. Then the ancient-looking gold ring with the dragon emblem . . .*

I froze, clutching it instead of placing it on the table. Why had Vlad included *this* with the things he'd had packed for me? Edgar didn't seem to notice my shock. He was too busy looking at the other pieces through a magnifying glass.

"No flaws in the stones . . . excellent workmanship and design . . . highest grade of gold and platinum." He glanced up at me while still holding the magnifier to one eye. "Whoever he was, you should've held on to him a little longer."

"Some things are more important than money,"

I replied, still reeling from the presence of the ring. Vlad said only vampires in his line had one of these. Had one of his servants made a mistake including this with the other pieces? Or was it a sign that his invitation to change me still stood?

Edgar finally noticed that I clutched something. "Whatcha got there?"

"Nothing." I'd starve on the street before I hocked this.

He grinned. "Trying to whet my appetite by pretending I can't have it? Nice try, but I've seen every trick before—"

A deafening roar cut him off. Then the whole trailer shuddered and the windows shattered. I didn't have time to scream before a wall of fire swallowed us both.

Chapter 7

"We've got a live one!"

I wish I hadn't heard the voice. Then I wouldn't have felt the pain that followed as consciousness reared its pitiless head. In addition to that, something so heavy was on top of me that it hurt to breathe. Then I regretted breathing as the scent of scorched meat filled my lungs.

I *really* regretted opening my eyes. A blackened skull wrapped in a hideous pale cloak was the first thing I saw. It pressed down on me, crushing my limbs and sending fissures of agony through me. I screamed, but it came out as a choked gasp.

"Don't move," an urgent voice instructed.

I craned my neck as much as I could. To the right of the skull, behind the twisted cloak, was a helmeted fireman.

"We're going to get you out," he went on, his voice muffled from the breathing device he wore. "Don't move."

I couldn't if I wanted to. My eyes burned, but after some hard blinking, I saw the skull on top of me wasn't wearing a cloak. What surrounded it was too thick and hard, like plastic . . .

The last vestige of confusion lifted. Not plastic. It was the white acrylic dinette table that had been between me and Edgar when the explosion went off, which meant the charred skull belonged to Edgar. The fire must've been so hot it melted the table around him like a grisly shroud. That—plus something else, from the heaviness—pinned me beneath it.

"What happened?" I managed. "Is anyone else hurt?"

The fireman didn't answer. I asked again, but my only response was an oxygen mask placed over my face. Then a flurry of activity began as more firemen arrived and tried to clear away the debris on top of me.

"Looks like the furniture melted *around* her," one of them muttered, disbelief clear in his tone. "How is she still alive?"

I knew the answer, but it was the least of my concerns. Marty and Dawn would've gone back to the RV to change after their final show. That was only a few trailers away. What if the explosion had reached them, too?

"My friend is a dwarf," I said despite how much it hurt to talk. "His trailer isn't far. Has anyone seen him?"

No response, but they exchanged pitying glances. Then I remembered the words I'd woken up to. *We've got a live one!* Fear mixed with pain shot through me. Marty was a vampire, yet he wasn't fireproof. Only I was. What if Edgar hadn't been the only person killed tonight?

I angled my head until I moved the oxygen mask partially aside. Then, forgetting the pain, I began to scream as loud as I could, hoping desperately that he was alive to hear me.

"Marty! Marty, where are you?"

Heavy hands forced the mask back in place. Someone said to give me a sedative. I kept screaming, anguish rising as only more medical workers appeared. Marty should've come by now. Even with all the other noises, he should've heard me. I screamed louder in desperation. *Please, Marty, please be okay!*

Suddenly a path cleared as the people clustered around me were shoved aside with inhuman force. Relief turned to confusion when I got a look at the vampire who knelt down next to me.

"Leila, you're alive," Maximus breathed.

He started to say something else, but my hearing faded and a cottony taste filled my mouth. The last thing I saw were his eyes changing to blazing green as he rose and turned around.

This time when I woke up, I wasn't in pain. That awful stench was still there, though, as if someone had overcooked a roast and rubbed it all over me. I coughed, relieved my lungs didn't feel like closed fists anymore. Then I opened my eyes.

Walls the color of old mustard met my gaze.

Not pretty, but better than a charred skull. I rolled over, seeing the rest of the tiny room in that single glance. It made the blond vampire on the opposite bed look even larger and more imposing.

I had so many questions, like why I was naked under the covers, but my primary concern hadn't changed.

"Marty. Is he . . . ?" I couldn't finish the sentence.

"He's gone, Leila."

Maximus's tone was gentle, but the words hit me with more force than the downed power line I'd touched when I was thirteen. I sucked in a breath that ended on a sob. At the same time, something dark rose in me, causing my right hand to spark. I wanted to do so much more than cry. I wanted to lash Maximus with all the voltage I had in me for saying such an awful thing that couldn't—couldn't!—be true, yet all I could do was fight for control while absorbing the news that my best friend was dead.

Maximus didn't attempt to comfort me. Either he could sense the danger in my sparking hand or he didn't care how I felt. Then my sobs subsided as suspicion broke through my grief.

"What happened? And what are *you* doing here? You were supposed to be back in Romania by now!"

His mouth twisted. "I didn't set the explosion, if that's what you're thinking. If I had, I would have killed you when I saw you survived. Your being alive proves I'm not behind it."

Currents still throbbed in my hand. "Who *is* behind it?"

"I don't know."

Maximus got up and began to pace, difficult since three of his strides covered the length of the room. His clothes were ripped and soot smeared, making me wonder again why he'd been Johnny-on-the-spot when the explosion went off.

"The fireman said a gas line ruptured," he continued. "They're calling it an accident. Since it ruptured right next to Marty's trailer, I doubt that."

"But why would anyone want to kill *Marty*?" I burst out.

He swung a hard glance my way. "I don't think anyone did."

The explosion was meant for me? If so, it almost worked. Despite my fireproofing, I'd nearly been crushed to death. Maximus must have given me some of his blood to heal me.

"If someone wanted to kill me, why didn't they just shoot me in the head?" I asked, grief making my voice dull.

"They must have wanted it to look like an accident."

I swiped my eyes. Tears wouldn't help me find who'd killed my best friend. "What does Vlad think?"

Maximus stopped pacing and turned around, an inscrutable look on his face. "I didn't tell him about the explosion, let alone that you survived it."

"Why not? We're broken up, but I doubt he'd be happy to hear that someone tried to *kill* me."

Maximus said nothing. Underneath those closed-off, rugged features, I caught a glimpse of pity. And understood.

"No," I whispered. "He wouldn't."

Maximus let out a grim snort. "Oh? You came as close to humiliating him as anyone has since Szilagyi faked his death centuries ago. And you saw how Vlad reacted to that."

"*I* humiliated *him*?" If I hadn't been so torn up over Marty's death, I would've laughed. "I told Vlad I loved him only to have him make it clear where I'd always rank in his life, which was just a few notches above 'undead bed buddy.'"

"True," Maximus replied without hesitation, "but that's more than he offered any of his other lovers, yet you turned him down. Then you had the temerity to leave him."

"Temerity?" I repeated in disbelief.

"No woman has ever left Vlad. Cynthiana, his lover before you, even seduced Shrapnel trying to make Vlad jealous after he ended things between them."

"Did it work?" I couldn't help but ask.

"Aside from cutting off his protection for Cynthiana because she callously used Shrapnel for her own gain, he didn't care."

"How long was Vlad with her?"

Maximus thought for a moment. "Around thirty years."

I was incredulous. "That's longer than I've been alive! If Vlad walked away from *that* relationship without a backward glance, he's probably forgotten me already."

Maximus slanted a look my way before resuming his pacing. "Not likely. Regardless of what he does or doesn't feel for you, your double rejection will burn him for years."

Enough to incite him to murder me? The thought made me feel like a drowning victim who'd been dunked under one more time.

"Let's say Vlad does want me dead. I doubt he'd be so cowardly as to fake a gas line explosion when he could've killed me while I was still at his castle."

"Yes, but then he'd have to kill Gretchen and your father, too, making the whole business look very emotional on his part." A weary sort of cynicism replaced the pity on his face. "Being emotional is seen as a weakness among vampires. Vlad knows his enemies would fall on him like wolves if they suspected that weakness in him."

First Marty's death, then realizing the explosion was meant for me, now the suggestion that my ex-boyfriend might be behind it. I closed my eyes. How much more could I take?

"You're Vlad's right-hand man" was what I said after an extended pause. "Wouldn't he tell you if he planned to kill me?"

Maximus was silent so long, I opened my eyes. "What now?"

"I don't think he would," Maximus finally said. "He'd know I would have a problem with it, and why strain my loyalty if he didn't have to? Instead, he could've ordered someone else to make your death look like an accident. If I hadn't been here, I might've even believed it."

Back to that question. "Why *were* you here?"

He sighed, returning to the bed across from mine. "Partly because I wanted to make sure Marty really did let you stay with him even though he'd replaced you with that other girl. You need vampire blood to keep your electricity levels from killing you. If Marty wouldn't have kept providing it, I would have made other arrangements. But mostly, Leila, I didn't go back to Romania because of how I feel about you."

If I wasn't overloaded from grief, I would've been shocked. As it was, I could only muster up faint surprise.

Maximus leaned forward, brushing my hair back.

"I told you when we met, you're beautiful, ballsy, and your abilities fascinate me. I've also seen your courage, your loyalty, and your strength in leaving a man you loved because you knew he'd never love you."

More surprise, but that was trivial compared to my anguish and the growing need I had to avenge my best friend and the young girl who'd never had a real chance at life.

"Maximus, you're very attractive and I'm flattered, but I can't even think about this right now."

He leaned back, a hard little smile curving his mouth. "I know, but we *are* having this conversation again."

I didn't argue. I was too busy trying to figure out who was behind that explosion. I still doubted it was Vlad, but if Maximus thought it was possible, I shouldn't throw caution to the wind by automatically discounting the idea.

Besides, even if I was right and Vlad wasn't behind this, I doubted news of my alleged death would rock him. He'd gone out of his way to prove that I didn't mean much to him.

I shook off that thought before it brought me even lower than my rock-bottom state. "I need some clothes."

Maximus got up and rummaged through the suitcase on the dresser. Then he pulled out a shirt and a pair of boxer shorts.

"These won't fit, but the fire burned your clothes off and I haven't had time to get you new ones."

"This is fine," I said, accepting the bundle. As soon as I touched it, colorless images exploded across my mind.

I stuffed my clothes in the suitcase and then slammed it shut. Time to take Leila home. No one expected her to leave Vlad, yet she had, and soon she'd be an ocean away from him. I smiled at the thought. She might have refused me once, but that was before she realized Vlad couldn't give her what she needed. I could, and now I finally had a real chance to show her that.

"Maximus," I whispered once the hotel room with its putrid yellow walls surrounded me once again. "It's *back*!"

Chapter 8

Maximus pulled out a lighter, turning the flame up. I held my hand over it—and immediately snatched it back with a yelp.

"That hurts!"

He flipped the lighter closed. "You're saying for several weeks it didn't, because Vlad's aura rendered you fireproof?"

"That's right. Fire skipped over me like it does with him. How else do you explain me surviving an explosion that was so intense, it destroyed the trailer I was in?"

And killed another vampire, I didn't say aloud. If I dwelled on Marty's death, I'd start sobbing and wouldn't stop.

"Being in such intense flames must have used up the remains of his aura in you," Maximus said in a thoughtful tone. Then he frowned. "Vlad told me about your psychic abilities malfunctioning. Why didn't he tell me this?"

I sighed. I didn't want to think about Vlad now. "Maybe because he'd never done it before and he wanted to keep his ability to render someone temporarily fireproof a secret?"

"Perhaps," he mused.

I didn't care why Vlad hadn't told anyone. My fireproofing was gone, my abilities were back, and someone who'd tried to kill me had murdered my closest friend, an innocent girl, and many others, too. Finding that person and making him pay was my new goal in life.

"Okay, picking up impressions from an object works. Let's see if I can still find someone in the present."

So saying, I stroked the nightstand with my right hand. Tables, doorknobs, and other fixtures were high-traffic areas for emotional imprints. At once, multiple images flashed across my mind. I weeded through them until I found the strongest thread. Then I concentrated on it, seeking the person at the other end of that invisible essence trail.

The hotel room morphed into an office decorated in shades of beige. A fortysomething man sat behind a desk, balancing the phone with his shoulder as he grabbed a notepad.

"No, that's not what we agreed on," he said as he scribbled away. "I don't care what her lawyer wants . . . for fuck's sake, she's already getting half my check in alimony and child support!"

Even though everything was slightly hazy as images in the present were, the word *BITCH* on the notepad was clear. *You shouldn't have kept cheating on your wife in no-tell motels*, I thought, dropping the link and willing myself back to reality.

Maximus stared at me without blinking. "Did it work?"

"Yes."

A ruthless anticipation began to swell in me. Now I could start hunting for the person who killed Marty. I still didn't believe it was Vlad, but if I was wrong . . .

"Maximus, thank you for pulling me out from under the wreckage, healing me, and bringing me here. I owe you my life." I paused to take in a deep breath. "But now you need to go."

Both golden brows rose. "What?"

"If Vlad *is* behind this, I can't trust you," I said bluntly. "You might like me, but we both know you're not going to betray centuries of allegiance over a passing fancy."

I expected a lot of responses. Laughter that sounded like stones grinding together wasn't one of them.

"You don't know me as much as you think you do," he said, and then grabbed my right hand. My power responded, yanking me out of the present into his past.

Multiple wounds covered me, but I was jubilant. The Holy City was once again ours.

"Allah Akbar!" a voice wailed above our shouts of victory.

Fools. If their god truly was great, we wouldn't

have retaken Jerusalem. The survivors of the battle, mostly women and children, stared at us with frightened loathing.

Then my cousin Godfrey's voice rang out. "Men of God! Destroy the filth that befouled Jerusalem. Let none survive!"

I froze. Sunlight glinted off hundreds of swords as the other soldiers raised their weapons. Then the swords fell to the accompaniment of high-pitched screams.

"Obey!" the knight closest to me urged. He showed no hesitation as he hacked at those in front of him.

"God wills it!" Godfrey continued to roar while he joined in the destruction. "We must cleanse this city!"

A form hurtled toward me. By reflex, I caught it, looking down on the tearstained face of a boy, his brown eyes wide as he sobbed out a plea for mercy in his native tongue.

Abruptly, he sagged, blood spurting from his mouth. The knight next to me yanked his dripping sword from the boy's back.

"We have orders," he barked. "Do not refuse. God wills it!"

I dropped the lifeless boy. Then, jaw clenched, I raised my sword and started toward the survivors.

I snapped back from that gruesome memory with slivers of electricity shooting from my hand. At some point, Maximus had let go, wise since I now wanted to aim those currents at him.

"I know what you saw," he said flatly. "It's forever burned into my nightmares. For the sake of allegiance, I once followed a terrible order. Afterward, the guilt nearly destroyed me. I will *not* be that man again. Vlad is ruthless when protecting his line and casualties of war happen, but he's never murdered innocent women or children. If that has changed, then so has my loyalty to him, but not for your sake. For mine."

I stared at Maximus. I'd expected he had a dark sin—most people did, especially centuries-old vampires—but I hadn't anticipated what he'd shown me.

"How could you have fought in that battle *and* been changed into a vampire by Vlad?" I finally asked. "Didn't the Crusades take place hundreds of years before Vlad was born?"

He smiled tightly. "They did, but the Knighthood of the Temple of Solomon had secret rituals. One of them involved drinking blood instead of wine in a mimicry of the Last Supper. For members of the original eight Templars, as I was, the blood wasn't human, though we didn't know it. We thought our increased strength and accelerated healing came from God."

"You were tricked into drinking vampire blood?" Wry snort. "I've been there. When did you find out what it was?"

"Centuries later when I met Vlad. In truth, it was a relief. I thought I couldn't age because God wanted to keep punishing me for spilling innocent blood in His name."

Some of the anger I'd felt melted away. What Maximus had done was awful, but he'd lived with the guilt for longer than I could imagine. He didn't need more recriminations from me.

"Um . . . all right."

Such a trivial response, but too much had happened the past several hours. I rubbed my head, feeling Vlad's essence flare underneath my fingers. He'd left imprints all over me. I dropped my hand, not wanting to accidentally link to him. With his mind reading, he was one of the few people who could tell when he was being psychically spied upon. It was how we met, and in the unlikely event that he *had* tried to kill me, I wasn't about to let him know he'd failed.

My eyes burned at the thought, but I forced the pain back. *Survival first, then heartbreak*, I reminded myself bleakly.

"I need to go back to the carnival," I said to Maximus, "and you can't come with me."

Chapter 9

"I look *ridiculous*."

I didn't turn, but continued to stride through the remains of the employee parking lot as though I belonged. We passed a few reporters mixed in with the throng of onlookers. The explosion brought out the gawkers as well as the bereaved.

"You're the one who insisted on coming." Spoken low so only he would hear me. "At least you no longer look like a reincarnation of Eric the Red, which is noticeable, by the way."

A scoff. "And this isn't?"

Now I did glance at him, taking in the thick black hair covering every inch of his exposed skin and the pronounced brows I'd applied with glue and some modeling clay. Considering the time crunch, I'd done a good job making him look like he had hypertrichosis, more commonly known as wolfman's disease.

"Not at a carnival it isn't."

My disguise was less dramatic. I wore a short

blond wig that matched the color of my new shaggy beard, plus about two pounds of gel inserts to give me the double-D's that nature never intended. My waist and butt were similarly padded, rounding out my figure into unrecognizable proportions. Stage makeup covered my scar where the beard didn't, and dark glasses completed my incognito look. Well, incognito for a carnival. Most of them had at least one bearded lady.

From the glare the barrel-bellied policeman threw Maximus and me, we succeeded at blending in.

"I told you people to stay back," he barked.

I hefted my fake boobs higher in their corseted confines. "My trailer was barely damaged," I said, pointing at an RV that had the least amount of soot. "Why can't I go in to get my purse? I need money to pay for a hotel room!"

"You noticed the big explosion, right? Once we finish *our* job, everyone can come get their stuff. Until then, stay with a friend. Doesn't wolfie have a pack he can call?"

The officer turned to go after his caustic rebuttal, but Maximus's growl stopped him. Guess he was taking his new disguise seriously.

"You want me to—" the officer began, only to fall silent as Maximus's gaze flared, mesmerizing him at once.

"Let us through," he said in a low, resonant voice.

The officer bobbed a nod. "Absolutely."

There were days when I envied vampires. This

was one of them. "Good thing you came. I'd hate to wait and risk them erasing all traces of the killer's essence," I murmured as Maximus and I ducked under bright crime scene tape.

Even with the fake hair, I caught his grim expression. "So would I." Then to the newly compliant officer, he said, "Walk with us. If anyone asks, we're witnesses you're interviewing."

Considering all the policemen, firemen, gas company employees, and other personnel hurrying about, we had a few minutes before we were stopped. With our new escort, we headed to Marty's trailer.

Even several hours after the explosion, the air was still thick with a mixture of gas, burnt rubber, and other, unspeakable things. I forced myself not to gag, but the urge was strong. So was the urge to burst into tears when I saw the blackened, hollowed shell that had served as my and Marty's home for years. Half of it was gone, either disintegrated from the ferocious heat or blasted into innumerable parts.

Staring at the ruined husk made the full reality of Marty's death hit me. A small, foolish part had secretly hoped he'd survived and hadn't heard me when I was yelling for him last night. That hope extinguished as thoroughly as his life would have when the explosion went off. The destruction was so complete, I doubted they would find enough remains for me to bury. Despite my resolve, a warm, wet trail slid down my cheek.

"Don't," Maximus said softly. "This isn't the time."

I swiped at the errant tear and squared my shoulders. He was right. Grieving would come later. Now, I had to find out who snuffed out Marty's life. Yet looking around, I wasn't sure where to start. The large crater in front of what used to be Marty's trailer? Farther up the gas line?

"What have you found so far?" Maximus asked. I turned, but the question wasn't directed at me.

"Last of the fires were only put out a couple hours ago, so not much," the officer replied in a monotone. His light brown eyes were fixed on Maximus as if glued. "Five dead, three more missing. Gas company's got the power off so we're checking the pipes. Found something in the pit near a twisted hunk of pipe—"

"Show me," Maximus interrupted.

The officer began to walk toward a tented area swarming with people wearing ATF jackets. I tugged at Maximus's sleeve.

"There's too many of them," I whispered.

"Come back," Maximus told the officer, who obeyed at once. "Get the object and meet us outside the east section of the barricade. Don't let anyone know what you're doing."

The officer left. I followed Maximus to the section of the barricade where there was the least amount of spectators. After ten minutes, the portly officer was back.

"Here," he said, pulling a bag out from under his shirt.

I took it, my bulky rubber gloves dispelling any fingerprint concerns. Those had been the next priority after Maximus purchased all the necessities for our disguises. Then I held up the bag, frowning. The clear cellophane revealed a few crumpled bits of wire and what looked to be a shard of plastic.

"That's it?"

The officer nodded. Maximus drew me to a lone hut about thirty yards away. Before last night, it had been a concession stand. Now it was empty, the harsh scent of chemical smoke replacing the popcorn, cotton candy, and funnel cake aromas. I took my right glove off with a sigh. I'd leave fingerprints this time, but I had no choice. Then I stroked the piece of plastic.

The first thing I relived was an investigator finding this shard. From his thoughts, I knew it wasn't plastic, but titanium, a material sometimes used in bomb making. Underneath that, I had the faintest impression of another person digging in the dark, but the essence trail was too weak. The fire must've burned most of the traces away.

"You were right. Doesn't look like an accident," I said.

"I knew it," Maximus muttered. "Did you see who did it?"

"No."

I stroked one of the wires next, disappointed

when the only impressions were from another crime scene investigator. Then I touched the final wire and the concession stand vanished.

I whistled as I pressed the wires into the plastique, then used thin surgical forceps to twine the ends around the trigger. After examining them, I closed the shell over the device and leaned back, taking off my mask. Finished. I gazed proudly at the bomb. By far my best work. Pity no one would appreciate its intricate design, but most of it would disintegrate on detonation. Just as the client wanted.

That image dissolved and I was back in the concession stand with a huge vampire disguised as the wolfman. I smiled at Maximus with a coldness I hadn't thought myself capable of.

"I've got the bomb maker."

Chapter 10

His name was Adrian, and it took two days of linking to him to discover where he lived. One of the drawbacks to finding people in the present was not being inside their heads. People didn't have their addresses tattooed onto their forearms, so determining their location wasn't always easy. Adrian didn't help me out that first day, either. He mostly slept.

The next morning, he walked to his local Starbucks, ordered a double shot of espresso, and then read the news on his iPhone. Twenty minutes later, Maximus and I were on our way to Chicago.

He drove. Chivalry or control freak, I didn't know, and after several hours, I didn't care. I'd stayed up most of the previous night trying to determine Adrian's location. On top of lost sleep, linking to someone for long periods of time drained me. I'd been determined to stay awake in case Maximus changed his mind about splitting up the drive, but at some point between Atlanta and Chicago, I nodded off.

I floated above a white hallway. Doors were at either end, one wide with a computer keypad that a curly-haired woman sat beside, the others so nondescript as to be drab.

That second set of doors opened and Vlad strode through. His trench coat was open, the sides fluttering like dark wings. I gasped, trying to disappear into the ceiling, but he didn't seem to notice me. He continued down the hallway at a pace that had the doctor behind him running to keep up.

The curly-haired guard rose. "Who are you?"

"Shut up and open that door," Vlad snarled.

He'd passed by me, so I couldn't see if his eyes were lit up. Even if they weren't, the barely restrained violence in his tone must've been enough for the female guard. She punched in a few numbers on the keypad and the wide door swung open.

As soon as the doctor caught up, Vlad grasped him by the collar, lifting him off his feet. "Now, show me her body."

Another snarl that throbbed with the promise of the grave. The doctor nodded as much as Vlad's fist around his neck allowed. Vlad dropped him, and once he righted himself, the doctor hurried inside the room, Vlad right behind him.

I knew I should leave, but I couldn't stop myself from floating toward the open doorway. Before I reached it, I heard a metallic creak and then Vlad's harsh "Now get out."

The doctor ran from the room, his head pass-

ing through my legs as his body briefly converged with mine. My formless state should have worried me, yet I was oddly unconcerned. If I was dead, there was nothing I could do to change that. Plus, as long as I didn't have a real body, then Vlad wouldn't know I was here. I floated past the guard, who was huddled behind her chair, mumbling something that sounded like a prayer.

Even though no one had been able to see me thus far, I only peeked into the room beyond. It had several metal tables, a long sink with multiple basins, and a wall made up entirely of what appeared to be square steel cabinets.

Vlad stood next to an open cabinet in the wall. A slab holding a black plastic bag jutted out in front of him. His head was bowed, dark hair hiding his expression as he unzipped the bag. Fire engulfed him from hands to shoulders as he stared at its contents. Then, very slowly, those flames extinguished as he reached inside.

Now I knew where I was. A morgue, and though I had a good idea of what was in the bag, I had to be sure. I floated over, keeping close to the ceiling, and peered down.

My first surprise was how little it contained. A skull, two femurs, and a spine comprised the pieces big enough for me to identify. After that, it was anyone's guess as to what the other charred, smaller bits were. My next surprise was seeing Vlad stroke the bones. He traced the curve of the spine, the length of the femurs, and then the skull,

*all with a touch so gentle it barely disturbed them.
I still couldn't see his face, but the light piercing
through his hair was so intense that I half expected
it to burn the bones like twin emerald lasers.*

*My biggest shock was hearing him sigh, "Leila,"
as he stroked the bones. He thought these were
mine? But Vlad was in Romania and I'd suppos-
edly been blown to bits in Georgia—*

*Wait. Vlad had spoken to the guard and the
doctor in* English. *I looked around. The signs were
in English, too. Had Vlad gone to Georgia upon
hearing of my purported demise?*

*If so, I wished I knew what he was feeling at
this moment! Satisfaction, if he really was behind
the gas line bomb? Or grief, if someone else had
planted it and he thought this bag's contents was
all that was left of me?*

*His head remained bowed, hiding his expres-
sion.* Look up, Vlad! *I silently roared. If he smiled
as he stroked the remains, it would confirm my
worst suspicions, but what if grief was etched on
his face instead?*

*Suddenly, he did look up—and seemed to be
staring right at me. It still didn't answer my question. His gaze was so bright that his expression
blurred by comparison.*

"Leila."

I jerked, but it wasn't Vlad who said my name.
It was another man's voice, accompanied by a hard
jostle. I snapped into alertness, the morgue trans-
forming into the front seat of a car. Maximus let

go of my shoulder, frowning before he returned his attention back to the road.

"Must've been some dream. You started trembling."

I didn't doubt it. My hands still shook and I kept looking around the car as if expecting Vlad to magically appear. I'd had vivid dreams before, but none had ever felt *this* real.

I glanced at my hands, relieved that I still had my gloves on. They not only kept my currents in, they also kept my ability to accidentally connect to someone *out*. Not that I'd ever linked to anyone in my sleep before. Linking took concentration, and sleep was the antithesis of concentration.

"You're still trembling. Are you all right?"

"Yeah," I replied. "It's nothing. I don't even remember what the dream was about."

His raised brow said, *Bullshit*, more eloquently than words, but he didn't push and I pretended that I hadn't lied.

"Now that you're up, link to the bomber. We're only an hour from Chicago. If he's not home, I want to know where he went."

Good idea. I pulled out the pouch I'd stuck in the drink holder and then took off my right glove. We'd returned the plastic evidence bag to the officer minus one piece of wire.

I rubbed that wire, bypassing the first images to focus on the replay of Adrian whistling as he made the bomb. His imprint was as strong as before, but when I attempted to follow it back to its source, I came up against a brick wall of . . . nothingness.

I tried again, concentrating until the traffic sounds faded into soft white noise. Though I focused with all of my might, I couldn't find anything at the end of that essence trail.

"Is he still home?" Maximus pressed.

Frustration mingled with a sense of foreboding. "I don't know. I can't see him. Either I'm temporarily out of juice, or . . ."

I didn't need to finish the sentence. Maximus's lips thinned into a hard line. Then he stomped on the gas pedal.

The flashing lights, crime scene tape, and stench of smoke were becoming all too familiar. We'd had to park over a block away since the street Adrian lived on was cordoned off. Though I couldn't see any house numbers at this distance, I'd bet Adrian's was the one that the firemen were still hosing down.

"Son of a bitch," Maximus spat.

"Whoever's behind this must not like loose ends," I replied, while inside, I cursed. I doubted this was a case of a bomb accidentally detonating while Adrian tinkered with it, though I was sure it had been staged to look that way.

We still had a chance to see what really happened, but we needed to hurry. Even if the killer was still in the area, he wouldn't be for long.

"Maximus, go down there and get me a bone off the body."

Confusion flashed across his face. Then he smiled. That was the last thing I saw before he sped away, reminding me of a large, charging lion. Less than a minute later, I heard a gunshot and the whoop of a police siren. Then he was back with a charred hunk of something in his hand.

"Let's go," he said at once.

I grimaced at the burnt meat smell. If I survived all this, I might become a vegetarian. The reek didn't seem to bother Maximus. He tucked the chunk into his coat and walked me back to our car as more sirens went off. The cops probably hadn't seen every detail of what just happened, but from the sounds, they knew enough to be alarmed.

I got into the car, forcing back a gag as the closed interior made the stench worse. Maximus quickly sped us away. After a few minutes, he took the blackened chunk out of his coat and plunked it onto my lap with a muttered "Here."

I couldn't help it—I shrieked. He slammed on the brakes, causing the thing to hit the windshield with a splat. I shrieked again when it smacked back onto my lap, smearing my pants with soot and thicker, grosser things.

He looked around, one hand on the wheel, another holding a large silver knife.

"What's wrong?"

"What's wrong?" I repeated, days of pent-up grief and stress making my voice shrill. "You slapped a smoldering body part onto me without even a warning, *that's* what's wrong!"

His brows drew together. "But you asked me to get that."

"I know I did!"

Frustrated, I swiped my hair off my face only to feel something slimy. A glance at my gloved hand was the final straw. I'd just smeared blackened bomber goo onto my cheek.

I flung the body part in Maximus's direction and got out of the car. My slimy gloves came off next as I ran to the nearest sidewalk. Then off came my jacket, but before I threw it away, I wadded it up and scrubbed furiously at my cheek. My shirt also had revolting smears on it, so it went flying, too, leaving me in nothing but a bra, jeans, and sneakers. I dashed down the sidewalk without any real idea what I was doing or where I was going. All I knew was that I couldn't stand to be covered in my attempted murderer's stinking goo for another second.

"Leila!"

I ignored the shout, not that it mattered. Maximus caught me in the next heartbeat, spinning me around to face him.

"Don't touch me," I snapped, rational thought replaced by a wounded animal mentality. "You've got him all over you!"

His coat and shirt were on the ground before I could blink. At this hour, the stores around us were closed, but streetlights threw every inch of his upper body into stark relief. Like Vlad, Maximus had many faded marks from old scars, but unlike

Vlad, his chest was smooth. No crisp dark hair, just pale, taut skin stretched over muscles that rippled when he folded me into his arms. He didn't flinch as currents slid into him from touching my bare flesh. He drew me closer instead.

"It's all right," he said softly. "You're safe now."

I hadn't realized how much I needed to hear that until he said it. All the pain, loneliness, and grief from the past two weeks reared up, seeking solace anywhere it could be found. I don't know if he bent his head or if I lifted mine. All I knew was he was kissing me, and for the first time since this whole terrible ordeal began, I didn't feel alone and rejected.

When his tongue slid into my mouth, I welcomed it. He'd kissed me before, months ago, and back then, I'd felt mild enjoyment but no real emotion. This time, I was filled with such aching loneliness that I explored his mouth as thoroughly as he did mine. It didn't matter that he wasn't the man I loved. All that mattered was he was here.

After several moments, Maximus pulled away.

"I wish I didn't care about you so much."

"What?" I asked breathlessly. Vampires might not need oxygen, but I couldn't kiss like that without paying a price.

His eyes resembled the nearby traffic light with how green they were. "You're overstressed, overtired, and emotionally vulnerable. I won't take advantage of that, but if I cared less about you, Leila"—his voice deepened—"we'd be in the nearest alley with your legs wrapped around my waist right now."

Heat should have swelled at that explicit image. Instead, an icy bucket of shame washed over me. What was I *doing*? Despite my actions, I didn't want to start anything with Maximus. I wanted to find Marty's killer—who hopefully wouldn't turn out to be Vlad—murder that person, and then grieve for my best friend while putting my life back together. Getting involved with my ex's right-hand man wasn't anywhere on my list.

Maximus must have sensed the change because he let me go, his gaze turning from glowing emerald back to smoky gray.

"My point exactly," he said, dryness etching each word.

I crossed my arms over my chest, wishing I hadn't thrown my coat *and* shirt away. "Sorry. I didn't mean to, ah—"

"Save it," he interrupted crisply. Then his voice softened. "I understand. You needed to feel something good in the midst of everything crumbling around you, even if it was only for a moment. Humans don't have a monopoly on that, Leila. Vampires need it sometimes, too."

Then he picked up his discarded shirt and coat, giving me a single hard stare before he turned away.

"But right now, we need to get back to the car and then *you* need to find out who killed that bomb maker."

Chapter II

 It didn't take long to find the images I sought. Although nothing was more densely packed with memories than a person's bones, death was a stand-out event for everyone. Pity the images only played like clips from a film reel instead of me being inside Adrian's head when his murderer came calling.

"Who is it?" Adrian replied to the knock, as if he wasn't looking at the other side of the door through a security feed.

"Don't be boring, dearie" was the reply he received.

My brows went up. Adrian's killer was a woman. She didn't have an accent so much as a pretty lilt to her speech, but I doubted her nationality was American.

Adrian minimized the screen before he opened the door. The woman walked in, wearing dark glasses and a scarf around her head. To make matters worse, what I could see of her face seemed blurry. What a time for my psychic vision to need a tune-up.

"Make yourself at home," Adrian drawled, shutting the door behind her. "You thirsty?"

"Of course," she purred.

That tone would've screamed, Danger! *to me, but Adrian didn't seem to notice.* "What'll it be?" he asked.

"When we're done, your blood," she replied pleasantly.

He turned, startled, and then froze as she took her glasses off. Though her face was still blurred, the inhuman glow from her eyes came through clearly. I could almost see Adrian's willpower being hijacked under that hypnotic gaze. If he hadn't made a bomb that killed my best friend, I would've pitied him.

"You will erase all records of our dealings, from bank transactions to the camera feed at your door," the woman stated.

No! *I thought, but of course that didn't change Adrian's actions. He went to his computer, booted up a bunch of files, and then methodically deleted them. He even erased secondary backups and ghost files, too, much to my dismay.*

"It's done," he said woodenly once he was finished.

The woman took off her scarf. I caught a flash of rich, dark hair before everything blurred again.

"Time for that drink now, dearie."

Then she yanked Adrian's head to the side and

*bit down on his neck. When his death ended the
vision, my frustration grew.*

Not once had I gotten a good look at her face.

"Five foot four, about a hundred and twenty
pounds, dark hair, and a slight accent that could
be Welsh, English, Scottish, or Irish."

Maximus scowled. "That's all you got? A female
vampire that *might* be from the UK?"

I knew how useless that information was. "I'll
try linking to her again, see if it works better this
time."

Despite my disgust, for a second time I rubbed
the burnt piece that Maximus had yanked off of
Adrian's body. Flashes of lights followed a rocking
sensation, but when I concentrated harder, those
images faded and I began to feel dizzy.

"Leila? Are you all right?"

"Fine. Just a little carsick," I muttered, trying
again. After a few moments, I caught a glimpse
of a woman wearing the same outfit as Adrian's
killer, but that and the thick spill of walnut-colored
hair was the only way I could be sure it was her.
Her features were completely indistinguishable.
The tiny blue room she was in rocked, which was
odd. Then all my attention focused on what she
was saying.

" . . . no, it wasn't too risky . . . I took care of it,
dearie. He's dead, ending any chance this will be
traced back to us."

From how she spoke, she must be on the phone.

I stared at the blurred spot where her face would be, concentrating, but instead of getting better, it made the haziness worse.

"You're overreacting," she went on. "Even if there are suspicions, they won't lead anywhere. Whatever she might have been worth to him alive, she's less dangerous to us dead . . ."

I tried to focus on her more, but then my dizziness came back with a vengeance. My ears rang, too, and I felt something wet trickle out of them.

Maximus swore. Then the car swung so sharply that it fishtailed, adding crashing to my list of concerns. I couldn't seem to voice a complaint, though, and now the only thing I saw were large black spots. *That can't be good*, I thought, right before something hard smacked me in the forehead.

I had a few minutes of blissful nothingness until I became aware that I was choking on coppery-tasting liquid. I tried to spit it out, but a hand clamped over my mouth.

"Swallow, dammit!"

Left with no other choice, I did, grimacing as I recognized the taste. Vampire blood. Pureed pennies would've been less repugnant. I opened my eyes to find Maximus crouched over me. My seat belt was off and my seat was all the way reclined. At least he'd pulled over before utterly ignoring the road.

"Yuck," I said once he finally dropped his hand.

He didn't look offended so much as relieved. That's when I noticed both his hands were smeared in red and so was the front of my shirt. This couldn't all be from Maximus forcing me to drink his blood. That whole lack of a pulse meant vampires didn't bleed much even when they were cut. Add that to the steering wheel being ripped off, and I'd missed something big.

"What happened?"

He tossed the steering wheel into the back before flopping back into the driver's seat. "You started hemorrhaging from your eyes, ears, and nose. Then your heart stopped. I had to give you CPR and blood to bring you back."

Hearing that I'd come so close to dying should've terrified me, but all I could muster up was a weary "This day sucks."

Maximus's incredulous expression made me want to laugh, an even more irrational response, but what was I supposed to do? I couldn't cry because that wouldn't fix anything and we didn't have time for me to slowly rock myself while shaking, which was the only other thing that sounded appealing.

"I must be using too much power within too short a time," I said. "Plus, I'm not fireproof anymore, but remnants of Vlad's aura might still be messing with my system. Between the two, I should've guessed that my body couldn't handle it."

Maximus still stared at me as though he couldn't believe my nonchalance over almost dying. I ignored that, directing my attention to more important issues.

"What happened to the steering wheel?"

"It was in my way when you needed help" was his reply.

"Well." I forced a smile that must've been lopsided at best. "Thanks. Too bad we have to get another car now."

His teeth flashed in a matching humorless grin. "That's the least of our problems."

Great. "What's the worst of them?"

Maximus pulled out his cell phone and wagged it at me. It didn't ring but the screen was lit up, showing an incoming call.

"This is the third time Vlad's tried to reach me. I have to answer or he'll get suspicious."

"Don't you—!"

Maximus held up a finger. "Don't even breathe loud," he muttered before answering his phone with a brief "Yes?"

I froze when I heard Vlad's voice. That familiar, cultured cadence affected me so much that for a few moments, I didn't breathe at all.

"Maximus," my ex said coolly. "Am I interrupting anything?"

Smoky gray eyes bored into mine as Maximus replied, "No, why?" in a tone so casual that I blinked. Good liar, I noted for future reference.

"Because this is my third call" was Vlad's implacable reply. Guess it was too late to keep him from being suspicious.

"I left my phone in the car while I found someone to eat," Maximus said glibly. "Everything all right?"

Even if I wasn't a couple feet away in a closed space, I still would've heard Vlad's whiplike reply. "No, everything is not all right. When did you last see Leila?"

I couldn't help it—I sucked in an audible breath. Maximus frowned at me before responding with "Last week, when I dropped her off at Marty's trailer in Atlanta."

Nothing from Vlad for so long, I wondered if he was speaking too softly for a nonvampire to overhear. Then Maximus asked, "Are you still there?" dispelling that idea.

"Yes."

One word, bit out so harshly that I flinched. Something had Vlad furious. I wanted to grab the phone and demand to know if he'd tried to kill me, but of course, I didn't. I waited, breathing as shallowly as I could despite my heart racing.

"Why did you ask about Leila?" Maximus prodded, still doing a great job of sounding guileless.

Another loaded silence. Then Vlad replied, "She's dead," in a tone so casual that tears sprang to my eyes. Even if he hadn't ordered it, he didn't care. Hearing the apathy in his voice cut me in places I didn't even know I had.

I must've made some sound because Maximus scowled while holding his finger to his lips in the universal command for silence. Then he said, "What? How?" with such believable shock that I mentally upgraded him from Good Liar to Fantastic One.

"A gas line ruptured near Martin's trailer. I'm told both of them were killed instantly in the explosion. I leave for America tonight to return Leila's remains to her family."

Oh shit! In the midst of everything, I'd forgotten Gretchen and my father would also think I'd been killed. I began to mime at Maximus that we needed to stop Vlad, but he clapped a hand over my mouth, tightening it when I grunted.

"That's terrible," he said, rolling down the car window with his other hand. Traffic noises soon merged with my grunts, muffling them. If he hadn't saved my life twice in the past week, I would've taken off my gloves and dosed him with enough electricity to make him glow, but he had so all I did was glare.

Well, that and I bit him. He deserved it.

"Yes, tragic," Vlad said, sounding bored this time. "Meet me in Atlanta tomorrow. We'll fly from there to Gretchen's."

"That might be difficult," Maximus replied, flashing his fangs at me when I continued to chomp on the fleshy part of his hand. I took that as *Keep it up and I'll bite you back* so I stopped after one final, angry nip.

Iciness returned to Vlad's voice. "Why?"

"I told you I was checking on some of my people while I was in the States. Seems a couple of the younger ones have taken to feeding in the open. I have to deal with that, of course."

"Of course," Vlad all but purred. "If you don't

punish their disobedience now, who knows what betrayals they'll inflict on you in the future?"

From the way Maximus's features hardened, he, too, thought those comments were more warning than instruction.

"Pass on my condolences to Leila's family," he said, mouthing, *Don't make a sound* at me.

Since his hand was still clamped over my mouth, I couldn't, but my glare promised that we weren't done with this.

"I will," Vlad replied.

Then they hung up. Vampires weren't big on saying good-bye, as I'd learned after years of living with Marty. Once he double-checked that the call had truly ended, Maximus took his hand away from my mouth.

"We can't let my family believe I'm dead" were my first words. "That's too cruel."

"What's more important? Their safety, or their temporary sadness?" he retorted, nailing me with a hard stare.

"Safety? They have nothing to do with this!"

"Not yet," he countered ruthlessly, "but they will, if you reveal that you're alive. You think they can fool Vlad? One *sniff* and he'll know they're only faking grief."

Despite his logic, I was torn. My dad was strong, but I didn't know how much Gretchen could take. She still had emotional scars from finding me after a failed suicide attempt a decade ago when my new abilities had nearly broken me.

"I still don't think Vlad is behind the bomb. He might not care that I'm dead, but if we play on his pride, he'd be a hell of an ally while we looked for the real person responsible."

The look Maximus gave me was both annoyed and pitying. "He'd also be a worse enemy if you're wrong, and then what do you think will happen to your family?"

I banged my fists against the car seat. Yeah, I knew. Vlad would use them against me. Even if he wasn't behind this, the real killer would, if it leaked that I was alive. The best way to protect my family was to let them think I'd died—and hope one day they'd forgive me for the deception.

I sighed. "They're going to hate me for this."

"But they'll be alive to hate you," Maximus pointed out, and that was the most important thing.

I shot him a grim look as something else dawned on me.

"Even if Vlad isn't responsible, what are you going to do when he discovers you've been lying to him this whole time?"

From the way Maximus's expression closed off, he'd already thought of this. "I'll have to convince him not to kill me," he said, voice light as if he were discussing a game.

I closed my eyes, struck with a sudden, irrational urge to pray. That would be easier said than done, as we both knew.

Chapter 12

 Maximus green-eyed a passing motorist into taking us to a Motel 6 inside the Indiana border. Once there, I forced myself to eat the drive-through food Maximus had gotten me even though traveling with a body part had killed my appetite. Then I showered before tumbling into the unoccupied second bed.

Despite having slept only a few hours the past couple days, I was wide awake. Maximus, on the other hand, seemed to fall asleep as soon as his head hit the pillow.

I glanced at the plastic baggie on the table between us. At least the smell from Adrian's crispy . . . whatever was contained. I couldn't risk using it to link to the female vampire again for a few days. I needed regular doses of vampire blood to stay alive even when I *wasn't* overusing my abilities, or dealing with the lingering aftermath of a pyrokinetic aura embedded in me.

Once again, I found myself envying vampires, this time for their instant healing. If I wasn't human, I could start tracking Adrian's killer now instead of in a few days. Being limited by my fragile mortality was frustrating, but I'd turned down my chance to switch sides. With Marty gone and Vlad and I broken up, there wasn't another vampire I'd trust enough to "sire" me. Vlad had been right about it being an unbreakable bond. I doubted I'd ever feel close enough to another vampire to want that permanent connection with them.

Still, some rest, regular nutrition, and vampire blood should recuperate me enough to track down my would-be killer without risking another hemorrhage and heart attack. Even if it didn't, I'd try again in a few days. The brunette vampire's pretty face flashed across my mind, bringing a fresh surge of determination. Marty and Dawn deserved to be avenged and my family deserved to be safe. Stopping that woman—and whoever had sent her—was worth the risk.

I floated inside a luxurious private aircraft, knowing at once where I was. Vlad's plane. He was only a few feet away, wearing a charcoal trench coat over black pants and a black shirt. It was the same outfit I'd imagined him in at the morgue, but he wasn't threatening anyone now. His eyes were closed, hair spilling over his shoulders to blend into his dark clothes.

This had to be another dream. Since none of this was real, I could do what I'd secretly longed to do the past couple weeks. I floated over to Vlad and lowered myself until I hovered next to him, reaching out to stroke his face.

I didn't feel the stubble that clung to his jaw. Instead, my hand disappeared through his face. Still, touching him fulfilled a need that had clawed at me night and day since I left him. Even though everything had gone to hell and Vlad might be the very person I was running from, I couldn't stop myself from stroking his cheek, his brows, and finally his lips. Part of me hated him for his callous treatment, but the rest of me still missed him so much it hurt.

"I see your powers are back, Leila."

I jerked away, fleeing to the far side of the aircraft. Vlad's eyes were still closed, but the sardonic curl to his mouth told me I hadn't imagined the words.

"This is only a dream," I stated, more to myself than him. "And we're on your plane because you told Maximus you were flying to America, so my subconscious used that detail."

See? Nothing to worry about, I reassured myself. Too bad he wouldn't shut up so I could siphon off a few more moments of solace. Figures even in a dream, Vlad wouldn't be cooperative.

"You're with Maximus." A statement, not a question.

I shrugged even though he couldn't see it. "That's none of your business."

Flames appeared, crawling up from his hands to his upper arms. "Oh, but it is."

Then his eyes opened and he sat up, looking around as if to pinpoint my location. I waved my hand back and forth, pleased when he didn't so much as glance in my direction. Vlad always seemed to know where I was before when I spied on him, further proof that none of this was real.

"It ceased to become your business when you walked away from us without a backward glance," I said, relishing the chance to unload some hurt. Thank you, subconscious!

"I *walked away?*" His snort managed to be both contemptuous and elegant. "I offered you everything, yet you spurned it all. I've had enemies be less merciless in their dealings."

I grabbed his shoulders but my hands went right through. So much for shaking some sense into him!

"Me merciless? All I wanted was for you to love me, but according to you, THAT was asking too much."

Those flames extinguished. Good. I didn't want to dream about him accidentally blowing up his plane.

"Words." His tone sharpened. "I shared my house, my bed, and my blood with you, as well as offered you a place in my life forever. What are words compared to that?"

I sighed, my anger dissipating as quickly as his flames had. "Oh, Vlad, if you believed that, you would've told me what I wanted to hear to just ap-

pease me. You didn't, which proves saying 'I love you' means more to you than everything else."

His brows drew together like thunderclouds. "Enough of this. Tell me where you are."

I almost said, "South Bend, Indiana" because what was the harm in telling Dream Vlad? Then I paused. Why would I gratify Dream Vlad, either?

"I'm at the corner of None of Your Business and Screw You."

His fist slammed down, knocking the armrest off. "Don't test me. You know the gas line explosion wasn't an accident."

"And I also know who might've been behind it," I countered nastily even though I didn't believe it.

His fists clenched and unclenched. If this wasn't a dream, I'd swear I smelled smoke. "You can't think it was me."

Another shrug he couldn't see. "Maximus says your pride might have prompted a little payback for me leaving you."

A noise escaped Vlad that was too visceral to be called a snarl. "He's signed his own death warrant twice, then."

Even imaginary, there was no reasoning with him. "I need to wake up. This dream sucks."

"You're asleep? Is that why your voice is fainter and I can't catch most of your thoughts?"

Alarm bells began to ring. This better be my subconscious being VERY creative.

He must have taken my silence as a yes. Vlad smiled, foreboding expression changing to infuriating satisfaction.

"You won't contact me when you're awake, but you reach out to me in your sleep. That should tell you who you really trust."

I began pinching my arm. Hard. Dream or not, it was too upsetting to keep talking to him.

"Think on this when you wake," he continued, honeyed steel dripping off each word. "Maximus has always wanted you. Since the explosion, he has you believing he's your savior and you can't trust anyone else. A happy coincidence?"

Wake up, wake up! *I mentally chanted. Out loud, I said,* "Maximus wouldn't hurt me, whereas you kept doing that even when you weren't trying to."

Vlad's smile faded, though his lips remained drawn back, revealing fangs longer than I'd ever seen before.

"I'm coming for you, Leila. If you care for Maximus, then you'll leave him and then contact me with your location. That will give him a chance to run. Otherwise, you'll watch me kill him when I catch up with you."

You wouldn't dare! *trembled on my lips, but I didn't say it out loud because I knew very well that he would.*

"I don't know why I ever thought I loved you" *was what I barked instead, fear and anger making my tone brutal.*

Something flashed across Vlad's face that, on

any other man, I would've said was pain. But that was impossible. Even in a dream, Vlad didn't care enough for me to hurt him.

That proved true when his expression became detached again. "I'll see you soon," he said, waving as if in dismissal.

A surge of fury had me bolting upright in bed. My abrupt movement startled Maximus, who awoke with far more alertness. I was still processing the fact that my dream was over when he was right in front of me, big hands framing my face.

"Not again," he muttered, cutting his wrist with a fang.

"Stop," I protested when he held his bloody wrist against my mouth, but that and swatting at his arm made no difference.

"Swallow," he said sternly.

I did, cursing vampires and their highhandedness the whole time. When he finally removed his wrist, I shoved him, but it had as much effect as a fly trying to bring down a brick wall.

"What the hell?" I snapped.

He flicked my nose before showing me his red finger. "You started bleeding. I wasn't waiting to see if your heart stopped again, too."

Another nosebleed? But I hadn't been using my powers—

My gaze darted down. Yep, the gloves were still on, plus there was that whole impossibility factor with connecting to someone in my sleep. Still, the coincidences were piling up.

"Call Vlad," I said, seized with a near desperate urge to be proven wrong.

Both his brows shot up. "Why?"

"To see if he"—*threatens your life, tells you to put me on the phone, anything like that*—"sounds weird," I finished lamely.

Maximus stared at me, skepticism written all over his face.

"It's important," I said, gripping his upper arm.

After another penetrating stare, he went over to where he'd thrown his coat and pulled out his cell phone.

"Vlad," he said after a brief pause. "Sorry. I must've unintentionally redialed the last number that called me . . ."

I waited with indrawn breath, expecting to hear my name amidst an explosion of threats. But although I could make out Vlad's voice on the other line, he spoke too softly for the words to be clear. After a minute, Maximus hung up and shrugged.

"He sounds fine."

I let out my breath in a sigh that seemed to come from my soul. *Only a dream!* trumpeted across my mind. No matter how it felt or my spontaneous nosebleed, if it had been real, Vlad would've torn into Maximus as soon as he heard his voice—

I froze, claws of doubt skittering up my spine. *Or would he?* Vlad told me to get away from Maximus and then contact him. If Maximus knew the jig surrounding my purported death was up, he wouldn't let me out of his sight long enough for me to do that. Vlad also insinuated that *Maximus* might be the one behind the gas line bomb. If he believed that, would he tip his hand about my ability to contact him in my sleep?

No. Vlad was cunning to the point of being a sociopath. He'd never reveal such an advantage until it was too late.

Of course, there was another possibility. Vlad might not reveal that I'd contacted him in my dreams just to mess with me.

"Going to tell me why I just crank-called my sire?"

Maximus's wry voice cut through my musings. Even though I didn't believe the insinuations Dream Vlad had levied, niggling doubts kept me from replying with the truth.

"I, um, had a dream that his plane crashed," I said, managing to hold his gaze despite feeling like I had "Liar!" written in neon lights on my forehead.

A grunt. "You need to get over him. You'll only make yourself crazy if you don't."

Make myself crazy? I thought bleakly. All signs indicated that I was already there.

Chapter 13

 Sweat dampened my clothes and my muscles screamed, but I kept lifting and lowering my legs in a smooth, controlled rhythm. One hundred thirty-nine . . . one hundred forty . . .

"You've got to stop. This isn't healthy."

Maximus's arms were crossed, his handsome features creased into a scowl. I ignored him, continuing my leg lifts.

Cool hands locked around my ankles, keeping me from my next set of lifts. "I mean it, Leila. Stop."

I glared up at him. "Let me go."

His grip only tightened. "Not until you tell me what's been eating you the past few days."

Laughter came out in pants from my exertions. "Should I start with my best friend being blown to smithereens, or skip to the part where you think his killer may be my ex-boyfriend?"

Or maybe even you? my nasty inner voice added.

I tried to ignore that voice, but it had been growing louder. Maximus claimed he hadn't known about my being fireproof, but he could've overheard that while I'd been living at Vlad's. He'd helped me find the bomber, but what if that was because he knew Adrian would already be dead? Since then, he'd been adamant about me holding off on looking for the female vampire, citing concerns for my health. But what if the heart attack never happened? What if the only repercussions from me overusing my powers were a nosebleed?

"Something else is bothering you," Maximus said, letting go of my ankles. I sat up and carefully picked my words.

"Exercise helps keep me strong and I'll need that to link to the female vampire tomorrow. I've waited long enough."

Maximus grunted. "Some days, you remind me of Vlad."

"Meaning?" I asked sharply.

"Your obsession with revenge. Next you'll want to drive a pole through that vampire once you find her."

The thought *was* appealing, but . . .

"It's not just revenge. My family will have targets on their backs as soon as the killers find out I'm alive." Then I switched tactics. "Besides, I keep having nightmares about Vlad finding us. Exercise helps me sleep without those."

All true. I'd let myself off easy last night and regretted it when Dream Vlad told me he was closing in on me. It wasn't real, but I woke up with a nosebleed and a sense of foreboding anyway, both of which I hid from Maximus.

His gray gaze became tinged with green. "There are other ways to tire yourself out before sleeping."

This was the first time since our sidewalk kiss that he'd made a pass; pretty chivalrous considering we'd been locked in the same room for the past three days. I was about to let him down gently when that inner voice roared to the surface.

Now's your chance! Take your gloves off and touch him. If the brunette's essence is anywhere on him, he's guilty as hell.

I paused. Could I be so ruthless?

You're swimming with sharks, that pitiless voice snapped. *Either grow some teeth or get eaten.*

Maximus's gaze grew brighter. Little did he know *why* I was considering his offer. Guilt competed with cold practicality. Maximus had been nothing but kind to me, but how well did I truly know him? For that matter, Vlad had known him for centuries, yet Maximus was still going behind his back now.

Marty's face flashed in my mind, followed by my dad's and Gretchen's. Someone had murdered my best friend and would hurt my family to lure me out. I couldn't afford to be naively trusting when I could be sure instead.

Very slowly, I stripped off my gloves. Maximus's eyes gleamed brighter, bathing the room in a soft emerald glow. Then he came over and knelt, each movement deliberate, as if anything sudden would startle me into bolting.

It might. My heart beat so fast it made me slightly

dizzy. I was about to play a sensual version of Russian roulette with the nearly thousand-year-old, six-and-a-half-foot vampire crouched in front of me. There was a fine line between survival and recklessness, and right now, I wasn't sure which side my actions fell on.

Maximus came closer with that slow, leonine crawl. When he was only inches away, he inhaled, and a frown stitched his brow.

"What's wrong?"

Damn vampires and their ability to decipher emotions by scent. I glanced at my hands and then back at him. Lies were more convincing when peppered with the truth.

"I don't want to hurt you, but I don't want to put my gloves back on." I swallowed a lump that wasn't entirely made up of nervousness. "I—I want to touch you."

A low growl sent icy-hot chills up my spine. Before my next breath, I was in his arms. He kissed me with an intensity that briefly made me forget my objective. Then he pulled me onto his lap, shifting until I straddled him.

A large bulge jutted between my thighs. He grasped my hips and rocked me against it, that hard length rubbing my most sensitive spot. I gasped, but with a touch of despair. It felt good, but also . . . meaningless. With sudden clarity, I understood the difference between lust and lovemaking. If I had sex with Maximus, I'd enjoy it the same way I enjoyed Chinese food—with the knowledge that too soon, I'd feel empty inside again.

Damn Vlad! Even in another man's arms, the memory of that hardhearted vampire tormented me. I tore my mouth away.

"Maximus, stop."

His hands stilled, but he gave my neck a long, hungry lick.

"What's wrong?"

For starters, you're not the man I'm still in love with. Besides that, I'm not sure I can trust you. "I . . . it's too soon."

I dropped my head as I said the words, letting my fingers play over his shoulders as if in apology. *No trace of foreign essences there.* Then I sat back with a sigh, trailing my hands down his arms. An all-too-familiar essence thread popped up, making me silently curse Vlad again. He wasn't only embedded in my skin; he was in Maximus's, too.

His hands slid over my thigh. "Too soon for sex, perhaps, but there are other things we can do."

I stopped his hands by working down his arms to grip them.

"Sorry. It's, ah, too soon for that, too."

His disappointed sigh made me feel guilty. *Tease!* my conscience mocked. That devious inner voice didn't care. It urged me to grasp Maximus's hands in a pretense of concern while I searched them for incriminating essence traces.

"It's fine." Wry smile. "I'm not getting any older."

Another essence trail *was* imprinted on his right

hand, but it didn't belong to the brunette vampire or to Vlad. Whoever it was felt very guilty when he—or she—touched Maximus, but if it wasn't the female killer, it wasn't my business.

"Thanks for understanding," I said before dropping my hands and rising. "I, ah, think I'll hit the shower now."

I wouldn't even need to make it a cold one. For the third time, I cursed Vlad. It wasn't fair that he'd been the only man to inflame my heart *and* my body. Wherever he was, I hoped my memory still burned him inside and out, too.

Maximus got up, too. Then his head cocked as if listening—and I was on the floor, his big body protecting mine from an explosion of glass. Over the noise from our window shattering, I heard him groan. Felt him shudder so violently that his grip became excruciating, but before I could scream, he let go. Then he grabbed several knives and leapt up.

I did, too, voltage surging to my right hand from a double shot of fear and adrenaline. Vlad must have found us! This was the same way he'd stormed a hotel room when we first met. I expected fire to soon surround us, but it didn't. Instead, another volley of gunfire sounded. Maximus knocked me down and shielded me once again, but this time, he didn't leap up after the barrage stopped. He slumped forward, agony streaking his face as vividly as the bloody holes all over his body.

"Bullets are liquid silver," he rasped. "Run!"

I was horrified. Even a vampire's regenerative abilities wouldn't be able to expel that, and not only would it near-paralyze Maximus, it would feel like acid burning all through him. I shoved him off me, but not to run. To slice an electric bolt through whoever tried to shoot him with that poison again. I yanked my gloves off, grimly satisfied at the unearthly glow suffusing my right hand. Then I held it up while letting loose a snarl of my own.

"You want to kill him, Vlad? You'll have to go through me!"

Mocking laughter met this statement. The door didn't open—it flew across the room to smash against the bed. A cloaked figure appeared in the door frame, face in shadows, but I caught a glimpse of dark hair. I tensed, my heart twisting even as the electricity channeling into my hand became more intense. Could I kill the man I loved to protect the man I didn't?

"If you want him to live, don't move."

Moonlight fell onto the cloaked man's face, revealing short black hair, a smooth jaw, and a wide, full mouth. Not Vlad, I realized, or anyone else I recognized. Who the hell was he?

The stranger smiled, showing fangs. "You have questions, but we only have time to answer one. Will he live or die?" Belittling nod at Maximus, who writhed in agony. "If you want him to die, fight me. You'll lose because I didn't come alone, and then we'll take you anyway and kill him. Leave with me willingly, however, and I'll let him live."

"Don't listen to him," Maximus managed to grit out.

I didn't glance his way because that would require taking my eyes off this stranger; a mistake I wouldn't make.

"I should trust you why?" I asked with heavy sarcasm.

His eyes flashed green. "Because I'd rather not lose my best leverage over you."

That single sentence spoke volumes. Whoever he was, he wasn't stupid. He also wasn't one of Vlad's men. Vlad wouldn't attempt to use Maximus as leverage against me. He'd know it was pointless since he'd already told me he was going to kill him.

Sirens sounded in the distance. The stranger sighed. "Time's up, little bird. Which will it be?"

My hand ached with the overload of currents coursing into it, but slowly, I lowered it. Now wasn't the time. Maximus cursed between ragged moans of pain. The stranger smiled.

"I heard you were smart. Let's hope your friend is, too."

Something hard jabbed me in the chest. I glanced down, seeing what looked like a dart sticking out of me. By the time I glanced back at the stranger, my vision was already starting to blur and my legs felt like they'd been replaced with jelly.

"Make sure you get her gloves" was the last thing I heard before everything went dark.

Chapter 14

When I came to, I didn't open my eyes or alter my breathing. Instead, I took inventory while pretending I was still unconscious. Headache, no surprise, but other than that I felt okay. My arms were behind my back. Thickness around my fingers was gloves, tightness around my wrists and ankles was restraints. Uncomfortable gag in my mouth, self-explanatory.

Then I moved on to my surroundings. The pitch and roll beneath me had to be waves, which meant I was on a boat. Some of my captors were topside, from the voices, but I could tell someone was in the room with me.

So when I opened my eyes, my gaze landed unerringly on the black-haired vampire who'd shot up the hotel last night. The only surprise he showed was to blink.

"Didn't expect you to be up already," he drawled.

I glanced down at my gag and back at him, raising a brow.

He translated the silent message. "Do I need to tell you that screaming is useless?"

I rolled my eyes. What was this, amateur day? He smiled before rising from the opposite berth. "I thought not."

The vampire looked to be around my age, but I judged him to be less than a hundred in undead years. Really old vampires had a certain . . . weight in their stares, as if the passing centuries had left a tangible heaviness. My nameless captor didn't have that, and if I was lucky, neither did anyone else on this boat.

Young vampires were easier to kill.

"Water," I said once the gag was removed. Between that and the aftereffects from being drugged, my mouth was so dry that my tongue felt like a wadded-up sock.

The vampire disappeared and then returned with a can of Coke. Even better. The caffeine would help my headache, and watching him pop the soda can tab meant he hadn't doctored the contents, so I wasn't about to be drugged again.

I gulped at it when the vampire held it to my lips, which meant that I let out an extended burp when I stopped swallowing. If that burp happened to be aimed in my captor's face, well, it wasn't my fault. I was tied up.

"Charming," he said dryly.

"I lost my concern for social niceties when you shot my friend up with liquid silver," I replied in an even tone. "Speaking of, I want to see him."

The vampire's mouth quirked. "You're not in a position to make demands, but yes, he's still alive."

"You don't want to take me to him, fine," I said, thinking fast. "I assume you know I pick up psychic impressions from touch, so take these gloves off and let me touch you. Then I'll know if you're telling the truth."

The vampire chuckled, a brighter green swarming in the peat-moss color of his eyes. "Touch me? Don't you mean use that deadly electrical whip you can manifest to cut me in half?"

I stiffened. How did he know about that? Aside from Vlad, Maximus, and a handful of Vlad's guards, everyone who'd seen me wield that power was dead.

"That's why those rubber gloves are duct-taped onto you," he went on, unperturbed. "Just in case."

"What's your name again?" I asked, glad I sounded casual.

Those wide lips stretched further. "Call me Hannibal."

I smiled back. "Okay, Hannibal, what do you want me to do? Use my abilities to find one of your enemies? Tell you if someone is betraying you? Or read the past from an object?"

Hannibal laughed, and though it was more Dr. Evil caliber than chilling, it was still foreboding enough to creep me out.

"I don't want you to do anything, little bird. I'm merely the delivery boy. I don't even know who I'm delivering you to. All I know is you're worth three times as much alive, but if you try anything, dead is still a good payday for me."

Hannibal gave me a cheery wave before leaving the room. I said nothing, trying to think of a way out of my predicament. I was *not* going to let myself or Maximus be delivered to some unknown baddie. I'd find a way out of this if it killed me.

The fact that it might didn't deter me. After everything that had happened, I'd rather an early death while fighting than living with more regret than I already had.

Every ten minutes, one of my captors would check in on me. I'd seen four different faces in addition to Hannibal's, and from the paneled walls, queen-sized bed, curtained windows, and the size of the room, whoever hired them had deep pockets. If I weren't trussed up to the handicapped railing, I'd have enjoyed traveling in such a nice vessel.

The only window had the drapes drawn, but from the lack of light peeking out, it was still night. Guess Hannibal had been telling the truth about me not being out that long. Lake Michigan was the closest large body of water to the hotel and it was larger than some seas, so it might be a while until we arrived at our destination. Or we might arrive in minutes.

That's why I was concentrating, trying to channel all the currents in my body to my right hand. After several moments, the overload of electricity began to form into what felt like a spike. It pushed against my glove, seeking the smallest crack to free itself from its heavy rubberized cage.

No such crack existed, but my goal was to make one. Better to be killed trying to escape than meekly be delivered to whoever wanted me dead or alive. I should never have surrendered to Hannibal, but I hadn't anticipated him knowing the full extent of my abilities, and Maximus's life had been on the line.

He's probably dead already, my nasty inner voice whispered. *You gave yourself up for nothing!*

My teeth ground together. How I hated the dark part of me that continually foretold failure or futility. It had driven me to a suicide attempt at sixteen, but it would *not* defeat me now. Dismal odds or no dismal odds, I was getting out of this.

I refocused on my right hand, willing more currents into it. If that spike of energy became sharp and strong enough, it would punch through the rubber and I *would* get free. *Come on*, I silently urged it. *Drill, baby, drill!*

Was it my imagination, or did the layer of rubber around that energy spike feel like it suddenly . . . dented?

My heart pounded, either from excitement or from being overly strained. I didn't need a doctor to tell me that building up so much electricity was hazardous to my health, but I kept concentrating, willing those inner currents to grow and strengthen. Sweat beaded on my upper lip, my vision blurred, and my whole body started to tremble, yet I kept focusing—

White light briefly suffused the room and I heard a *zzzt!* right before an ominous cracking at my feet. I looked down, both elated and mildly terrified to see a small but distinct hole. Good news: I'd broken through my glove. Bad news: I might've punched a hole all the way through the boat's hull, too.

I didn't hear any footsteps, but I hadn't expected any strange sounds to go uninvestigated. Seconds later when the guard with the thick beard and long black hair appeared in the doorway, I'd already covered the hole with my foot.

Of course, if that hole started spurting water, I was dead.

"You've got to let me out!" I improvised, banging against the pole and making more of a ruckus. "I, um, I have to pee!"

The guard, who I'd nicknamed Captain Morgan because of his looks, shook his head in disgust.

"Humans," he muttered. Then he disappeared.

I waited, breath sucked in, but he didn't reappear and water didn't start shooting up beneath my foot. Then I exhaled with relief and ruthless determination. Ten more minutes until the next guard checked in with me. In that time, I'd have to get free, and once I did, I'd have to kill them all.

Chapter 15

 Thankfully, I got loose without punching more holes into the floor, but I barely made it to the blind spot behind the door before the next guard came to check on me. I cursed my heartbeat as I heard those light footsteps come nearer. Could the guard hear that I was no longer secured to the railing? If so, I was signing my own death warrant. Hannibal's warning echoed through my thoughts. *Dead is still a good payday for me . . .*

Nerves and fear added to the electricity shooting into my hand, making a tiny shower of sparks rain from it. The air felt thicker and I caught a whiff of ozone. Then the guard paused at the doorway before rushing forward with a muttered "What?"

My wrist snapped, the currents arcing out as though they had a will of their own. The blond guard didn't utter another word, but his mouth was still moving when his head hit the floor. The rest of him stayed upright for a few seconds, arms flailing as though he was trying to get his balance.

I was too worked up to be sickened. Fear-fueled

adrenaline surged through me, acting like jumper cables to my currents. I peeked down the hallway, saw no one, and at once seized on a way to lure another guard in the room without arousing suspicion.

"What are you doing?" I asked in a shrill voice. "Stop! Get your filthy hands off me!"

I punctuated that by making a slapping sound and then crying out as though in pain. After that, I made ragged whimpering noises interspersed with cries of "Don't, no, stop!"

Moments later, Hannibal muttered, "I told you not to damage the merchandise, Stephen. Fuck someone in the hold instead—"

My wrist snapped as soon as Hannibal crossed the threshold, but he took one look at the body and slammed the door back into me. The whiplike current sliced into his waist instead of his neck, but not deeply enough. He was still standing.

"Bitch," Hannibal snarled as something red hit the floor.

Part of me was screaming in disgusted horror, but survival instinct trumped everything else. Hannibal lunged at me and I whipped another sizzling current at him. It cut through his shoulder all the way down to his side, blanketing me in a veil of red as his momentum carried him into me.

I shoved him away. He fell, but the half of him that had a head kept flopping toward me. Only a few inches of flesh attached his left side to his torso, yet he still wasn't dead?

"Bitch," he rasped.

My eyes bugged. He could *talk*, too?

I didn't want to see what else Hannibal could do. Another burst of current turned him from a large Y shape into a dotted i, but I didn't have time to breathe a sigh of relief. More footsteps sounded in the hallway.

"Not inviting me to the party?" an amused voice asked.

I didn't wait for him to see that the "party" had taken a lethal turn. As soon as those footsteps got close, I whipped a bolt into the hallway, hitting the Captain Morgan look-alike. He stared at me with the oddest expression on his face. Then everything north of his jaw slid off, hitting the floor with a thud that was echoed by his body moments later.

"What the *fuck*."

A fresh surge of adrenaline shot through me. The fourth guard stared at the remains of Captain Morgan with disbelief. Then he disappeared up the stairs with vampiric speed.

I ran after him, desperation or overexertion making my heart feel like it would burst. The vampire was already at the controls, punching a button as he glanced back at me—

The bolt cut him across the face, but I was too far away for it to kill. I lashed another one at him as I scrabbled up the deck so fast that I fell. Immediately, something heavy smashed into me, pinning me down before it bashed my head against the thick fiberglass.

The fifth guard had joined the fight.

My vision swam while pain seared my mind, but if I focused on that, I was dead. Instead of protecting my head as I instinctively wanted to do, I laid my right hand against the vampire, shooting everything I had left into him.

Immediately, his weight was gone. I crawled backward so fast that I almost pitched myself overboard, but I grabbed the railing just in time. Then I held on, looking around with frantic resolve for my attacker.

No one rushed toward me. Nothing moved at all, in fact. I used the railing to hoist myself to my feet, my head continuing to ring while nausea and the pitching waves made it hard to find my footing. I hadn't taken one step before I tripped, cursing my clumsiness. Then I looked down . . . and stared.

I hadn't tripped because I was dealing with the aftereffects of getting my head bashed against the hull. I'd tripped because the deck was covered in what looked like lasagna. It took a few seconds to translate the sight.

Not lasagna. The remains of the vampire who jumped me. Had to be; the other vampire was slumped over the controls, slowly withering as all vampires did when they truly died. I'd shoved so much electricity into my attacker that he had exploded.

I was torn between wanting to laugh from relief and wanting to crawl back to the railing and throw up until I passed out. I'd wanted to kill my captors and I had, yet I hadn't been ready to know the full extent of my abilities. As usual, life hadn't waited until I was ready to show me what it had in store.

The sound of several hard thumps yanked my focus from the terrible sight around me. They came from below deck, and caution mingled with hope. Was that Maximus? Or another guard trying to lure me down to the same lethal trap I'd used on his buddies?

I went over to the narrow staircase, looking at it with resignation. My whole body was drained but the fight might not be over. Bad guys didn't stop for time-outs and neither could I.

I didn't bother to creep down the staircase. At my stealthiest, I couldn't sneak up on a vampire who knew I was coming. My only defense was my right hand, and it felt like a light bulb that was one switch flip away from burning out. The thumps continued, coming from underneath the floor despite me being below deck now. Did this boat have another level to it?

I flinched at every pitch and roll of the boat, anticipating a sixth attacker about to pounce on me. The only open door along the narrow hallway was the one filled with bodies, but I wasn't alone. The continued sounds proved that.

I'd reached the end of the hallway when a thump vibrated right underneath my foot. I jumped back, weak sparks shooting from my hand, before noticing the latch in the floor.

A cargo hold locked from the outside. That

ruled out an imminent attack by a sixth guard. Another thump sounded. Maximus, I thought, relief making me drop to my knees. I pulled out the bolt, flung open the trap door . . . and stared.

"Please," a red-streaked girl mumbled. Her eyes were closed and more bloody forms were beside her.

I wanted to pull her up but didn't touch her. Even drained, the juice in me would harm her and she looked near death already. Hannibal's directive to Stephen rang across my mind. *Fuck someone in the hold instead.* I hadn't been the only cargo Hannibal had picked up.

"It's going to be all right."

Fury made my voice sound stronger than I felt. The girl's eyes fluttered open.

"Who're you?" she mumbled.

"I'm the person who killed every last vampire on this boat," I told her. After seeing the contents of the cargo hold, I was no longer repelled by my abilities. In fact, I was glad I'd blasted the fifth guard to smithereens.

She smiled weakly, then that faded and her eyes closed. I rattled the door to get her attention.

"Don't. You need to stay awake, and if anyone else is alive, you need to wake them, too. Tell me you understand."

Her eyes opened, their blue color reminding me of Gretchen's. They looked to be the same ago, too. My anger grew.

"Got it." Then she began to shake the closest form to her.

"Get up, Janice. Help is on the way."

I rose, filled with fresh determination. Damn right it was.

Then I opened every door in the tiny hallway. Two were storage closets, one was a bathroom, and the fourth . . .

I rushed forward. Maximus was on the floor in a tiny bedroom, duct tape around his mouth and something that looked like silver razor wire binding him from ankles to neck. It wrapped so tightly around him that it disappeared into his skin in places, as if his struggles had driven it deeper.

I'd cut my fingers off if I tried to mess with that wire, but I could help with the gag. I ripped it off, slapping his face when he still didn't open his eyes.

"Maximus, wake up!"

No response. If not for the fact that vampires turned into withered husks when they died, I would've sworn that I was too late. Then, with excruciating slowness, he opened his eyes.

I stared at him in horror. The whites were streaked with dark gray lines. A closer look revealed that underneath all the dried blood, his skin bore similar streaks.

"They never got the liquid silver out of you," I whispered.

No response from Maximus. His eyes rolled back and he shuddered so hard that the wire tore away chunks of flesh. Marty had told me what would happen to a vampire if liquid silver stayed in their system long enough. It wouldn't kill Maximus. It would do something worse: degrade his brain until he became a madman, and once it reached that stage, it couldn't be reversed. Even if I cut the razor wire off him, the real poison would still be destroying him from the inside out.

Maximus couldn't help me save the dying humans in the cargo hold. He couldn't even save himself.

Chapter 16

 I searched the dead vampires' bodies. Hannibal had the only cell phone, yet it was cut in half along with the rest of his upper body. Then I spent a futile several minutes trying the boat's communications system, but I'd overloaded that when I killed the vampire slumped over it. Even if a 1–900-VAMPIRE helpline existed, I had no way to reach it. I didn't see lights from nearby boats, either, not that I could steer toward them. The engine was as fried as the communications system.

I wanted to scream out of sheer frustration. There had to be *something* I could do!

Then my frustration began to fade as logic took over. I could wait until I eventually drifted to land or the path of another boat, but that would be too late for everyone else. There was, however, one vampire I could reach without the aid of technology, and despite the many reasons why I didn't want to, unless I was willing to let Maximus go mad and the humans die, I had no choice.

I sat down on a section of the deck that wasn't covered in body parts. With the cool breeze whipping my hair, I ran my right hand over my skin until I found a familiar essence trail and followed it. Within seconds, the deck vanished and I found myself looking at the parking lot of the Motel 6 in South Bend.

Lights from three police cars cast a red and blue glow over the ruined exterior of my former hotel room. Most of the window was gone and bullet holes pockmarked the outer walls. With all the gunfire, the inside must look like Swiss cheese, too. Then I noticed the dark-haired figure on the edge of the parking lot, barking furiously into his cell phone in Romanian.

Seeing him at the site of my kidnapping didn't bode well, but if I doomed Maximus and those poor people by not taking this chance, I couldn't live with myself anyway.

"Hang up, Vlad," I said shortly. "We need to talk."

Shock flashed over his face. He whirled as if trying to pinpoint my location, hanging up without saying another word.

"Leila. Where—"

"Are you here to admire your lackey's handiwork?" I cut him off, going on the offensive. "If so, you'd be proud. Hannibal shot up this place with an utter disregard for innocent peoples' lives, all to make sure Maximus was pumped full of enough liquid silver to make him barely able to move."

Fire erupted from his hands. "I had nothing to do with this, so tell me where you are. Right now."

He could be trying to find my location in case he realized I'd managed to free myself, but as I told Maximus, if Vlad wanted to kill me, I expected him to be a lot less cowardly about it. I was still asking the most obvious question, though.

"Then why are you here? And put out your hands, cops are crawling all over the place."

To punctuate my point, a police officer walked up, looking at Vlad in the suspicious way any sane person would. "You. What's wrong with your hands—"

"Shut up and leave," Vlad said with a flash of his gaze, though he did extinguish the flames. The officer headed back to the hotel and Vlad continued as if we hadn't been interrupted.

"I'm here because I tracked Maximus's cell phone to this area, but I'm not behind this attack."

"Then we've got another problem, because the vampire who grabbed me knew things about my abilities that only you and a few of your guards knew."

Vlad's features hardened into diamondlike planes. "Oh?"

"First things first. You're not surprised that I'm alive, so I really did connect to you in my dreams before, didn't I?"

His hands didn't light up again, but they briefly turned orange, as if the fire tried to free itself but he held it back.

"Yes. Perhaps you don't need to physically touch anything to link to me because we've shared each other's blood, perhaps it's because your powers are stronger than you realize. Either way, your 'dreams' were real."

I sighed. Deep down, I'd always known that, even when I desperately wanted to deny it. Of course, that meant I had a bargain to work out first.

"Promise me you won't kill Maximus and I'll tell you what I know of my location."

Vlad growled out something in Romanian. I couldn't translate all of it, but I recognized several curses.

"We don't have time for games," he finished.

"I know," I shot back. "I've got several humans who need medical attention and a vampire going insane from silver poisoning, but you said you were going to kill Maximus. So unless you swear on your father's and son's graves that you're not, I won't give up my location. Oh, and you can't torture him, either," I added, remembering the backhanded way he'd kept his promise not to kill Marty.

Vlad's eyes changed from copper to green, glowing so hotly that I found myself thinking if dragons were real, they'd have eyes just like his. My next thought was We're screwed, because then he smiled in that lethally genial way I'd seen him do right before he burned someone to ash.

"On the graves of my father and son, I, Vladislav Dracul, swear not to torture or kill

Rossal de Payen, the man you know as Maximus."
He paused a moment as if letting those words sink
in. "Now, Leila. Where are you?"

Vlad was infamous for his honesty, yet that
smile made me feel like I'd overlooked something.
Still, I'd done the best I could, and Vlad was the
only chance Maximus and those humans had.

"I'm on a boat, and since I wasn't unconscious
long, we've got to be on Lake Michigan . . ."

The sun rose three hours ago, but I had yet to see
another boat. In some ways, that was good. I'd
never explain the mess on the deck to the Coast
Guard, and it meant Hannibal's boss hadn't discovered his "package" had killed her delivery boys.

I was below deck, alternating between checking on Maximus and doing what I could for the
critically drained victims. That didn't consist of
much beyond dropping down blankets, duct tape
and fabric for bandages, and cups of water for the
conscious ones. I'd considered cutting Maximus
to give them some of his blood, but the last time
I got close, only a quick leap backward kept him
from biting off a hunk of my leg. Either the pain
made him lash out instinctively or the madness had
started to set in.

I found myself praying to anyone who might be
listening that help wouldn't arrive too late.

I was on my way back to the cargo hold when
all of a sudden, I couldn't *move*. It was as if an invisible, massive fist squeezed me from head to toe,

choking off my breath as instantly as it had frozen me in place. Panic had me mentally screaming, but I couldn't twitch or draw a breath. It even felt like the currents inside me came to a screeching halt.

Buzzing started to sound in my ears, growing louder as the seconds stretched longer. Then, just as abruptly as it had come, that terrible squeezing sensation vanished. I fell forward, sucking in huge gulps of air. I had to blink repeatedly to chase away the tears and black spots in my vision. Once I could see straight again, I looked up—and then froze for a different reason this time.

Vlad loomed over me, dark hair wildly tangled, lean stubbled features a thunderous mixture of fierceness and triumph. His pants and shirt were soaked, their light blue color making them almost see-through. I blinked, wondering if I'd fallen over the edge of consciousness without realizing it.

A faint smile twisted his mouth. "I'm real, Leila. See?"

He grasped my arms and pulled me up. My legs trembled but held, and with ragged pieces of rubber still dangling from my hands, I touched his bare wrists. Heat scalded my flesh at the same instant that a current sizzled into him.

Oh yes, he was definitely real.

Of all the thoughts to cross my mind in that instant, *He looks even better than I remembered* was the last one I wanted Vlad to hear. It didn't matter. His widening smile told me he'd caught it. I let go, seizing on a more important topic.

"What just happened? I couldn't move."

"Mencheres is with me," he said, as if that explained it.

My brow rose. "*And?*"

He dropped one hand but tightened the other. "Come."

I followed Vlad up the narrow steps. Once topside, I saw the Egyptian vampire, also soaking wet, surveying the remains of my captors with detached admiration. Then Mencheres turned, shading his gaze against the bright, mid-morning sun.

"My apologies for using my power on you, Leila. We thought it necessary to immobilize the entire boat in case some of your captors had survived."

You think I wouldn't notice someone else trying to kill me? I thought jadedly.

"One could have jumped overboard and then waited to catch you unawares," Mencheres replied, reminding me that Vlad wasn't the only mind reader on board. "That's why we swam the last few miles. Less to notice when we're under water."

"So you're the reason I felt like I was encased in invisible carbonite?"

The vampire shrugged. "I can control things with my mind," he said, his tone implying that it wasn't a big deal.

With that incredible ability, Vlad should take Mencheres with him on all his rescue missions. All his assaults, too.

A growl made me glance up. Vlad's expression

was closed off, reminding me that this wasn't a happy reunion.

"Thank you both for coming," I said, my voice turning businesslike. "The injured people are in the cargo hold and Maximus is in one of the rooms below.

Another ominous sound from Vlad. "I know. I smelled him."

"The humans need blood for healing," I said, ignoring that. "And Maximus needs that silver out of him. He's already showing signs of . . . mental instability."

With that, I headed downstairs, making sure to sing anything that came to mind as I went. Being near Vlad was so much harder than seeing him in a dream. Every emotion I'd tried to suppress resurfaced with pitiless intensity, and that was only how he affected my heart. My hands still tingled from their brief contact with his skin, and if his wet clothes molded any more explicitly to his body, I'd soon smell like eau de slut to any vampire within sniffing distance.

He'll be gone soon, I consoled myself. Then I could go back to burying those traitorous emotions by hunting for Marty's killer. Hannibal said he didn't know who hired him, but a search through the memories in his bones would show if he was lying.

I'd gone into Maximus's room without thinking about it. He lay exactly as he had before, but with one marked difference. His eyes were open, silver streaking them like hideous veins, and they were fixed on a point over my shoulder.

I turned. Vlad was in the doorway behind me. He stared down at Maximus, his face coldly expressionless. Then, almost casually, he withdrew a knife.

Maximus's eyes fluttered shut, either from resignation or insensibleness. Without my even needing to concentrate, a whipcord of electricity shot from my hand.

"You promised!"

Vlad glanced at the glowing strand and his eyes went green.

"Are you threatening me?"

His voice was buttery smooth—and deadly. My gut twisted from a mixture of fear and resolve. He could burn me to death before I snapped this whip, but I wasn't about to back down.

"I am if you're about to break your word."

My wrist was suddenly seized in an iron grip. Any other vampire would've been knocked backward from touching my right hand when it was fully charged, but Vlad absorbed the voltage like it was mere static electricity. Then he leaned down, brushing my hair back with his free hand.

The one that still held a knife.

"I told you before—I dislike being called a liar." Breath from his words fell like the softest of blows against my neck. "But more importantly, if I had decided to go back on my word, you wouldn't be able to stop me."

Just as blindingly fast, he was kneeling in front of Maximus, slicing through that razor wire with brutal efficiency. The cord of electricity I'd summoned curled up into itself before disappearing into my hand like a turtle seeking the shelter of its shell.

No, he'd proved that I couldn't stop him even if his pyrokinesis was out of the equation. At that moment, I felt like exactly what I was: a woman who was in way over her head with the creatures around her. All at once, loneliness overwhelmed me. I didn't belong in the vampire world, but thanks to my own oddities, I didn't fit into the human one, either.

I turned on my heel and left the room. I couldn't do anything about being an outcast in every society that existed, but I could at least let the terrified survivors know that help had arrived at last.

Chapter 17

 Mencheres and Vlad stood close together, talking too softly for me to
overhear. Still, they stopped as soon
as I came back on deck.

Weariness helped me hold back
my snort. They weren't even trying to be subtle,
were they?

"My associate will be here shortly to transport
us," Mencheres stated.

Good. I'd checked on Maximus again, too, since
he looked in worse shape than the humans, which
was saying something.

"Just drop me anywhere after you take care of
them," I said, giving the dead bodies a calculated
look. I hadn't cared before in my search for cell
phones, but a few of them carried cash. I'd need
that to keep up my hunt for the female vampire.

"Robbing them won't be necessary. You're
coming with me."

Disbelief snapped my head up. Vlad flashed me
a smile that was both charming and challenging,
while his expression almost dared me to argue.

I took that dare.

"I'm not coming with you because my problems no longer concern you." Ice was warmer than my tone. "So thanks for the arrogant assumption, but no thanks."

"But they do concern me," he replied, his tone as pleasant as mine had been cold. "If I do nothing when someone attempts to blow up and then kidnap my former lover, my enemies will think I'm weak and attack more of my people."

"I'm not one of your people and I don't need your protection, as all the bodies on this boat should attest."

Vlad's charming smile never slipped. I stiffened, remembering he was never more dangerous than when he smiled.

"As you wish." Then he glanced at the door leading to the cargo hold. "Their heartbeats are faint, and they might not live long enough to make it to the hospital. Pity."

My fists clenched, the only sign of the fury coursing through me. "You promised to heal them."

"No," he replied instantly. "You made me swear not to kill or torture Maximus, but you never bargained for them. Dropping them off at a hospital is free, but my blood comes at a price."

I hadn't thought to bargain for them because Vlad normally wouldn't need to be bribed to help innocent victims. Yet from his expression, he would do nothing more than bring them to a hospital if I didn't go with him, and that might not be enough. Only vampire blood could guarantee their survival.

I glanced at Mencheres, but the other vampire appeared to be fascinated by the waves lapping against the boat. *Really?* I thought in disgust.

His oblique shrug was my answer. I'd get no help from him, either. Once more, I found myself cursing the limitations of my humanity. Vlad had me cornered and we both knew it.

"Heal them and make sure they're safe, and I'll come with you," I said, jaw clenched so tight I could barely speak.

His teeth flashed in something too feral to be called a grin. "Wise choice."

Probably not, but unless I wanted to kill those people myself, I didn't have any other option.

I stared down at the boat from the helicopter. We were up high enough that the water was no longer white from the churning rotors. Vlad sat up front with Mencheres, but I was in the back with the humans, trying to convince the crying ones that *these* vampires wouldn't eat them.

My attempts at comfort were interrupted when an eerie blue light suffused the entire boat. For a few seconds, I couldn't figure out what it was. Then a flash of color yanked my attention over to Vlad. He sat as if completely relaxed, a half smile curling his mouth, but his hands were engulfed in flames.

My gaze flew back to the boat. Now I knew what that blue light was. Fire. Vlad never changed his relaxed position, even when the boat exploded with a spectacular *boom!* that shook the chopper and littered the lake with flaming debris.

"We can go now," he said to the pilot, a muscular blond vampire Mencheres had addressed as Gorgon.

I closed my mouth with an audible click. Vlad hadn't rigged the boat with explosives. He'd destroyed it with his power, and while I'd seen him burn people to death, I hadn't known the full extent of his abilities. Since he'd just made a forty-foot craft go up like a Roman candle, I suppose I should be flattered that he hadn't laughed when I threatened him earlier. The boat explosion was as devastating as the gas line bomb—

"Shit," I burst out as something occurred to me. "We didn't grab any bones off of those vamps."

I'd also lost Adrian's charred body part. Not that Hannibal would have taken it with us even if I'd asked. Kidnappers were notoriously uncooperative.

"They were hired mercenaries; I doubt their bones would contain anything useful," Vlad stated. He didn't ask me to explain the context behind my thought about Adrian. He must have figured out why Maximus and I had carted around a body part.

"I exploded the boat to hide the evidence of what you did, and to send a message to whoever hired Hannibal that now he'll have to deal with me. Or she," he added reflectively.

He must have read that from my thoughts, too. Then Maximus let out an extended moan, turning my attention to him.

"Why haven't you started to get the silver out?"

Vlad's smile remained but his features hardened.

"It will require extensive cutting. If I do it, then I'm guilty of torturing him. Gorgon is flying the helicopter, and while Mencheres could hold him down, you don't have the experience to remove it properly."

I swallowed. Much as I hated the thought of Maximus continuing to suffer, I didn't want to release Vlad from his word not to torture him. Wait it was, then.

"Where are we going?" *Please don't say back to your castle, please don't say back to your castle . . .*

"Fine." Glints of emerald appeared in his burnished copper eyes. "I won't say it."

For the second time in ten minutes, the word *shit* flew out of my mouth. Vlad only chuckled, the sound as enticing and merciless as the man himself.

Mencheres and his wife, Kira, lived near Chicago, which explained how quickly he'd rendezvoused with Vlad. We stopped by his house first, which relieved me for several reasons. For one, several of Mencheres's staff immediately went to work on Maximus. Two, I got to shower and change out of the oversized wetsuit Hannibal had dressed me in. Kira kindly let me borrow one of her outfits, and judging from the grandeur of their home, she'd be in no hurry to get it back.

I was barely done getting dressed when it was time to leave. Gorgon flew Vlad and me to a nearby private airport where Vlad's jet was fueled and waiting. Maximus . . . well, Vlad was keeping his word, but he obviously hadn't forgiven him. I didn't even get a chance to say good-bye, but insisting on that would only make matters worse. I hadn't meant to cause the rift between them, but I was the reason for it nonetheless.

It was only when we boarded Vlad's sleek Learjet that the full weight of my circumstances hit me. For the second time in my life, I was being hustled to Vlad's home because some unknown person was trying to use me or kill me, in whatever order proved most opportune. And Vlad was only protecting me because it was in his best interest. Talk about déjà vu.

When he sat down and held out his hand as he had on my first trip to Romania, something inside me snapped.

"No."

His brow rose. "You'd rather take down the plane if you accidentally short-circuit the electrical system? Don't be childish, you know it's this or gloves and we don't have any."

"I don't care."

To my horror, tears sprang to my eyes, but I'd used up all my strength freeing myself and then killing my captors, so I didn't have anything left to fight them.

"In the past month, I've been rejected, blown

up, shot at, drugged, and kidnapped, but I'd rather go through all of that again than hold your hand while acting like . . . like everything that happened between us doesn't matter." My voice cracked. "Maybe it doesn't to you, but even being around you hurts and I can't pretend that touching you won't be a thousand times worse."

As I swiped at those treacherous tears, I braced for mockery. Or another coolly practical admonition about how my condition necessitated this action, but Vlad said nothing. He stared at me, his expression slowly changing from cynical detachment to an almost pathological intentness.

"I don't want to touch you, either."

The words hit me like a slap, but before I could respond, he went on.

"No one feels like you do, so every brush of your skin is a cruel reminder of what I've lost. I can barely stand the sight of you because you're more beautiful than I've allowed myself to remember, and when I cut that wire off Maximus and smelled you all over him, I wanted to kill him more than I've wanted to kill anyone in my life, yet I couldn't because of my promise to you."

His voice thickened. "Now sit down and take my hand, Leila. The pilots are waiting for my command to leave."

Slow tears continued to trickle down my cheeks, but for a different reason this time.

"You care."

The words were whispered with a despairing sort

of wonder. He wasn't willing to rescind his loveless vow, clearly, but I was wrong about the apathy I'd thought he felt. That he admitted all the above was surprising enough; the fact he'd done it within earshot of his pilots was no less than shocking.

Vlad grunted. "Don't worry. I intend to kill them as soon as we land."

I laughed, something I wouldn't have thought possible five minutes ago. "No you won't."

"I will if they repeat any of this."

That I believed, and though it only highlighted all the reasons why I should flee from this lethal, arrogant, maddeningly complex man, I sat down and took his hand. I could pretend I didn't have a choice, but that would be a lie. He could send one of the pilots to get gloves. Hell, he could've sent someone to do that when we were back at Mencheres's. For that matter, I could've brought the rubberized body suit my kidnappers had clothed me in; it's not like flying complications were a surprise to me. But neither of us had done those things. Deep down, we both must have wanted this no matter how much it hurt.

His hand tightened around mine and currents sparked into him as though they'd missed him, too. I met his gaze and something else flared between us, not tangible like the electricity coursing from my flesh into his, but just as real. I barely noticed him directing the pilots to take off, and the rumbling of the engines couldn't compare with my heartbeat when he brushed my hair back to stroke my face.

"You should never have left me."

I reached out as well, tracing my fingers over the stubble on his jaw before moving higher to the smoothness of his cheekbone. "You shouldn't have made me."

His lips curled into something that wasn't quite a smile. "You don't really want me to love you, Leila."

I let out a soft scoff. "Is that what you tell yourself?"

"It's what I know," he said, a touch of anger coloring his tone.

"You remember the dream I kept having?" I whispered. "The one with the waterfall of fire? I finally figured out whose voice kept warning me to leave. It was mine, and you're the flames I couldn't hold on to no matter how hard I tried. That's why I had to leave, Vlad. If I'd stayed, your refusal to even consider loving me would've ended up destroying me."

Then I closed my eyes, putting a finger to his lips when he drew in a breath to respond.

"I don't want to argue. Right now, I want to do what I tried to do when I dreamed myself onto this plane several days ago."

With that, I rested my head inside the crook of his shoulder, draping my other arm across his chest. He stiffened, but made no move to push me away.

"This is what you sought to do when you came to me that night?" His voice was rough.

I nodded, wondering if he was angry. True, it was a violation of his personal space and Vlad was picky about people touching him, but in my defense, I thought I'd been dreaming . . .

His free arm slid around me and the stiffness left his frame. Then something brushed the top of my head, too briefly for me to tell if it was his chin or his lips. Somewhere deep inside me, that twisted, pain-filled knot began to loosen.

All at once, I wished the flight to Romania was longer than twelve hours.

Chapter 18

Either the drugs Hannibal pumped into me were long-lasting, or I hadn't realized how exhausted I was. Whatever it was, I ended up sleeping almost the entire flight. When I awoke, Vlad was back to his usual aloofness, which was for the best, I told myself. Nothing had really changed except the knowledge that I wasn't the only one upset over our breakup—cold comfort for my pride, of no use to my still-wounded heart. We passed the last couple hours in strained silence. Once we landed and transferred to a car, I couldn't wait to get to his house so I could put some distance between us.

Of course, like all of my wishes, this one turned out to be topped with a stink bomb instead of a cherry when it came true.

I'd seen his house many times, but when we pulled up and I got out, my breath still caught. Over four stories of gleaming white and gray stone towered above me, made even more imposing by the triangular turrets that rose from each corner.

Ornate carvings adorned every pillar, balcony, and exterior window, while stone gargoyles kept watch on top of soaring towers. The limousine could've fit through the house's twelve-foot-high, fifteen-foot-wide doors with their ancient-looking dragon knockers, not that they were needed. As soon as our vehicle came to a stop, the doors opened wide and stayed open, a guard appearing on each side.

I was admiring how green all the trees had become when a petite girl with shoulder-length black hair came charging through the entryway.

"Gretchen," I said, both surprised and delighted to see my sister. "What are you doing he—?"

My question was cut off by a ringing slap. Stunned, I gaped at her while cradling my cheek.

"How *could* you?" she shouted. "You let us think you were *dead*! Dad and I were planning your frigging *funeral* when he"—a wild wave at Vlad—"showed up to say you're alive and we have to come back here for our own safety! Then you don't call *once* and no one tells us anything until ten minutes ago when they say you'll be here soon!"

"Dad's here, too?"

"Yes, I'm here," a steely voice said from behind Gretchen.

I gulped, feeling like time rewound and turned me into a child awaiting punishment. A slim man with salt-and-pepper hair appeared in the doorway, his bearing erect despite leaning more heavily on his cane than the last time I'd seen him.

"You kept your word," my dad said, but he wasn't looking at me. He stared at Vlad.

"I always keep my word," he replied before striding by my father and entering the main hall of the house.

"What do you have to say for yourself?" Gretchen demanded, yanking my attention back to her.

I opened my mouth . . . and nothing came out. What *could* I say? That I hadn't told them I was alive because I was afraid Vlad would use them against me if he was the one behind the bombing? It had seemed viable at the time, but fell flat now considering that Vlad had been the one to rush them to safety instead.

Guilt hit me harder than my sister's slap moments ago. I hadn't just let my family believe I was dead. I'd let Vlad believe it, too, and while I was off with Maximus doubting him, he was making sure my family was safe while searching for me.

The word *sorry* didn't even begin to cover this one.

"I didn't mean to hurt you" was what I said, and it sounded as inadequate as it was.

Gretchen gave me a withering glare. Then she turned on her heel and stomped away. Moments later, I thought I heard a door slam.

That left me with my father and the two vampires who continued to hold the massive front doors open, their faces expressionless. Hugh Dalton treated me to a long, wordless stare and then he sighed.

"Vlad said you probably thought you were protecting us by this deception. Is that true?"

"Yes." A lump rocketed its way up my throat. *He knew why I did it, too.* I couldn't have felt more ashamed.

"Well." My father gave me a wintry smile. "I'd say more, but I think Gretchen's slap covered it. Try to use better judgment next time, will you?"

I swallowed hard, regretting so many things that I didn't know where to start with the self-recriminations.

"I will."

A vampire named Oscar escorted me to the same room I'd stayed in before Vlad and I started dating. It was on the second floor, a full two levels below Vlad's room. The sight of the lace canopied bed, marble fireplace, enormous antique wardrobe, and indigo walls shouldn't have been depressing, but it was. Months ago, I'd dubbed this the Blue Room because of its color and the psychic impression I'd picked up from the crying woman who'd stayed here before me. Her relationship problems ended up being resolved, as I found out after meeting her and her husband. Mine were irreparable.

It was just after ten a.m., Romanian time, but convert that to Greenwich Vampire Time and it was practically the middle of the night. Therefore, I made no attempt to talk to Vlad. I might have slept on the flight over, but he could've been awake the whole time making sure my hand didn't short-circuit the jet. Besides, I wasn't sure what I was going to say.

I showered and changed into an outfit I selected from the packed wardrobe, not surprised to find it was my size. Vlad's house was always stocked with all the amenities. Then I went down to the first floor, passing by several magnificent rooms in search of one on the farthest eastern corner.

Once inside the kitchen, I was glad to see a familiar face.

"Hi, Isha," I greeted the rotund, gray-haired woman who was one of the house's several cooks. Vlad's guards were vampires and so was his staff, but he made sure that the human blood donors who lived here ate like kings. So did his guests. I could've ordered room service, but I didn't want to put on airs.

Isha stopped chopping. "Miss Dalton," she replied in her heavy Romanian accent. "How may I assist you?"

I blinked. It had been "Leila" before, and was it my imagination, or was she politely glaring at me?

"Don't mind me. I just came to grab some fruit and cheese."

Isha blocked the front of the huge refrigerator before I made it two steps into the kitchen.

"Miss Dalton, please indicate where you would like your breakfast served, and I will be happy to have it sent there."

Now I stared at her in disbelief. I couldn't count all the times I'd helped myself when I lived here, usually while having a pleasant chat with Isha or one of the other chefs.

"It's no trouble, I'll get it myself," I tried again.

Isha's gaze narrowed even as she smiled, crinkling lines that showed she'd been in her sixties when she was changed.

"Nonsense, it will be my pleasure. Shall I send a plate to your bedroom, or to the second-floor lounge?"

Her tone couldn't have been more civil. Same with her words, and still, I felt like I'd been reprimanded.

"The lounge is fine. Ah, thank you, Ms. . . ." Crap, I didn't know her last name. "Call me Isha, dear!" she'd said when we met, and we'd been on a first-name basis ever since.

She turned away without another word, going back to her cutting board. Faster than a machine, she julienned a pile of vegetables, the morning light glinting off her knife.

I left, but decided to take the long way back to my room. There was something I wanted to test first.

As I wandered around downstairs, I made it a point to greet every person I recognized. They were all impeccably polite, but people I'd once counted as friends now made Stepford Wives seem warmer by comparison. If I had undead senses, I'd bet the scent of disapproval would've clogged up my nostrils.

No great stretch to figure out why. Guess I'd done

the unforgivable by breaking up with their Master. Even if they'd overheard my reasons, obviously they thought I should've been grateful to accept whatever crumbs of affection Vlad offered me.

Now I knew how a pinball in a machine felt—everything I touched seemed to bounce me away as fast as it could. His staff's coldness shouldn't bother me, but it did. My stomach growled, reminding me I hadn't eaten in over a day, but instead of going to the second floor, I went to the small stairway behind the interior garden. Then I followed it to an enclosed stone hallway and opened the second door past the chapel.

The gymnasium. I'd spent most of my childhood in one of these, so the pulleys, mats, weights, trampoline, and uneven bars meant more than exercise. They were time machines transporting me to a carefree past before I touched that downed power line. I went to the trampoline and started a series of flips, but they reminded me too much of my act with Marty. I jumped off and went to a mat, fighting a surge of grief.

There, I began to do the routine I'd perfected back when I was thirteen and had a shot at making the Olympic gymnastics team. My body wasn't as conditioned nor was I wearing the right clothes, but I did the entire set of floor exercises anyway. Then another one, and another. Soon my jeans and T-shirt were sweaty, but I didn't stop. Some days, if I pushed myself hard enough, I could almost hear my mother's voice.

Who's my little champion? I'm so proud of you, sweetheart . . .

"Leila!"

The feminine voice didn't come from my imagination. It came from a strawberry blonde across the room.

"Everyone, Leila's back!" Sandra called down the hallway. Then she rushed forward with a grin. "Why didn't you tell us?"

Her genuine happiness was like a balm on a stinging burn. If it wouldn't have electrocuted her to death, I might have hugged her for an hour.

"I, ah . . ."—*was afraid I'd get yelled at or rejected again*—"wasn't sure if you'd be awake," I finished lamely.

Sandra laughed. "I wasn't an hour ago, but that would have been fine. Why are you back? Did you and Vlad—"

"There she is!" Joe called, cutting off Sandra's question. In no time at all, I found myself saying hi to old friends and meeting the new live-in donors for the a.m. shift of the house's feeding schedule.

"Come, you must tell us everything," Sandra commanded. Then she grinned. "I didn't really want to exercise anyway."

I couldn't tell her *every*thing, but I could give her some details. Besides, there was a kitchen down here, too, and unlike the one upstairs, it didn't have any vampires who held a grudge against me in it.

Chapter 19

After a pleasant couple hours where I caught up with Sandra and the others, I went back upstairs. There, I spent a not-so-pleasant couple hours with Gretchen and my dad, trying to explain that *someone* had planted the gas line bomb and that same person would've considered my family excellent bait if he—or she—realized I'd survived. My father, a retired lieutenant colonel, understood and seemed willing to forgive me. I wondered if Gretchen ever would.

At last, I went back to my room and took another shower. Once clean and redressed, I looked out my window at the darkening sky and tried not to wonder if Vlad was waking up. Out of all the people who were angry at me, he had the most right to be. Despite how coldly he'd ended our relationship and how hard it was to be near him, I still owed him an apology for believing that he'd been behind the carnival bomb. The next time I saw him, I'd pay up on that debt.

Until then, I distracted myself by wondering

how Maximus was doing. I wasn't about to ask the staff, and asking Vlad might make him blow his lighter fluid. However, I had another way to see if Maximus had recovered.

I ran my right hand over my skin, finding the essence trail Maximus had left. Then I focused on it until the Blue Room vanished and complete darkness surrounded me. For a second, I was confused. Then I saw a green glow and heard Vlad's voice.

"—wasn't my preference. I'd rather kill you."

A heavy sigh. "Then why don't you?"

Maximus's voice. I still couldn't see him, but he sounded sane, to my vast relief. Where were they that the only light came from Vlad's eyes?

"Leila." My name hung in the stygian air. Vlad let out a short laugh. "She refused to tell me where she was until I swore an oath not to torture or kill you."

Maximus laughed, too, and it sounded equally humorless. "She left a few things out, like eternal imprisonment."

"She's young," Vlad said, "and it may not be eternal. In a century or two, I might get over my anger and let you out."

Something clanked together, and then another flash of green filled the blackness. Maximus's eyes, illuminating enough for me to see that his face was pressed against thick metal bars.

"She'll be long dead by then," he rasped.

Vlad's gaze gleamed brighter. "Will she?"

Now I knew where the two of them were, and rage shot through me. Maximus wasn't back at

Mencheres's house. He was about a hundred feet below me in Vlad's underground dungeon!

"Leila refused your offer to turn her into a vampire." Maximus's tone hardened. "She's done with you, remember?"

Vlad's laughter rolled out, low yet relentless, like thunder during a spring storm. "If you believed that, you wouldn't have lied to me about her being alive. You must have guessed that I was letting her leave me, but I wasn't letting her *go*. That's why you kept her from contacting me by convincing her that I might be the one behind the bomb."

"You could have been," Maximus growled.

Vlad's hands flashed out, closing over Maximus's. Only those thick rods of metal separated their faces as he leaned in.

"That, you must want to believe," he said softly. "Otherwise, you betrayed me for nothing."

Their matching glowing gazes showed every nuance of their flinty expressions. Finally, Maximus's mouth curled and he yanked his hands out from under Vlad's.

"Oh, I wouldn't say it was for *nothing*."

My jaw dropped. His insinuation was clear, as Vlad's hands bursting into flames proved. Part of me was offended by the false intimation while the other cheered Maximus for scoring a hit despite his helpless circumstances.

Which I was going to do something about. Locking him away in a dungeon counted as torture in my book, especially since Vlad intended Maximus to stay there a century or two.

Vlad barked out something in reply, but the room swam around me, blackness giving way to an avalanche of blue as I lost the link. After I was reoriented, I felt dizzy and didn't need a mirror to know what the warmth trickling from my nose was. Fury made that irrelevant. Vlad might think he'd pulled one over on me, but I was about to show him otherwise.

I swiped the blood off my upper lip and stormed out of my room, practically running down the stairs to the interior garden and the staircase behind it. Those steps I took two at a time, making a left turn at the tunnel instead of my usual right. My footsteps echoed in the enclosed space, but I slowed down the last twenty yards. I had a plan to get past the guards, and running up to them wouldn't help.

The hallway curved and narrowed, dead-ending with two vampires in front of an iron door a foot thick.

"I'm sorry, Miss Dalton, you can't be here," the sandy-haired one said. Then he frowned. "You're bleeding."

I gave him my best helpless-female smile, hoping he'd mistake the rage wafting off me for something else.

"I know, that's why you have to let me through. I need Vlad to heal me. It might be serious."

The guards exchanged a wary glance. "He didn't authorize you to come down here," the beefy, red-headed guard stated. "However, I would be glad to give you my blood—"

"Wouldn't that make him angry?" I interrupted, widening my eyes. "If I drank your blood when he was so close by?"

The guards exchanged an even warier look while inwardly, I smiled. *That's right. Think about how territorial you vampires are and how I only drank Vlad's blood when I lived here before.* For further effect, I swayed, and though the sandy-haired guard steadied me, as soon as I straightened, he snatched his hands away while looking around guiltily.

Checkmate.

"I'll secure permission to let you through," the redhead guard said. *He* wasn't so easily deceived. Must be married.

In response, I let myself go entirely limp. As expected, I didn't hit the floor before strong arms caught me. Then I was lifted up, the wind rushing past me from how fast whoever had grabbed me ran down the narrow staircase that led to the dungeon. I kept my eyes shut and my head drooping as we were ushered through more checkpoints. None of Vlad's guards wanted to be responsible for me dying, yet they were all too afraid of him to give me their blood.

By the time the fourth and final door creaked open, I sat up and pushed at the arms supporting me. No need to make it easier for me to be hauled away once the jig was up.

"Let me down," I told the guard, who turned out to be the blond instead of the redhead. No surprise.

My feet had barely hit the ground before Vlad's voice thundered through the cavernous darkness around us.

"What the hell is she doing here?"

Chapter 20

 An orange glow preceded his appearance, showing the stone monolith in the center wasn't empty like the last time I'd been in the dungeon. Two vampires hung from the spiked silver chains embedded in the rock, a third impaled in front of them. When Vlad came closer, more light from his flaming hands showed which part of him the long wooden pole had entered by first.

"That's *sick*," I breathed, temporarily distracted.

He ignored that, stabbing a flaming finger at the guard. "You've bought yourself some painful time to think, Jameson."

"But she's bleeding!" the guard protested, giving me a little push forward.

"So you come and *get* me," Vlad said icily. The flames on his hands vanished as he seized my jaw, turning my head and forcibly preventing me from looking at his prisoners.

"You don't bring her down here without permission, ever," he continued, still speaking to Jameson while he stared at me. "A week on the pole will remind you of that."

"I wasn't about to let you pull one of your usual disappearing acts, so I tricked him by pretending I'd fainted," I snapped, trying without success to knock his hand away. "You want to punish someone? Punish me."

He grasped a handful of my hair. Between that and his grip on my jaw, I couldn't move as he leaned down, placing his lips directly over my ear.

"I *am* punishing you," he whispered. "You'll suffer from guilt every day he's on that pole. Then perhaps next time, you'll think twice before tricking my guards."

I shoved at his chest the same instant he released me, so I ended up pushing away only air. Vlad stood a few feet off, almost invisible against the darkness with his charcoal-gray shirt and black pants. If not for the emerald glow coming from his eyes, I wouldn't have known where he was.

"Now, apologize for intruding."

Not whispered. Instead, the command resounded in the cavernlike interior. Despite that, I couldn't contain my snort.

"I'd rather bleed to death."

"If you were anyone else, those would be your last words."

All of a sudden, I was reminded that the dungeon was a place where most people that entered never left. I'd looked at storming in here from my perspective: I was going to tear my ex-boyfriend a new one for his underhanded way of breaking a promise, and I had to get through a few of his cronies first.

From a *vampire's* perspective, I'd deceived highly trained guards into betraying their Master by taking me into what was supposed to be the most secure area of his house. That I'd done so in front of enemy combatants probably made it worse. I suppose the human equivalent would be bitch slapping my ex-boyfriend at his wedding while telling everyone what a small penis he had, though that would have short-term consequences. With the fear-based, feudalistic system vampires lived under, the repercussions from this might reverberate for centuries, and I couldn't even claim the girlfriend exemption anymore.

"At last, you begin to understand," Vlad said, irony threading into his tone.

I no longer saw the blond guard I'd duped into taking me down here, but even if Jameson had left, he was still listening. *All* the guards I'd fooled would be listening, and they'd repeat my next words to the rest of Vlad's staff, who'd repeat them to other vampires, who'd eventually repeat them to his enemies. I might prefer whatever retaliation Vlad would be forced to dish out to apologizing, but this was about more than me.

That didn't mean I was overlooking what he'd done to Maximus. *I'll play along now, but if you refuse to see me after this, I'll make you impale me with the fit I throw*, I thought defiantly. Then

I cleared my throat and uttered an apology I never intended to give.

"Please forgive the intrusion. I shouldn't have come down here and I'm sorry."

My tone was good, but if tiny sparks shot out of my right hand in protest, I couldn't do anything about that.

A smile flitted across Vlad's face.

"I forgive you, but only because you said 'please.'"

Smartass, I thought. Then I groaned at the instant chorus of "Please!" mixed with cries for release from Vlad's prisoners. No wonder he got so sick of the word.

"I'm only merciful to one person a day," he threw over his shoulder. "As the saying goes, today isn't your day and tomorrow doesn't look good, either."

Then his gaze landed back on me. "Now, ask me to heal you."

You are REALLY pushing it, I thought, glaring at him.

He bared his teeth in a charmingly ferocious grin. "My dungeon, my rules."

Mentally, I cursed him in English *and* Romanian, but out loud I said, "Would you give me some of your blood to heal me?"

Another flash of teeth, now with fangs. "Come and get it."

I approached him the same way I would a swaying, upright cobra—with extreme caution. Being in close proximity to Vlad was dangerous, especially since we both still had feelings for each other. The odd sort of "time out" we'd experienced on the plane was over, so touching him now was playing with fire—literally—and he'd made sure that I had no choice.

Yes you do, my inner voice hissed. *Take a beating instead!*

I paused, considering that, and Vlad yanked me to him. Despite my anger, I was the one who felt like shocks of electricity sizzled into me when his body touched mine. For the briefest second, I closed my eyes, savoring the sensation. Then I snapped them open and stared up at him in challenge.

"Going to give me your blood or not?"

His grin was gone, replaced with a tight-lipped, savage intensity. Then he brought his wrist up, bit down deeply on it, and held it over my mouth.

I didn't look away as I parted my lips, taking in that warm, sharply flavored liquid. I never thought I'd miss the taste of blood, but with one swallow, I knew I'd missed his. My eyelids felt heavy with the strangest sort of bliss, yet I refused to close them. Keeping them open proved almost as treacherous. The look in his eyes when I sealed my lips over the punctures and sucked sent heat rocketing straight to my core.

Have you missed this, too? a dark part of me whispered. It wasn't my hated inner voice; it came from somewhere else. A place that felt like it only flared to life when Vlad was near.

His lips parted, showing the tips of his fangs. "Ask me again and I'll show you."

A threat? A sensual promise? Both? I moistened my lips. Even both would give me more pleasure than I could stand—

"No," I said, the single word echoing from my vehemence.

His embrace was my drug of choice, and as any addict knew, one sampling was too many—and a thousand never enough.

Then I pushed him away. Something dangerous smoldered in his gaze but he did nothing to stop me. Several torches flared to life, allowing me to find my way to the exit without tripping or groping about. Once I reached it, I turned back to him.

"I meant what I said. We still need to talk."

"Be in my private lounge at ten tonight. Otherwise, I'll consider the matter closed."

His private lounge, the same place I used to cross every morning because it bridged his bedroom with my old room. I'd sooner face a firing squad than go there, but if I refused, Maximus could stay locked in this dungeon for centuries.

The smile Vlad flashed me before he disappeared into the darkness said he already knew what I'd choose.

Chapter 21

 I entered the lounge at exactly ten p.m. Vlad was on the sofa, two wineglasses and a bottle on the obsidian table in front of him. The TV was off and the light from the fireplace cast a soft glow over the rust-colored couch.

Memories assailed me as mercilessly as I'd feared. Vlad and I had spent many evenings unwinding with a bottle of wine on that couch. We'd done other things there, too. Unbidden, warmth crept through me that had nothing to do with the blazing fire.

I tried to squelch it with bluntness. "You didn't misunderstand why I wanted to see you, did you?"

He laughed, and that half growl, half-amused purr played havoc with my senses even as my hackles rose.

"You think I'm trying to seduce you? How presumptuous, considering I've never allowed an ex-lover back into my bed."

I glanced at the wineglasses, the romantic lighting, and finally back at him. If Vlad wasn't trying to seduce me, then he was taunting me with what

I couldn't have. I'd dressed in a simple navy sheath that rose no higher than my knees. His black pants molded to his lower body, while his white shirt contrasted like snow against his tailored ebony jacket. That shirt was open, revealing all of his throat and the first few inches of his chest. Platinum cuff links winked when they caught the firelight, and his long, dark hair was combed back, all the better to highlight his lean, sensual features and arresting copper eyes.

The only thing missing was him slowly pouring hot fudge onto that bare expanse of chest. Then any court in the world would consider this sexual entrapment.

His smile widened. Crap, I'd forgotten to sing to keep him out of my thoughts.

"Fine. We're both here for platonic reasons and we'll leave it at that," I said, hating how husky my voice had become.

"Fine."

All of a sudden he was inches away, bringing me eye level to his open collar and the skin I'd just imagined drizzling with chocolate. I swallowed. *Think of the dungeon and his broken promise, not how intoxicating he tastes even when he's not covered in dessert!*

The dungeon image helped. "You need to let Maximus go," I stated, my voice stronger now.

"No. Wine?"

I blinked, anger covering my desire. "You promised you wouldn't torture him, but being imprisoned in a dungeon for centuries counts as torture."

Vlad held out a glass and then drank from it himself when I refused with a sharp shake of my head.

"No it doesn't," he said, still in that damnably unruffled tone. "Since I've firsthand experience with both, I assure you that torture and imprisonment are very different."

"You're splitting hairs. You knew *exactly* what I meant when I asked for your promise."

A shrug. "I've honored my word as it was given. If you wanted more, you should have specified."

"I was drugged!"

"And I was coerced," he replied, his gaze narrowing. "Many would consider that reason enough to invalidate a promise. I don't, and Maximus knew that betraying me would cost him. Because of you, it hasn't cost him as much as it should."

"This is just what you did with Marty," I seethed. "Giving me a promise that's useless after you're done playing word games with it, then you get offended when I call you a liar!"

Vlad set his glass down so hard I was amazed the stem didn't snap. Then he went to the door. When he opened it, I thought he was going to order me out. Instead, he left.

"Where are you going?" I called.

"To kill Maximus" was the reply that drifted back. "If I'm a liar, I may as well get full value out of it."

"Wait!"

He'd already made it to the end of the hall by

the time I ran out to him, but at my frantic call, he turned around.

"You can't have it both ways, Leila. Either I'm a liar or I'm not, and if I'm not, then you have no cause to cry foul over what I've done to Maximus."

Frustration made me go right for the jugular. "He's the only reason I survived after that gas line bomb. Doesn't that mean *any*thing to you?"

He came toward me with the unhurried gait of a true predator, making the hallway feel like it shrank around me. The closer he got, the more I instinctively moved away. It wasn't until I saw the mahogany paneled walls that I realized he'd maneuvered me back into the parlor.

"Yes, it does. That's why I forgave him for telling me he was checking on his people when in reality, he was stalking you. I won't, however, forgive his repeated lies after the explosion. Those weren't to save you. They were to keep you from me because he wanted you for himself."

"He really thought you might've been behind it," I muttered.

Vlad rolled his eyes. "*You* believed that, but Maximus knew I wouldn't murder an innocent woman out of spite."

"He thought your injured pride might've made you more homicidal than usual."

"No, he wanted to fuck you."

His even tone vanished, replaced with one that sounded like razors over shattered glass.

"If he believed any of what he told you, it was

only to assuage his guilt for betraying me." His eyes changed from copper to emerald in a blink. "He's wanted you since the first. When I discovered you were alive, I wondered if he'd succeeded and the two of you rigged that explosion in order to disappear together."

"You thought I killed a bunch of people to fake my own death so I could run off with Maximus?" If my voice got any higher, all of the nearby glass would shatter.

"You believed I ordered your death out of injured pride because you left me." His gaze raked me. "Don't pretend to be the injured party when you also leapt to the wrong conclusion."

At that, my temper snapped. "Of the two of us, who's more likely to have killed those people?"

His smile was sharklike; all teeth, no humor. "Me, but you still should've known better. Martin, who I tortured the day we met, contacted me after the explosion because he knew I hadn't done it. Yet you, my once-treasured lover, were so convinced I might that you let me believe you were dead."

I barely heard the last sentence. My mind seized upon one thing, shock replacing my anger.

"Marty contacted you *after* the bombing? But that would mean he . . . he wasn't . . ."

"Wasn't killed in the blast," Vlad supplied, his lips curling. "Terribly cruel of me to let you believe that someone you cared about was dead, wasn't it?"

Rage collided with a tidal wave of joy. Those wildly contrasting emotions proved too much.

I lunged at Vlad, snarling, "Damn you!" while happy tears sprang to my eyes.

He caught me, lifting me several inches off the ground. At this height, we were eye level, and the look on his face would've made me take a step backward if I could.

"Don't," he said, the word falling like a hammer. "You're the only one who's struck me without retaliation, but you're not my lover anymore so I won't be as lenient again."

I hadn't intended to hit him. True, I'd wanted to shake him until his fangs rattled for letting me believe my best friend was dead—and wait until I got ahold of Marty!—but that urge drained away as I stared into his eyes. His expression was so thunderous I should have been afraid, but something other than fear began to fill me. Unable to help myself, I glanced at his mouth. It looked hard, but if I leaned forward a few inches, I knew it wouldn't feel that way . . .

Suddenly his mouth was on mine, proving that I was wrong. It *did* feel hard. The stubble on his face felt rougher, too, plus I'd have bruises from how forcefully he yanked me down to him.

And nothing had ever felt better. Rapture burst forth, scorching everything else in its path. I kissed him back so fiercely that I tore my lip on his fangs, yet the sting didn't register. All I knew was his taste, like spiced wine mulled with the darkest of fantasies. How his arms crushed me closer while his heat seared through my clothing. The sensually brutal way his tongue twined with mine, and the overwhelming urge I had to touch him as fast as my hands could race over his body. I needed him as much as the jagged breaths I snuck in between kisses, but another emotion proved stronger, giving me the strength to push him away despite every cell in my body howling in protest.

"What are you doing?" I managed.

His expression was nothing short of ferocious, and if his gaze grew any hotter, I'd burn beneath it.

"You've never had angry sex. I'm about to show you what you've been missing."

At those words, the throbbing between my legs became painfully intense. In spite of that, I stopped him when he swooped down to kiss me again.

"You said you'd never take an ex-lover back."

His mouth descended to my neck with devastating effect. "You've proven to be the exception to my rules."

Those burning lips made the cool pressure of his fangs feel that much more erotic. Still, a deep-seated hurt overrode the passion slamming into me.

"Not *all* of your rules."

Vlad made a sound too harsh to be a growl. "You won't be satisfied until you've brought me to my knees, is that it?"

"Why not?" It shot out of me with all the recklessness of my still-broken heart. "You brought me to mine."

He released me so abruptly I had to use the couch to steady myself. Without his body against mine, I felt cold despite the pleasant warmth of the room.

"I told you that you can't have it both ways, and that's true for us as well."

Did I miss something? "What are you talking about?"

"I'm Vlad the Impaler," he said, biting off each word. "I've survived for over five hundred years because if someone crosses me, I kill him, and if I am betrayed, I exact my revenge. I told you this when we met, yet you're still upset when I act on it."

"Oh, you don't have to remind me how merciless you are," I said, bitterness leaping to the surface.

"Obviously I do," he replied. Then he cupped my face with hands so heated they felt like brands.

"You claim to love me, but the man you love doesn't exist. That man wouldn't have survived years of beatings and rape as a boy because sheer hatred kept him from breaking. That man wouldn't have impaled twenty thousand prisoners to terrorize a larger advancing army because fear was the only tactical advantage he had, and that man wouldn't have imprisoned one of his closest friends for lying to him over a woman he was enamored with. I am not that man."

His hands dropped and he stepped back, his expression still frighteningly intense.

"You see, you don't want *me* to love you. You want the version you've made up. The knight, even though I'm the dragon and I always will be."

Then he left. This time, despite my calling out, he didn't stop. In the seconds it took me to get to the hallway, he was gone, the two open windows at the far end still vibrating from his exit through them.

Chapter 22

I went down to the second floor, so upset over Vlad's accusations, I walked right by my family without seeing them.

"Leila," Gretchen snapped, jerking my attention to the sitting room I'd just passed. "What is your problem?"

"What's my problem?" Hysterical laughter bubbled, but I choked it back. "I wouldn't know where to begin."

My father's gaze swept over me, taking in my mussed hair, swollen mouth, and sparking right hand.

"Gretchen, I want to have a word with your sister."

She shrugged. "Go ahead, I'm not stopping you."

"He means leave," I said wearily.

This was the last thing I needed, but I'd put him through hell recently, and everyone knew how paybacks worked.

She got up, muttering, "You're lucky Vlad covered my expenses for the year," under her breath.

"What?"

"Gretchen, go," my dad ordered.

She did, leaving me alone with my father. I plopped onto the couch opposite his, noting the differences between this sitting room and the one I'd left. The colors were lighter and there were no weapons or barbaric shields over the fireplace. All at once, I hated the apricot and cream decor and the white hearth with the insipid oil landscape above it. This room lacked complexity, fierceness, passion . . .

It lacked everything that Vlad was.

"So he's covering Gretchen's expenses for the year." Of course he hadn't told me that. Vlad seldom mentioned his thoughtful deeds. "That's very generous of him."

My dad glanced around pointedly. "He can afford it."

"He can also mesmerize her into forgetting she ever met him and drop her back at her apartment without a cent," I said in a crisp tone. "Come on, Dad. Give credit where it's due."

That salt-and-pepper head snapped up. "I do. He promised to bring you back safely and he did. He promised to let us return to our lives when the danger had passed and I believe him. But he refused to promise to leave you alone, and from how you look now, he's made good on his intentions not to."

I was a grown woman, but I didn't think I would ever feel comfortable discussing my sex life with my dad. In this case, though, he had nothing to worry about.

"It's not what you think. We're not back together."

"You're still in love with him," he said flatly.

Not according to Vlad! my inner voice mocked. *He thinks I'm in love with a version of him that doesn't exist.*

I drew in a deep breath. If I could pull that voice out, I'd send it to the moon with all the currents I'd shoot into it. But thinking that way made me one step up from Gollum in *The Lord of the Rings*. Soon I'd be arguing with my own reflection.

"When does love solve anything?" was what I replied.

My father grunted. "You're too young to be so jaded."

I held up my right hand with a short laugh. "You remember what I see with this, right? Everyone's worst sins, so I might only be twenty-five, but I haven't been *young* for a long time."

He was silent for several moments. At last, he nodded.

"I suppose you haven't."

Then he leaned forward, lowering his voice to a whisper. "But, baby, you've got to stay away from Vlad. In my decades in the military, I've met all types of hardened men, yet I've never looked into any of their eyes and felt afraid. When I look into *his*, it's like someone just walked over my grave."

A rational reaction considering Vlad wasn't

your average soldier, mercenary, warlord, or anything else my dad could compare him to. In many
ways, he was a slice of history's untamed past
among us, yet I had only one response. While it
was the last thing my father wanted to hear, it was
also the truth.

"I don't feel that way when I look at him."

Then I rose, filled with renewed determination.
Vlad thought I loved a faux version of him because I couldn't handle the full Dracula? I'd prove
to him—and my hated inner voice—that he was
wrong.

"Good night, Dad. There's something I need
to do."

I made sure to mentally sing the most annoying
song I could think of in case Vlad had come back.
What I was about to do might be risky, but when
was my life *not* risky? Besides, the last two times
I'd used my powers, I'd only gotten a nosebleed.
I'd also had Vlad's blood today, so that further de-
creased the danger. In short, it was now or never.

Once on the first floor, I bypassed the dining
room, library, and conservatory for a room I usually avoided. The Weapons Room, as I called it.

This room was second only to the dungeon in
bloody mementos. It was filled with chain mail,
suits of armor, swords, long curving knives, mal-
lets, shields, spears, crossbows, and spikes, most
bearing dents, stains, and other evidence of use.
Even being close to them made my right hand

tingle, as if the essences in those objects were reaching out to me.

The last time I'd been here, I kept my right hand glued to my side because I hadn't wanted to know the grisly stories these objects contained. This time, I stretched it out, seeking the events that had made Vlad into the man he thought I couldn't love. The first thing I touched was a long spear.

I hoisted my spear with a shout that was echoed by thousands of soldiers behind me. Outnumbered or no, we would rather die than allow Wallachia to be conquered. Then I urged my horse down the steep hill, hearing the thunder of hooves as my men followed me . . .

That image faded and I went for the shield next, touching the dragon emblem hammered into the metal.

A cloud of arrows blackened the sky. I raised my shield and braced, waiting to see if I lived or died. Once my shield stopped shuddering, I rose, slicing the arrows sticking from it with a rough swipe of my sword. Then I grinned despite the blood streaming from my forehead. Not dead yet . . .

My heart had begun to race from those battle echoes, but I wasn't about to stop. I stroked a wicked-looking mallet next.

I sat on my throne, showing no sign of the rage coursing through me. Mehmed thought to cow me by choosing three of my former jailers to accompany his envoy. He was mistaken.

"Your piety prevents you from removing your turbans in my presence?" I repeated. *Then I smiled at my boyhood torturers. "Let me assist you in ensuring they stay on. Hold them."*

My guards seized the officials while I fetched a mallet and several long spikes. Then, my rage turning to cold resolve, I nailed their turbans onto their heads. After the third one fell lifeless to the floor, I flung the bloody mallet at the horrified envoy.

"Here is my response to the sultan's terms."

I fell out of that memory into another one faster than I registered what I touched next. My vision swam as more images from the past overtook the present. Once I glimpsed a woman with luxuriant brown hair, but when I tried to see her face, it blurred. Then she was gone as I touched something else in my determination to see everything Vlad thought I couldn't handle. Phantom pains and emotions blasted into me with each new object, coming so fast and violently that I began to lose focus on what was real. I was no longer a woman seeking validation about her feelings for her ex-lover.

I was Vladislav Basarab Dracul, bartered by my father into hellish political imprisonment as a boy, then as a young man, fighting war after war to keep my country free, only to be betrayed by my nobles, the church, and even my own brother. Then I was abandoned by the vampire who sired me, widowed by a woman who'd shunned me for my deeds, and imprisoned again by Mihaly Szilagyi, a vampire who sought to rule Wallachia through me. Betrayal, pain, and death were my constant companions, yet I would not let them break me. I would use them to break my enemies instead.

"Leila!"

As if from a long way off, I heard Vlad's voice. Felt him grab me, but I couldn't see him. My vision had been replaced with red.

Vlad called my name again, but his voice became fainter. Soon I couldn't hear or feel him. Good. Couldn't he see that I was trying to sleep?

Something poured down my throat and consciousness returned. Through a red haze, I saw Vlad's face. Felt his strong arms around me while his wrist pressed to my mouth.

"Leila, can you hear me?" he asked, moving his wrist to allow me to answer.

I blinked, but the red didn't leave my vision. Then I handed him the object that was still clutched in my hand, dimly noting that it was an ancient-looking crown.

"You're wrong," I whispered. "I do love the real you."

If Vlad responded, I didn't hear it. A surge of dizziness followed by a blinding pain tore across my mind, and then I felt nothing at all.

Chapter 23

Ever been awake enough to hear snippets of what was going on around you, but too groggy to react to any of it? For what seemed like the next several hours, I remained in that strange, semiconscious state, hearing fragments of Gretchen's voice, my father's, Vlad's, and even Marty's. At one point, they got into a shouting match, but right when things became intelligible, I fell into oblivion again.

When I climbed back out, I was acutely aware of two things: the scent of blood and the sound of drums. Between the smell and the annoying *buh-boom, buh-boom*s, there was no way I could sleep, which sucked because I was *really* tired. With great reluctance, I opened my eyes, seeing a bright, fuzzy whiteness with silver branches above me.

"Stop . . . drumming," I rasped.

Something dark filled my vision. It took several blinks before I realized it was Vlad's face. His stubble was thicker and his hair clumpy and stiff in places. I'd seen that same unkempt look on people after a night drinking, but it surprised me to see Vlad looking like he'd been on the losing end of a bout with tequila. And—*sniff*—HE was the one who smelled like blood? What had happened?

"Dad, Leila's awake!"

Gretchen's excited yell sliced through the air. The drums got louder, too, their beats overlapping as if more people had joined the band. I groaned, closing my eyes. *Someone, please, make them stop!*

"Both of you, leave," Vlad stated. "This is too much for her."

"She's my daughter, *you* leave," my father hollered.

That made me open my eyes. Hugh Dalton rarely raised his voice, and didn't anyone care that the damn band sounded like it had traded regular drums for steel ones?

"Go. Now," Vlad bit out, his eyes flashing green.

I would've argued about him using mind control on my family, except three more things became apparent. What I'd first thought were silver branches were tall IV poles, I was wearing new rubber gloves, and once my dad and Gretchen wordlessly left the room, the only drumming I heard came from inside my chest.

"What's going on?" I asked, wincing at how my voice boomed. "And why do you look like you rolled in the floor of a slaughterhouse?" I added, shocked that my attempt at whispering also came out so loud.

Vlad stared at me, his expression changing

from the intractable one he'd leveled at my family to something I could only describe as affectionate rage.

"I'm covered in blood because you hemorrhaged to death in my arms and I haven't changed my clothes yet."

My mouth fell open. "I died?" I yelled.

The briefest smile flitted across his face. "You're not yelling. You've had so much of my blood that your senses are hyper-elevated. That's why you thought your heartbeat was a drum, and why your family's heartbeats sounded like more drums."

I glanced at the IV poles again. A bag with clear liquid hung from one of them, but the other had thick red liquid.

"You're still giving me your blood?" I asked/yelled.

"You only now came out of a coma" was his even reply.

I'd died *and* been in a coma? Could this day get any worse?

"How long?" I asked, lowering my voice as much as possible.

He sat back in his chair, tapping the armrest while his gaze went from burnished copper to bright emerald.

"In a coma? Three days. Dead? Six minutes, forty seconds."

I didn't need super senses to hear the leashed fury in his voice, or to guess the reason behind it.

"Vlad—"

"Don't."

The single word reverberated in what I now realized looked like a very messy hospital room. A defibrillator with char marks was in the corner, hypodermic needles were strewn on the counter, and a darkened EKG machine was on its side by the door.

"The next time you're tempted to overuse your powers, remember this," he went on in that same steely tone. "I *will* bring you back by any means necessary, so if you value your humanity, don't do that again."

Then he rose, giving me a glimpse of the rest of his blood-smeared, wrinkled, and decidedly smelly outfit before leaning down and caressing my cheek.

"As for why you did it," he said, voice lower and throatier, "we'll discuss that once you've recovered. Another day of blood and bed rest should suffice. Now, I have business to attend to and you have another visitor."

Marty appeared in the doorway, his expression both relieved and sheepish.

"Hey, kid."

Vlad dropped his hand, leaving without another word. I wanted him to stay, but he probably wanted to shower and change clothes, not that I could blame him. Besides, I had someone to hug . . . and demand an explanation from.

"Come here, Marty," I said, and hoped it was my supersonic hearing that made it sound like I hollered it at him.

A lump rose in my throat as he approached. I'd never thought to see his stocky, four-foot frame or bushy black hair again, and when he used Vlad's chair so he could lean over and hug me, I couldn't stop a flow of tears.

"Missed you, kid," he murmured, swiping at my wet cheek. "And could you quit with the near-death experiences?"

"You should talk," I retorted, sniffing. "What happened? I saw the trailer. No one could have survived that."

He gave my shoulder a last pat before disentangling himself from my IV tubes and sitting back.

"You're right, but I wasn't in it when the gas line blew. After our last act, I was walking back to the trailer with Dawn. Then I saw this woman across the parking lot, all by herself, just *wolfing* down a tub of ice cream—"

I started to laugh even amidst a pang of sorrow over Dawn. Marty's love of sugar-flavored blood was well-known to me.

"So your sweet tooth—or fang—saved your life." My laughter faded and I couldn't keep the hurt from my voice when I asked, "Why didn't you look for me after the blast? I kept yelling for you but you didn't come. Only Maximus did."

He let out a sigh. "I knew you were in The Hammer's trailer because I saw you enter it. Then the explosion . . ."

His features tightened. "Everything within a fifty-yard radius was obliterated. Even at twice that distance, the woman I drank from was hurt. I knew it would've killed you but I tried to get to you anyway. The heat melted my skin before I could reach The Hammer's trailer, so I had to turn back. Then all the screams . . . people were trapped in their RVs or running while on fire. I couldn't save you, but I tried to save as many of them as I could. After ambulances took away the worst of the injured, I left. I couldn't stand to stay and watch them dig out your body."

His voice cracked at the last word. I took his hand, glad my new gloves allowed me to do that without shocking him. "And then you called Vlad," I finished, piecing it together.

Marty let out a grunt. "He didn't take the news well. Made me find out where they were transporting the bodies and then jumped on his jet. I told him there wouldn't be enough left of you to raise, but he wouldn't listen."

"Raise?" I repeated before comprehension dawned. Ghouls were made by having a person drink vampire blood, then killing that person and switching their heart with a ghoul's heart. Since I was on a regular diet of vampire blood and Vlad knew I was fireproof at the time, he'd know such a transformation was possible, if the explosion hadn't ripped me limb from limb—

That's what he was doing at the morgue when I dream-linked to him! He hadn't wanted to see my body to grieve or gloat, as I'd thought. He'd gone there to bring me back.

"Raise you into a ghoul," Marty said, not knowing I'd figured it out. He shrugged. "You'd look the same, but every so often, you'd need to eat the other, *other* white meat."

I was still reeling from this discovery. Had Vlad known as soon as he saw those bones that I was still alive? Or had he not realized it until he "heard" me spying on him? And the most important question: Why, if he cared enough to fly overseas and rush to a morgue to raise me from the dead, had he acted so indifferent when I left him?

"—look pale, Leila. I'm gonna go, let you get some rest."

That I heard, but whatever he said before had been lost.

"I slept for three days, you wouldn't think I'd be tired."

I was, though. Still, I had a few things to do first. "Can you find my dad and Gretchen? Vlad ordered them out, but I can handle their heartbeats now."

And their voices. I'd just remember that everything sounded like a shout at the moment.

"Sure." Then Marty cleared his throat. "You should know something. When you hemorrhaged so much your heart stopped, Vlad stuck IV lines in your arteries and flooded you with his blood. Then he broke the defibrillator shocking your heart back to life. If that didn't work, you were waking up undead, and there wasn't a thing your father could've done to stop him."

I closed my eyes. Was that the shouting match I'd heard in my semiconscious state? *I will bring you back by any means necessary*, Vlad had said, and apparently he meant it.

Which meant he cared far more than he'd admitted.

Was there hope for us after all?

Chapter 24

Dr. Natalia Romanov was Vlad's in-house physician, and unlike the other members of his staff, she couldn't have been nicer. When I jokingly asked if I was her first patient this year, thinking a doctor couldn't be called upon much in a mostly vampire house, Natalia replied that she monitored all of Vlad's humans to ensure they were healthy enough to feed from and assisted in tortures since she was an expert in neuromuscular manipulation.

Well, I'd asked.

After she left, my dad and Gretchen came back to see me. I apologized for Vlad putting the mind whammy on them, which mollified my father not at all. Gretchen, oddly enough, seemed more fascinated than angry.

"I didn't want to leave, but my legs took me right out of the room anyway. He could've made me do anything, couldn't he?"

"Yes," I said, hating the way my father's features tightened up as though he'd swallowed ground glass. Then he muttered something under his breath that, without my new super senses, I never would've heard.

"No, he doesn't use mind control on me. For one, all the vampire blood I drink makes me immune to it. For another, if he did, we wouldn't have broken up because he would've made me believe I was delighted with the way things were between us."

My father stared at me, suspicion replacing the disbelief in his expression. "That you heard me proves how dangerous this man is to you. He's changing you into something inhuman. Leaving him was the smartest decision you ever made."

Gretchen shrugged. "After seeing how he acted when she almost died, I'm starting to get why she's with him." Then her voice hardened. "And really, Leila. That's twice now."

I closed my eyes, guilt assailing me. Yes, this was the second time Gretchen had seen me teetering on the edge of death, but unlike my suicide attempt at sixteen, this had been an accident. Not that it made it less emotionally scarring. In many ways, that power line accident had put Gretchen through as much hell as it had me, only she didn't get the occasional perks.

"I'm sorry," I said, opening my eyes.

Another shrug as she acted like it didn't matter. "Have your boyfriend add therapy bills to my expense tab."

"You'll take nothing else from him, and he's not her boyfriend anymore."

My dad used his lieutenant colonel voice. It usually garnered instant obedience from Gretchen, but this time, it rolled right off her.

"I'm taking it, and if he's not her boyfriend, someone should tell *him* that. You saw how he freaked when she almost died. Then he wouldn't budge from her side until she woke up."

"Vlad stayed here the whole three days?" I was shocked.

She nodded. "Like one of his stone gargoyles."

My father gave Gretchen a look that, if she'd been anyone else, I'd swear was a prelude to him throwing a punch.

"That's enough," he ground out.

"No, it's not," I said sharply. "You have no right to shush her because you don't like the truth. Whatever problems Vlad and I have had, at worst he's been a loyal friend who's saved my life, yours, and Gretchen's more than once, so as Mom used to say, if you can't say anything nice . . ."

Then shut the hell up, my flinty expression finished.

My father rose, his lips compressed into a thin, tight line as he limped to the door.

"I'm glad you're better, but I don't want your sister ensnared in this walking dead underworld, and no matter how you dress it up, that's what it is."

I didn't reply because anger would've made me say something I'd regret. I hadn't asked for the abilities that made me a kidnap magnet for the undead and drew my family into danger because they made great bait for the bad guys. My dad knew that, yet he was still blaming me anyway.

Gretchen waited until he'd left before she spoke, too.

"Wow. That was bitchy of him."

For once, my little sister and I were in complete agreement.

Chapter 25

With some help from Gretchen, I took a shower, glad to wash away the results of three days of being comatose and briefly dying. Then I had a bowl of soup and napped, awakening to another checkup from Dr. Romanov and more visitors as Sandra, Joe, and the other humans I'd befriended stopped by. In the evening, Marty and Gretchen came by again. Even my father dropped off books so I had something to do aside from watch my IVs drip, but the person I most wanted to see never showed up.

The next morning, Dr. Romanov pronounced me well enough to leave the infirmary. I was thrilled. Being stuck in a small, windowless room while on saline-and-vampire-blood IVs might've healed my body to top condition, but it was hell on my overly stimulated mind. *Why* hadn't Vlad come back? He'd spent three days at my side when I was in a coma, but now that I was better, I didn't even warrant a drive-by wave?

Maybe he was only worried that he would lose

his psychic weapon, my inner voice taunted. *Now that you're better, he has no reason to be near you until he needs something.*

Shut up, I snapped in reply.

Vlad hadn't asked me to pull an impression from a single object since my return. True, I'd spent most of that time unconscious, but that didn't mean he was concerned only because of my abilities. My nasty little inner voice could whisper all the poison it wanted. It didn't take away from the fact that *something* still burned between Vlad and me. As for why he'd avoided me the past twenty-four hours, I intended to find out.

When I left the infirmary, I went to my bedroom, taking a shower after releasing my pent-up electricity in the lightning rod Vlad had set up outside my window. Then I went to the antique wardrobe, opened the doors—and stared.

Empty. Not even a single hanger remained. I went to the dressers next, opening each one with increasing disbelief.

Every last stitch of clothing was gone. If not for the towels and robe in the bathroom, I'd be naked.

I tightened that robe around me and pulled the long tassel by the door. After a couple minutes, the albino-looking vampire named Oscar appeared.

"How may I help you?" he asked with a bow.

"Do you know what happened to the clothes in this room?"

"Yes."

I waited, but when he said nothing else, I gritted my teeth and tried again.

"And they're not here anymore *because*?"

A slow blink. "Because you're not staying here any longer."

What?

"I'm not?" I repeated in case I'd briefly coma-d out and misheard him.

"That's correct," he said with another bow.

Vlad was kicking me out? Sure, he was angry I'd overused my powers, but I couldn't believe he'd do something so drastic.

Told you he didn't really care! my inner voice crowed.

Eat me! I roared back at it.

"Where is Vlad now?" I asked, hoping it was my overly sensitive hearing that made the question sound like a screech.

"In his room."

I brushed by Oscar with a muttered "Thanks" before marching to the staircase. Then I went up, holding the bottom of my robe together so I didn't flash anyone.

No one passed me on the staircase. The long slate hallway on the fourth floor was also empty. I took the fork on the left, mentally gearing up for the fight ahead. I was *not* letting Vlad do this. We had too much unfinished business between us.

I went into his room without knocking. He never locked his door, probably because anyone who entered without permission was tempting death. I'd already died once this week, so that wasn't about to stop me.

"We need to talk," I said.

Thankfully, the lights were on so he must be awake. Though I was determined to have this out, Vlad was *not* Mr. Sunshine when he first woke up. I shut the door, my gaze skipping around. His room was broken into four sections: the mini-library, as I called the part with couches and wall-to-wall bookshelves; the bedchamber; the bathroom; and his walk-in closet.

Vlad came out of that closet in pants and a jacket the color of storm clouds. His raw silk shirt was a few shades lighter, as was the thicker, long silk scarf that hung with casual elegance around his neck. I must've caught him before he was done dressing because his feet were bare, which made his approach even more soundless than usual.

I held up a hand. "Before you say anything, hear me out."

Not waiting to see if he agreed, I plowed ahead.

"I know you, the *real* you, and while I don't like everything because you've got a master's degree in medieval torture, not to mention a reluctance to admit to feelings beyond affection or lust, which any shrink would tell you were commitment issues"—deep breath for the next part—"I still love you, Vlad. You, the dragon, not the imaginary knight, and I'm not letting you kick me out because I—I think you love me, too."

I was out of breath from too many words with

too little oxygen in between them. Throughout my emphatic if ineloquent speech, Vlad kept coming toward me. The scent of cinnamon, spice, and smoke filled my nose. This must be his natural scent, something I hadn't noticed before my nose received its upgrade.

I stared at him, wishing I had his mind-reading abilities because his expression gave nothing away. All I gleaned from searching his face was that his stubble was back to its eight o'clock shadow length and his molten copper eyes were sprinkled with emerald.

"You're right," he said at last, his tone thick with things I couldn't name.

"About what? The excessive torturing, commitment issues, or the other thing?"

His smile was tantalizing and frightening, like being whipped and finding out you enjoyed the pain. I couldn't stop the shiver that ran through me as I looked at the man who still had such a dangerous hold over my heart.

"All of it."

He seized me as he spoke, one hand tangling in my hair while the other splayed across my back. Their heat was nothing compared to his lips when he pressed them to my throat.

"Do you know what happened the last time I loved someone?"

Growled against my skin with such tempered violence that my shiver turned into a shudder. I nodded.

"No you don't." Another lethal growl. "You only know how she died. Let me tell you how she lived—in fear. My actions horrified her, as they horrify you. My enemies exploited her, as they exploit you, so it was more than an advancing army that made her throw herself from our roof. It was me."

He'd made sure to say this while his fangs were at my throat, as if I needed a literal example of how precarious life would be with him. In response, my arms came up, crisscrossing around his neck. One at a time, I pulled my gloves off. Then I plunged my hands into his hair, letting the electricity surge through him as I held him closer to my neck.

"I am not her."

I was glad the words vibrated from my vehemence. I wanted him to be able to feel them as well as hear them.

"You're the scariest man I've ever met, but I am *not* afraid of you. As for your enemies, let them come. I've survived them before and I will again."

His laughter teased my neck—hot, harsh, and silkier than the rich material covering him. Then he lifted his head, and his stare held mine captive as if he'd mesmerized me.

"You should be afraid. Very afraid. Before, I told you if you wanted to end things between us, I would let you go, but, Leila"—his voice deepened—"I lied."

Chapter 26

The words sounded like a threat, yet I was unable to stop a grin from tugging at my mouth.

"Does that mean you're no longer trying to kick me out?"

He turned, glancing at the entrance to his closet. "Look."

With a questioning glance, I went over to the closet. Yes, it was still the size of the RV I'd lived in with Marty, and yes, I still thought the automated system that moved his outfits along with the flick of a switch was cool. So what was—

My indrawn breath coincided with him drawing me against him, his arms encircling me from behind.

"Does that answer your question?"

It did, and I'd completely misunderstood Oscar's statement, "You're not staying here any longer." I thought he meant Vlad's house. What he meant was that *room*. All the clothes that had been in my armoire and dressers were here, down to the bras that took up the section once occupied by Vlad's ties.

Even when I'd been his live-in girlfriend, none of my stuff had been kept here. It had been in the adjoining bedroom where I sometimes slept, too. Vlad couldn't have been clearer about wanting me back, but in his usual way, he'd assumed because he wanted something, it was his.

If we were going to work things out, that had to stop.

I turned around, trying to rein in my roiling emotions. "You can't move my stuff into your room without talking to me first. What if I don't want to take things that fast?"

A snort escaped him. "You nearly died to prove I am the man you love, yet *this* is excessive to you?"

I lifted my chin. "It only takes one person to love, but it takes two to make a relationship work. If we're going to try again, it needs to be more than your way or the highway, Vlad."

His hands slid down my arms while he looked at me in a way that made me think of rapturous cries and blood dripping off steel. Possessiveness was so trivial by comparison.

"I don't want to try anything. I want you to marry me."

I thought I had been surprised before. Now I truly knew what the word meant. For several moments, I was convinced I hadn't heard him correctly.

Vlad's smile held a hint of savageness. "Love is a terrible weakness. It gives your enemies a perfect target, clouds your judgment, makes you reckless . . . and that's on a good day."

His hands continued their caressing path to my waist, their heat barely diminished by the thin material of my robe.

"On a bad day," he went on, his voice turning harsh, "it can destroy you. I never wanted to subject myself to that again, so yes, I kept you at arm's length. I even let you leave to prove to myself that you meant no more to me than my previous lovers. And then Martin called, telling me you'd been killed."

His grip tightened painfully before he released me, his hands clenching into fists at his sides.

"I didn't care about anything then. Not crushing my enemies, protecting my people, or how maddening you were by expecting me to behave like a modern man, as if I could shrug off half a millennium of living, based on your whim."

That last comment was unfair, but I'd address it later.

"Then I went to the morgue and saw that those bones weren't yours, heard your voice again in my head"—his eyes closed—"and once more, nothing else mattered."

His mouth twisted as he opened his eyes. "Then, of course, I discovered you'd run off with Maximus because you thought I was the one who tried to kill you. It enraged me, but I was determined to find you. Once I did, you maddened me no less than before, yet over the past few days, I realized it was too late."

Vlad cupped my face as he stared down at me

with an intensity that made my heart beat like a trip-hammer.

"I love you, Leila, and nothing else matters."

I never knew joy could be a physical sensation, but I wasn't imagining the wave that swept me from head to toe. My throat contracted, my chest swelled, and my fingers tingled. Meanwhile, something long broken in my soul seemed to snap back in place, and though I didn't feel it physically, it was just as real—and powerful.

"I love you, too, Vlad."

I would have said more, except his mouth scorched mine with a kiss so passionate, I couldn't breathe. It was hard to even think beyond a fervent, jumbled mantra of *loveyouneedwantyou!*

He lifted his head and, incredibly, stopped me when I began unbuttoning his shirt.

"No time for that," he muttered.

I was incredulous. "You have more important things to do?"

I didn't. In fact, if my nipples got any harder, the fabric would split where my robe rubbed over them.

He looked down as if judging for himself and a harsh noise escaped him.

"Not more important, but we're both going to be very busy until the ceremony tonight."

"Ceremony?" What ceremony?

The smile he flashed me was part amused and part feral. "Our wedding ceremony."

I had a split second when I thought, *This is all a*

dream. It had to be, because he did *not* just say we were getting married tonight.

"I didn't agree to that."

His smile vanished. "You're saying no?"

"No. Er, not no, but not, you know . . ."

I knew I wasn't making sense, yet my mind was whirling with joy, shock, and disbelief. At the same time, the rational part of me snapped, *Get a grip, Leila!* One more sputter and I'd magically transform into a nineteenth-century Southern belle, fanning myself while gasping, "This is all so *sudden*!"

I gave myself a mental shake and tried again.

"I know my misunderstanding of the ring thing before led to our breakup, but as I said then, it wasn't about angling for a proposal. It was about you being open to love—"

He laughed, which stopped me mid-sentence because it wasn't his sensual chuckle or even his disdainful, I-mock-you-with-my-superiority laugh. It was something new, and if I had to label it, I'd say it had *You're in for it now* written all over it.

"What did you think would happen when you made me realize I'd fallen in love with you? I'd want to date more? Get engaged to be engaged?"

Another laugh that made gooseflesh ripple over me despite the heat from his body. Then his laughter faded away and he leaned down until his mouth was millimeters from mine.

"As if I'd settle for anything less than making you completely mine, as soon as possible."

He was so close his features were a blur, yet his eyes had never gleamed brighter. I closed mine and it made no difference. I could still see his through the shield of my lids.

"I am yours," I whispered, and it wasn't only a statement. It was a promise.

As I spoke, I rubbed against him, craving more than his hands on me. For a blistering few moments, he complied, kissing me with such intensity that my knees buckled. When I began unbuttoning his shirt again, he drew away, his lips curled into a sensually cruel smile.

"Not unless you marry me."

My mouth dropped. "You're using sex as blackmail?"

That smile widened. "Whoever told you I played nice?"

My lips twitched but this was too serious to joke about. "I do want to marry you, Vlad. Tonight is too soon, but—"

"Why?"

Not a hint of humor colored the question. Belatedly, I realized he was serious. With that knowledge, my inner antebellum Southern belle burst to the surface.

"Because all of this is so sudden!"

After an outburst that even Scarlett O'Hara would scorn, I tried to explain in a more articulate manner.

"I'd want our wedding to be special. I don't have

a dress, you don't have a best man, and instead of flowers, we have corpses on poles decorating the front of the house."

"Flowers are on the way, as is my best man, three seamstresses are ready to make any dress you desire, and I'll have the corpses taken down," he replied without missing a beat.

If he had seamstresses standing by plus flowers and a best man on the way, he wasn't just serious about wanting to get married tonight. He was *planning* on it.

A colossal tug-of-war began inside me. I loved Vlad and I wanted to spend the rest of my life with him; I had no doubts about that. His arrogance and complexity would drive me up a wall, plus I'd never get used to his impalement habit; I had no doubts about *that*, either. Would a long engagement change any of the above? No, but the saying "Marry in haste, repent at leisure" was famous for a reason . . .

"Did I mention I honor the custom of paying a bride price?" he asked in a casual tone, as if his gaze hadn't narrowed while listening to my thoughts.

"In case you aren't familiar, a bride price is where the groom bestows a gift to his new wife," he went on. "The gift is supposed to reflect the value a groom places on his bride. Because of your value to me, no matter what you asked for, if it was in my power to grant, it would be yours."

I'd stiffened upon first hearing his description, insulted that Vlad thought he could overcome my concerns with money. Then he caressed the words of that last sentence until they shone as brightly as the apple the serpent offered Eve. What did he think I wanted? He loved me—that had been my biggest wish, and I didn't remember singing "Material Girl" around him lately . . .

Comprehension dawned. Anything in his power to grant, no matter what it was. *You MERCILESSLY diabolical man*, I thought, aghast and admiring at the same time.

"Let me guess—you don't pay up until I marry you?"

A sly smile curled his lips. "Correct."

"You *really* don't play nice when it comes to something you want, do you?" I breathed.

His eyes gleamed. "You have no idea."

A promise and a threat. That described my decision now, which held the hope of incredible bliss as well as the potential for irreparable heartbreak.

"You told me you wanted to marry me," I said, voice throaty from all my surging emotions. "You didn't *ask* me."

He probably hadn't noticed. To him, there wouldn't be much difference between the two, and that exemplified so many issues in our relationship. *See? You can't marry him tonight or any other night, you two will NEVER last!* my inner voice snapped.

Vlad stared at me, copper swallowing up his gaze until not a trace of emerald remained. Then, his expression the same mixture of challenge and invitation, he slowly knelt before me.

"Leila Dalton, my one true love, will you do me the honor of becoming my wife?"

I might've brought Vlad to his knees at last, but in so many ways, he would never bend. I knew that as surely as I knew I'd always love him, and it left me with only one answer.

"Yes, Vlad, I *will* marry you. Tonight."

My hated inner voice had never steered me right before. I'd be damned if I started listening to it now.

Chapter 27

 I now knew what Vlad had been busy with yesterday when he hadn't come to see me: preparing for a wedding I hadn't known about yet. He hadn't been kidding about the seamstresses, the flowers, or anything else. His staff hustled about with blurring speed, setting up decorations, making enough food for an army judging from the chaos near the kitchen, and putting out so many candles that the nearby countryside would soon suffer from a wax shortage. Unlike the frostiness I'd experienced before, Vlad's people were all smiles now, and if one more person bowed to me, I'd expect a tiara to magically sprout from my head.

But before picking a dress or any of the other items on my now-urgent to-do list, I had to talk to my family. All my family, even the vampire I shared no biological ties to.

Vlad sat next to me in the Tapestry Room. Images of medieval life, battles, and nature were intricately woven into the huge wall coverings. The ceiling had interior boxes carved into designs that mirrored scenes from the tapestries. The effect was stunning, but I didn't think my father appreciated it at the moment. He was staring at me with the same horror I'd seen on people's faces right before they were executed.

"You're marrying him *tonight*?"

Gretchen, for once, was more urbane. "That explains why everyone's running around like you set their asses on fire."

Marty's face was carefully blank, but his gaze flicked between me and Vlad in a way that could hardly be called joyous.

"Why the rush?" Gretchen asked. Then she stared at my midsection. "You're not pregnant, are you?"

"Vampires are incapable of impregnating humans," I said.

Relief crossed my father's face but I was ambivalent. Even if Vlad was human, I'd known since my teens that I couldn't have children. No baby could survive in my high-voltage body.

Then my father's features hardened. "You can't expect my blessing on this disastrous mistake."

The words were directed at me, but Vlad responded.

"I wouldn't insult you by asking. We both know you disapprove and we both know that I don't care. Leila's opinion is the only one that matters and she said yes."

My father cast a calculated look at the items on

the silver serving tray in front of him. Vlad flashed him a charming smile.

"You'd never succeed."

For a second, I didn't understand. Then my mouth fell open.

"Dad! You were *not* thinking of stabbing my fiancé with a silver knife!"

Marty leapt over to my father. "Hugh, you need to settle down," he muttered while shooting wary looks at Vlad. "Let's go for a walk, hmm?"

"That's not necessary, I won't kill him," Vlad said in the same tone most people used to talk about the weather.

"This is too twisted," Gretchen muttered. "I'm about to have Dracula for a brother-in-law."

I ignored that, still glaring at my father.

"I didn't expect you to be happy about this. I did expect that you wouldn't get *homicidal*. I've lived with a vampire for years, remember? They're not so different from us."

"You think I object because he's a vampire?" my father snapped. "If you were marrying Marty, I'd give my blessing because he's a good man. He"—a finger stabbed in Vlad's direction—"is not."

I sighed. "You saw the corpses on the lawn, didn't you?"

My father let out a scoff. "As if I couldn't tell before that. I told you, Leila, I can read people, and without a doubt, Vlad is the most violent person I've ever met."

"You're right."

Vlad hadn't shifted from his relaxed position, nor had his genial smile slipped. He waved a hand at Gretchen and Marty.

"You're both resigned to this wedding, so give us the room."

Gretchen got up, casting a sideways look at my hand. "Still no diamond ring. This is what happens when you don't play hard to get, sis."

I rolled my eyes. "If you want to help me design the dress, meet me in the library in half an hour."

Marty gave me a long look. "I hope you know what you're doing, kid," he said. Then he followed Gretchen out of the room.

I glanced back at Vlad, noting that he and my father were engaged in a staring contest. Vlad's eyes were their normal deep copper color, but even without vampiric enhancement, Hugh Dalton didn't stand a chance.

"Dad, I know you have certain opinions about Vlad, but once you get to know him, I'm sure—" I began, only to have Vlad's chuckle stop me.

"That won't help because he's right. I am a violent man and I always have been. Why, when I was half his age and human, I invited the local nobles to my home for a feast. While they still had food hanging from their lips, I slaughtered them all and counted it an excellent evening."

"TMI," I muttered.

He ignored that, meeting my father's harsh blue stare.

"Here's what you don't know: I am never violent without cause. Those nobles had betrayed my father, resulting in him being blinded and buried alive. Some of them had walled him into his grave themselves, yet they still came to my home without fear because they underestimated me. You don't, which is one of the two reasons I respect you."

Then he leaned forward, his smile fading.

"The other reason is this: loyalty. You've seen the riches I possess and the power I wield, yet you've never thought of using your daughters to garner those things for yourself."

"That's not loyalty. It's being a father," my dad gritted.

"My father bartered me and my younger brother to his worst enemy in exchange for political security," Vlad said flatly. "I've seen far worse in the centuries since. Fatherhood isn't why you value your daughters more than money, power, or even healing your leg, which I can do. It's loyalty, and I expect you honor it more now because of the loss you suffered when you betrayed it before."

I didn't know which shocked me more—Vlad saying he could heal my father's crippled leg, or him throwing up my dad's former adultery. Vlad knew about it because of the guilt I still carried over my mother's death. I'd told her about the incriminating letters I found in my dad's bag because I was angry that she was moving us away from my trainer to join my dad in Germany. At thirteen, I cared more about making the Olympic team than my mother's heartache. Her leaving him put us at my aunt's, where she died trying to help me after I touched that downed power line.

My dad also looked stunned, but then he rose, jabbing the end of his cane at Vlad. "How dare you."

The words trembled with wrath. Vlad didn't even blink.

"I dare because I want no misunderstanding between us. I am everything you think I am, but I love your daughter, and what I love, I protect with all of the violence in me, which, as you've guessed, is considerable."

Silence fell when Vlad finished speaking. Even his staff must have paused in their frenetic preparations because I could've heard a pin drop in the next room. My dad's face remained set in hard lines while I engaged in an inner debate.

He could've left out all the people he'd killed—

Why? A Google search would reveal the same thing.

Fine, but bringing up Dad's affair—

He was impolite while making a point? This is Vlad the Impaler. His points usually come at the end of a long pole.

Yes, but the two of them are going to be family—

Did you hear Vlad describe his family? He didn't even get to the part where his younger brother kept trying to kill him.

And on and on. As I'd feared, I'd morphed into Gollum.

What I finally said after the seconds ticked by was this:

"I don't blame you for being upset, Dad. If my daughter told me she was marrying the undead Prince of Darkness, I'd flip out, too. You don't have to like it or approve, but you can't stop me, and I hope . . ." I swallowed to relieve the lump that suddenly shot into my throat. "I hope you'll be at my wedding."

Then I went over to him and kissed his cheek before leaving the room. Whatever my dad, Gretchen, or Marty decided to do, I had a wedding to get ready for.

Chapter 28

 At some point, I felt sure I'd wake up. I wasn't the girl who had an exquisite gown handmade with fairy godmother–like quickness for her wedding. I was the girl who lost her mother before I could really get to know her. Who had her dreams crushed, whose family harbored resentments, who couldn't touch anyone without risking their lives, and who drowned in darkness from all the sins her abilities forced her to relive.

That didn't look like the girl in the mirror. My dress had a creamy bodice overlapping at the bust to increase my modest curves. Under that, a multi-layered chiffon skirt was inlaid with lace clusters and tiny seed pearls. The lace bolero jacket left my décolleté bare but hugged my neck and shoulders before descending into sleeves as sheer as spider-webs. They came to my fingers, embroidery clusters concealing my long, zigzagging scar. My hair was up, a diamond-studded clip underneath the bun. That clip held up the back of a sheer cathedral veil with more pearl adornments. The front of the veil was currently thrown back in case I needed any final touch-ups on my makeup.

No, the girl in the mirror didn't look like she'd suffered from loneliness, isolation, or an influx of images from the worst deeds people inflicted upon each other. She looked happy. One might even dare to use the word *blessed*. Was it any wonder I had a hard time reconciling that she was me?

Gretchen appeared in the reflection. "Don't even think about crying during your vows. It'll ruin your makeup."

My sister's comment was a dash of reality in these unreal circumstances, but that was fine. She was here, dressed in a strapless amethyst satin gown that showed off curves I needed creative draping to duplicate. Her shoulder-length black hair was up, adding an air of sophistication, and her dark eye makeup made her appear older than her twenty-two years.

"You look amazing," I told her.

"No," she said, her voice becoming soft. "You do."

Then she shocked me by hugging me. Underneath the hairspray and body lotion, I caught her scent, like lemons and sea spray. I inhaled, knowing I'd never come across either of those without thinking of my sister.

She let me go with a snort. "Did you just *smell* me?"

Sheepish, I nodded. "All the blood Vlad gave me put more than my hearing into overdrive."

Another snort. "You get weirder by the day, you know that?" Then she glanced around, but the three genius seamstresses had left. "Well, do I smell okay? You can't beg, bribe, or steal perfume in this place."

A house of people with hyperactive olfactory senses? I didn't doubt it. Perfume would be like mace to vampires.

"You smell fine," I assured her.

Taps sounded at the door. Gretchen opened it, revealing Marty. He wore a black tuxedo that must have been recently made because he didn't own one, and it fit him like a glove. His bushy sideburns were now neatly trimmed and his thick black hair was slicked back, adding a hint of rakishness to his formal appearance.

"It's time," he said. Then he stared. "Wow, kid. Both of you," he hastily added.

I turned so Marty could see my entire dress, careful not to trip on my train. "I still can't believe Sinead, Frances, and Bertrice made this in six hours. Those vampires sewed so fast, they almost caught the threads on fire."

My voice trailed off as someone else appeared behind Marty. Hugh Dalton also wore a tuxedo, and his gray-black hair was freshly cut. The lines in his face looked sharper, but lips that had been drawn into a slit softened somewhat as he looked at me.

"No matter what I think about this, Leila, you're my daughter, so you are *not* walking down that aisle alone."

I swallowed hard. Gretchen hissed, "Eye makeup!"

and elbowed me, but her eyes had a new shine, too. It had been a long time since we'd done anything together as a family.

Marty took Gretchen's arm. "Come on, beautiful. I'll show you where to go."

She gave her hair a final pat and then blew me a kiss. "See you soon, sis."

The two of them left. My father continued to stare at me. Then he let out a sigh that seemed to come from deep inside him.

"You're sure you want to do this?"

"I'm sure," I said in a steady voice.

He took my arm. My new current-repelling, ivory gloves only came to my wrists so he absorbed a shock, yet he concealed his wince behind a strained smile.

"I was afraid you'd say that."

I barely recognized the third floor. The normal furnishings were gone and the dark walls were covered with white silk. More silk hung from the ceiling, creating an elegant tenting effect. The hallway had flowers wrapped around white stone torches that were spaced with polished shields between them. Those shields picked up the firelight and reflected it, bathing the entire hallway with a golden glow. The scent to my newly sensitive nose made the air heavier and sweeter. Walking through it was like traversing an enchanted tunnel.

Marty and Gretchen entered the main doors to the ballroom. My father and I followed, and when we appeared in the entryway, organ music swelled, snatching away my gasp.

It wasn't the ballroom's new look that took my breath away, though the aisle formed from towering pillars of white roses and the massive antique chandeliers ablaze with hundreds of candles had transformed the room into a gothic dreamscape. It was all the faces that turned toward us. There had to be two thousand people, the sea of black tuxedos broken occasionally by splashes of color from women in formal gowns.

Had Vlad invited the entire town? I wondered in disbelief.

That thought vanished as I caught a glimpse of the groom. Vlad stood on a raised white dais, a canopy of intertwining iron vines rising several feet above him. He wasn't wearing a tuxedo. How like him not to blend in. Instead, his ebony jacket had thick braiding around the shoulders, reminding me of what kings wore in official ceremonies. It buttoned to his neck, the high collar framing his strong, chiseled jaw line. His pants were also black, but the cloak that draped over his shoulders and pooled at his feet was scarlet. Its edges were trimmed with ermine, and a wide gold chain held it closed, a gold and jet pendant the size of Vlad's fist hanging from the center.

In short, he was magnificent.

I walked down the aisle, barely noticing anyone else. Even the pressure from my father's hand faded away. Vlad's hair was brushed completely back, revealing his slight widow's peak. The absence of those dark waves made his lean features, strong brows, and high cheekbones that much more striking, and his coppery-colored eyes seemed to penetrate into my very soul.

Come to me, they silently commanded. Even if I wanted to refuse, I didn't think I could.

I was twenty feet away when fire snaked up the iron canopy, winding through all those intricately carved vines. My father stopped, his grip tightening to hold me back.

"Leila—"

"It's all right," I said. I'd never fear fire with Vlad near.

Then I let my arm slip from my father's grip, walking those last few feet alone. The canopy continued to blaze but not a stray spark dropped to the ground. By the time I climbed to the top of the dais and took Vlad's hand, the iron had lightened from the intensity of the flames, until it looked like the metal canopy above us had turned into molten gold.

To say I'd always remember this moment would be an understatement.

I was so dazzled it took me a second to realize the dais had stairs behind it, too. A gray-haired man in a long white garment climbed up to us. Then he made the sign of the cross while intoning something in Latin. Once he was finished, everyone sat in near perfect unison. That sort of coordination told me the majority of our guests had to be vampires.

I had no idea you had so many friends! slipped through my mind before I realized how it sounded.

Vlad's mouth quirked. Then, the minister? officiator? began speaking in English so I finally understood him.

"Dearest friends," he said with a heavy Italian accent. "We are here to witness the joining of this man and this woman in the bonds of holy matrimony."

With my abilities, I'd relived a lot of weddings. I'd also relived enough divorces to know the vow we were about to make had more than a fifty percent chance of failure, but that didn't intimidate me. I'd faced longer odds before, and Vlad was well worth the fight.

He smiled at that: knowing, challenging, and oh so sensual.

"No fight," he murmured. "We are forever now. This first ceremony is only so that you and everyone else know it, too."

First ceremony? I wondered, but then the officiator said, "May we have the rings?" and I froze. With all the activity today, I'd forgotten we didn't have rings. Now what?

To my surprise, Gretchen ascended the dais escorted by Mencheres. The long-haired Egyptian must be Vlad's best man. He handed something to

Vlad, and my sister took my bouquet while pressing something into my hand.

I looked down, relieved to see twisting bands of gold forming an unusual-looking ring. Then curiosity had me glancing at Vlad's closed hand. What sort of ring had he gotten me?

"Put the ring on her hand," the officiator stated. "Will you, Vladislav Basarab, take this woman, Leila Dalton, to be your wife . . ."

The words blurred into white noise when I saw the wide gold ring Vlad slid onto my finger, a jeweled dragon emblazoned on its surface. I didn't need Vlad to tell me that this was no replica. I could feel it throbbing from the essences of the ancient princes who'd worn it before me, Vlad included.

He hadn't given me an ordinary diamond ring. He'd given me the royal seal of the Dracul line, resized to fit my finger.

I didn't hear the officiator finish, but Vlad said, "I will," first in English, then in Romanian. The instant roar from the audience startled me out of my shock. Wasn't the cheering supposed to come after *both* of us said our vows?

Then it was my turn, and I slid the ring onto Vlad's hand while vowing to love, honor, and cherish him. No roar sounded after I was done speaking. In fact, the place went absolutely silent when the officiator stated that if anyone objected to our union, they should speak now or forever hold their peace.

To my relief, neither my father nor Marty said anything. Otherwise, someone in this groom-oriented crowd might have "forever" silenced them on the spot.

Then came the words I never thought to hear—man and wife—followed by a soul-searing kiss I would never forget.

This time, the cheers were deafening.

Chapter 29

 I found out who ninety-five percent of the guests were while accepting their congratulations. First-generation members of Vlad's line, meaning vampires he'd changed over himself. Apparently, his lineage was so extensive that even his huge house couldn't hold all the vampires *his* people had changed over, too. From their assortment of accents, Vlad's undead offspring hailed from all over the world. They must have dropped everything to rush here tonight.

Then again, they might have been afraid not to. I couldn't see Vlad taking *I was chillaxin'* as an acceptable reason to miss his wedding.

The vast number of guests meant I spent the first three hours getting my gloved hand kissed and hearing names I'd never remember. The next hour consisted of sampling bites from a feast so massive the nearby town could eat leftovers for days. Then came an avalanche of toasts, until I had to fake drinking or risk getting hammered at my own wedding.

Gretchen had no such concerns. She'd passed the giggly stage and moved onto is-the-room-spinning-or-is-it-me? phase. My father stayed close, glaring at any undead male who looked twice at her. He hadn't offered a toast, but he was still here.

The gigantic clock struck two a.m. when Vlad rose and held out his hand. I took it, surprised at the cheers that followed. Was that the signal for *We're outta here*? I hoped so. My energy was starting to wane and I didn't want to spend the last of it here, stunningly lavish though the reception might be.

Vlad laughed low. "Believe me, you won't."

Then he swept me into his arms to the accompaniment of more cheers and quite a few knowing chuckles. I didn't even have a chance to say good night before we were out of the ballroom and up the stairs. Then the hallway was a blur that culminated in a door closing decisively behind us.

I wasn't the one who carried someone over a hundred yards in less than five seconds, yet my heart started to pound anyway. In a reversal of his prior speed, Vlad let my body slide down his, inch by tantalizing inch, as he set me on my feet. All the while he stared at me with an intensity that made words seem insultingly trivial by comparison.

I forgot the thousands of people with supernatural hearing one floor below us. Didn't care that somewhere, a female vampire and other would-be killers were finding out I was alive *and* that I'd married Vlad. Under the weight of his stare, all of that fell away until there was nothing except the two of us.

Vlad unhooked the gold chain that held his regal scarlet cloak together. It dropped to the floor with a muted thud. I pulled out the clip my veil was attached to and unwound my hair from its bun. The frothy lace fell to my feet at the same pace that my hair spilled over my shoulders.

His hands twined in that dark mass before sliding down to the hidden clasps at my back. I drew in a breath as lace and chiffon were replaced with the searing touch of his fingers. Then I tried to undo his jacket, but my gloves were too cumbersome. I took them off, yet before I could catch the ring that came off with them, Vlad did. Green rolled over his eyes as he slid it onto my bare finger.

Then his hand swept down his chest, the fastenings popping open as if by magic. I only had a second to see the shirt underneath before it, too, was gone and he was naked from the waist up. I drank in the sight of his muscled chest with its dusting of dark hair and numerous scars. Vlad looked like what he was—a warrior who'd hacked his way through battles that would've killed lesser men. Unclothed, his seething masculinity and inherent dangerousness weren't diminished. Instead, they increased, and I'd have it no other way. A groan escaped me as I reached out and touched his hard, heated flesh.

He slid my dress off my shoulders and each sleeve down my arms, leaving me in a bustier, panties, and silk stockings. I wasn't even naked, yet as his gaze moved over me, I felt more exposed than I ever had before. Vlad seemed to stare past my skin into places of my soul that I'd never shared with anyone, and in the space of those moments, he claimed them as his.

I gazed at him with equal possessiveness. Whatever he'd done, whoever he'd been before and whoever he would be in the future, he was mine. If he still had shields over parts of his heart, I'd tear them down or blast them open. *You can have all of me*, I silently told him, *but I'm taking all of you in return.*

His smile was sensual and challenging, a dare for me to keep that promise. Then he pulled me into his arms, his bare skin sending shock waves of heat into my flesh. He lifted me, kicking away the fallen dress as his mouth closed over mine.

He tasted like champagne and the blood he drew when he scored his tongue with a fang. Pain flared as he scored my tongue next, though his blood healed it almost instantly. That coppery flavor increased, yet when I pulled back in instinctive aversion, his grip tightened.

"I thought 'all of me' included sharing each other's blood."

Testing my vow already. I expected no less, but if he thought I'd wave the white flag, he was wrong.

"Don't hold anything back."

I felt him smile against my lips. "I don't intend to." Then he picked me up, taking us not to the bed, but the fireplace. He set me onto the thick fur rug in front of it, his eyes never leaving mine as he took off my shoes and stockings.

I reached for his pants, but he caught my hands, holding them over my head as he unhooked my bustier. My breathing quickened when it fell away, leaving me in nothing but my panties. The hunger in his gaze made my nipples harden, and when he dropped it lower, I could almost feel my blood rushing to follow. Desire plumped all the parts I wanted him to touch while my loins seemed to throb with a pulse of their own. It had been so long since I felt him inside me. I didn't want to wait another second.

I tried to pull him onto me, but his grip on my wrists tightened. "Not yet."

I disagreed, and he might have my hands restrained, but my legs weren't. I hooked one around his hip and rubbed our lower bodies together, a gasp escaping me at the feel of his thick, hard flesh. His low laugh was both erotic and threatening.

"You'll enjoy regretting that."

His mouth lowered then, his hot, wet tongue making my nipples tingle with its rapid flicks. He released my wrists to stroke my back before drawing my panties slowly down my legs. Every time I reached for his pants, though, he blocked me with a low chuckle. Once my panties were off, he pressed me back, his body covering mine. I had a few moments to revel in his weight, the feel of his muscles, and sensual way his chest hair teased my nipples before his mouth sealed over my breast. He sucked until tingles turned into throbs, and when I felt his fangs lengthen, I arched in silent invitation.

Pleasure followed the momentary sting in less time than it took me to moan. Then warmth spread, the effect from the tiny drops of venom in his fangs. He sucked harder before flipping me over and pulling me on top of him, switching to my other breast.

He drew on it strongly, making me clutch him with growing urgency. I let my legs slide down until I straddled him, and when that jutting hardness in his pants grazed my clitoris, sparks shot from my hand at the deluge of sensations.

He bit down the same instant, flooding my breast with warmth and making my nipple erotically burn. My head fell back while an animalistic sound came from my throat. Vlad grasped my hips, molding me closer. Then he arched forward, increasing the friction while his fangs penetrated more deeply.

The double assault of pleasure was too much. I cried out as thousands of nerve endings clenched at once. That cry turned into a moan as ecstasy washed over me, turning need into sweet release. My pulse, once thundering, seemed to slow while languorousness stole into my limbs, making them feel heavier.

Vlad's mouth left my breast after a final lick. It slid in a searing trail across my shoulder and up my neck before he kissed me, pressing me back against the silky fur. This time, I barely noticed the coppery flavor to his mouth. I was too focused on the way his tongue stroked mine, the feel of his hard chest against my overly sensitive nipples, and the desire that flared anew when he took off his pants.

I opened my legs, moaning as he grasped my thigh and pulled it against his hip. A delicious expectation caused my inner muscles to clench, making me even wetter. When he reached down and his fingers invaded my depths, I gripped him and arched with more demand than invitation.

His chuckle ended in another fiery kiss. Those fingers went deeper, intensifying the ache that had me moving against his hand. My breath came in muffled gasps as he continued to kiss me with increasing fierceness, ravening my mouth with his lips and tongue. Then his hand stopped its sensual torment and slid beneath my hips, lifting me.

I was more than ready, but he was big and it had been a while. Inner walls stretched as he moved deeper, and when his full length pushed inside me, I let out something like a sob.

His hand left my hip to tangle in my hair, thumb caressing my jaw. His kiss changed, too, matching his slowness as he began to withdraw. My body hadn't fully adjusted yet, but I wrapped my legs around him and sent him a single, fervent command.

Don't stop and don't hold back.

The sound he made. Harsher than a moan, more primal than a growl. Then he thrust forward while his fangs buried into my throat.

Both sites flared with quicksilver pain and then overwhelming, molten pleasure. I didn't have a chance to cry out before another thrust/bite, sending more shattering sensations through me. My nails raked down his back as the electricity I couldn't control surged into him. It only made him grip me tighter as he continued to move with those rapturously rough strokes. By the time I realized he'd stopped biting me, I didn't care. He could've kept drinking me until there was nothing left. As long as it felt like this, I'd welcome it.

My senses sharpened as pleasure built toward a crescendo. Vlad's smoke-and-spice scent had never been more intoxicating. His body was scorching, muscled thighs harder than stone against mine, and his mouth ravished everything it touched. I felt lost in him, and when those incredible spasms shook me from the inside out, the strangest sort of vulnerability filled me. He'd wanted all of me and that's what I'd given him. Did it mean I had nothing left?

"No," he muttered, voice thick with passion. "You have me, and I love you."

Then he kissed me, moving faster, and reality blurred once more. By the time his climax surged powerfully through him, I couldn't remember what I'd been concerned about. Losing myself was gaining him, and vice versa. That was well worth any cost.

Chapter 30

 Yesterday, I woke up in the infirmary still nursing a broken heart. Today, I woke up in Vlad's bed as Mrs. Dracula. What a difference a day made.

"If you introduce yourself to anyone as Mrs. Dracula, I'll bite you in a manner you won't enjoy."

I smiled without opening my eyes. Some things didn't change, like Vlad being grumpy when he first woke up.

"I'm quaking with fear."

"As you should be, and I've been up, my lovely bride."

Now I did open my eyes. Vlad was dressed, to my disappointment, sitting in a chair with an iPad on his lap. He rose and came toward me, expression so serious that I tensed.

"What's wrong?"

"Just reading some e-mails," he said while his fingers flashed across the tiny keyboard. Then he held it up to me.

Someone in this house has betrayed me.

I sucked in a breath. An ironic smile twisted his mouth as he typed something else and held it up again.

Aside from Maximus, that is.

I left that alone. *How do you know?* I thought.

More rapid typing. *I became suspicious when my staff tracked Maximus's cell phone to that hotel, yet Hannibal beat me there. You said Hannibal knew details about your powers that were privy only to members of this household. As final proof, an e-mail Mencheres just sent confirmed that more incriminating information leaked that could only come from someone here.*

I hadn't forgotten Hannibal's too-accurate knowledge, but getting kidnapped, dying, being comatose, and marrying Vlad, all in less than a week, had pushed it from the forefront for me.

Not for Vlad, obviously. *Do you know who it is?*

An eye roll preceded his next sentence. *Wouldn't I be torturing that person now if I did?*

True, and while details of my abilities could have accidentally reached the wrong ears, telling Hannibal's boss where me and Maximus were was no innocent slip of the tongue.

Then the significance of Vlad's typed messages hit me. *You think whoever did this is on this floor.*

Vampires had great hearing, but Vlad's bedroom was better insulated than most. Plus, his house was always full of people, which meant lots of background noise. Unless he thought the betrayer was very close, Vlad wouldn't type instead of speak.

And only his most trusted staff had rooms on this floor.

I winced. *I'm sorry.*

Don't pity me, he typed with lightning swiftness. *Pity the man who will die a terrible death once I discover who he is.*

I probably would pity that person then, but right now, we needed to find him. I held up my right hand with grim purpose.

I'll help you weed him out.

Vlad stared at me, his cold expression changing to an inscrutable one. When I saw his typed response, I read it three times, yet still couldn't believe what it said.

As long as you remain human, you won't.

I descended the narrow steps to the dungeon, guards I'd had to trick before now bowing to me as I passed. Marty walked in front of me, two curved silver scimitars attached to his belt. The knives reached his knees, making him look almost comical, but I knew how fast Marty was. Vlad knew it, too. That's why Marty was my bodyguard now.

I hadn't wanted Vlad to accompany me for more reasons than the fight we'd just had. I'd known our marriage would be tumultuous, but I hadn't anticipated the sparring to start less than twenty-four hours after we said I do.

What's that you were saying about the difference a day made? my cursed inner voice mocked.

I ignored it and kept walking, nodding at the

guard who let us through the entrance. Once inside, torches provided enough light that I could see where I was going. The manacle-laden stone monolith was now empty, as were the poles in front of it. Whatever that meant, I wasn't sure and didn't want to ask.

"This way," Marty said, taking the passage to the right.

I hadn't ventured to this part of the dungeon before, and when I saw the next chamber, I never wanted to come back. Torchlight revealed machines both ancient and high-tech, complete with grisly accessories that defied even my abilities-driven imagination as to their use. It made the part of the dungeon with the impalement poles look as benign as a waiting room.

"Freaky, isn't it?" Marty grunted. "When you're a prisoner, the first thing they do is give you the grand tour. Then you're manacled to that stone wall to think about what you saw. Next is the pole, where round one of questioning begins. If you don't answer to their satisfaction, you come here for more incentive."

I looked around with a shiver. Why would any of Vlad's people betray him, knowing they'd end up in this little slice of hell if they got caught?

Then again, I was here to see someone who'd done just that.

Marty led me past the chilling machinery room to another tight passageway. This one didn't open to a large antechamber. Instead, a string of cells were hewn into the rock. Most were only as tall as Marty, leaving those unlucky enough to be in one unable to stand. This part of the dungeon was colder, too. My turquoise skirt hung to my ankles and I had on a long-sleeved top, but I should've grabbed a coat, too.

As I passed the smaller cells, nothing stirred in them. They, like the rest of the dungeon so far, seemed empty.

I had to ask. "Do you know where the prisoners are?"

Marty opened his mouth, but another voice beat him to it.

"Vlad had them all executed in honor of his wedding."

Maximus's tone was harder than the stone walls surrounding us. I swallowed and then followed it to the end of the walkway, where the last few cells were regular-sized, at least.

"How magnanimous."

I wasn't being sarcastic. I'd prefer death to experiencing everything this dungeon had to offer, and if someone wronged Vlad enough to end up here, death was the only way out.

Well, almost the only way.

Maximus came into view as I got closer. At some point since I'd last seen him, he'd been given new clothes, but his hair was still reddish from all the dried blood in it. He leaned against his bars, his gray gaze lit up with green. Then he looked at the ring on my gloved finger and his mouth curled downward.

"I'd say congratulations, but we both know I'd be lying."

I rested my hands against the bars. "Considering where you are, I don't blame you."

"That's not why."

Quick as a striking snake, he had my hands in his. Then his fingers tightened, preventing me from pulling away.

"After your breakup, I thought Vlad was still fixated on you because *you* ended things. Then he brought Mencheres to the boat even though seeking another Master's assistance in rescuing his people makes him appear weak. That's when I knew."

"Knew what?"

"That he loved you," Maximus said in the same tone most people used to deliver terrible news.

My mouth quirked. "Yeah, he told me. Even if he hadn't, proposing would've been a big clue."

Maximus made a harsh sound, releasing my hands to turn in a short circle. "You're romanticizing it, but you're trapped now. He didn't allow his first wife to leave him. Why do you think she jumped off that roof?"

"Because she thought he was dead and an army was on its way to drag her off to captivity." Even Wikipedia knew that.

"So she left her young son to face them?" Maximus asked, spinning back around. "I think not. He was Clara's world."

I said nothing, absorbing two facts I hadn't known before. First, Vlad had never told me his first wife's name, and history had forgotten it. But the other detail was more significant.

"You knew her."

A bleak smile flitted across his lips. "I was one of the guards Clara brought with her to her new husband's home."

Vlad's words the day before rang in my mind. *My actions horrified her, as they horrify you . . . It was more than an advancing army that made her throw herself from our roof. It was me . . .*

Was Maximus right? Had Vlad's first wife killed herself because death was the only way she could escape him?

I took in a deep breath. "Whatever her reasons, I'm not her. I know Vlad's dark side and I can handle it."

Maximus sighed. "Can you? The scars on your wrists show that darkness broke you once before."

I stiffened. "If you think Vlad is such a horrible person, why have you stayed with him all these years?"

His laugh sounded hollow.

"You misunderstand. I love Vlad and I'd gladly die for him. But whenever *he* loves something, he ends up destroying it. He can't help it. It's just his nature."

Marty threw me a hard look. Clearly, he had

the same concerns, but all he said was "Do what you came here to do."

I stared at Maximus as I punched in numbers on the keypad outside his cell. The dungeon might look medieval, but it had all the conveniences of a modern jail. The bars disappeared into the rock floor with a soft swish.

Maximus didn't move. "What is this?"

"My bride price," I said coolly. "Vlad told me to name anything I wanted. I chose your freedom, as he knew I would."

Maximus still didn't move. I swept out my arm. "If you're waiting for a red carpet, I didn't include that."

Very slowly, he walked out of his cell, looking around as though expecting silver knives to rain down on him any moment. Objective accomplished, I turned on my heel and walked away.

"Since I probably won't see you again, thanks for saving my life. We're even now, so good luck with the rest of yours."

"Wait."

Cool fingers sank into my shoulder. I whirled, anger at his grim predictions making me whip my right glove off.

"Let go of me or I'll use this."

Maximus dropped his hand, a mixture of frustration and empathy skipping over his features. "Leila, had I known before how Vlad truly felt about you, I wouldn't have—"

"Convinced me he might be behind the bomb?

Lied to him about me being alive? Or kept trying to sleep with me?"

"All of it," he replied evenly. "But you still need to be wary. You don't know him as well as I do."

He's right, you don't, my hateful inner voice whispered.

I turned away again. Whether I was mad at Vlad or not, I wasn't going to listen to any more disparagements about him.

"He's letting you walk out of here, Maximus. Bet you didn't see that coming, so maybe *you're* the one who doesn't know him as well as you think."

Chapter 31

With all the wedding guests last night, the house should have been bulging with people. Instead, everything looked normal, which was a relief to me. I wasn't up to making small talk with several hundred strangers. Contrary to popular opinion, I *did* know what I could and couldn't handle. Even though I was a human surrounded by vampires who had napped for longer than I was alive, I was still the best judge of me.

"Thanks, Marty," I said when we reached the foot of the main staircase. "I'm going back to my room now."

"Straight there?" he asked, his gaze narrowing.

I hoped he didn't smell the lie when I said, "Of course."

Another suspicious look was my response, but he left.

As I hurried up the grand staircase, the song "Ice Ice Baby" blared away in my mind. Let Vlad try to force his way past *that* to hear my real intentions. Still, I didn't have much time. Soon Vlad would realize I'd ended my farewell visit with Maximus twenty minutes early.

I went straight to the fourth floor, but instead of heading to my new bedroom, I chose a hallway I'd never entered before. Somewhere on this level, the traitor had to have left an essence trail. Then I pulled my right glove off and trailed my bare hand over the first doorknob I passed.

Images of Oscar flooded my mind. Aside from gleaning that the albino vampire was usually tired when he entered his room, nothing notable stuck out. I released the handle, doing a quick inventory on myself. No dizziness or nosebleeds, good. My power hadn't hit the danger zone, so on to the next one.

That turned out to be Lachlan's old room, useless since he'd been killed in an ambush by Szilagyi months ago. After another health check, I still didn't exhibit any warning signs, so I felt safe enough to try the third doorknob.

It was Maximus's room, and the deep loneliness imprinted on that handle took the sting out of my anger over his dire predictions. Was that part of the reason he had lied to Vlad over me? Because being with the wrong woman was better than spending another aching night alone?

I let go of the handle. Whatever Maximus's reasons, what was done was done, and I didn't have time to ponder why. I went to the fourth door, but before I could touch the handle, it opened. Shrapnel stared at me, surprise creasing his features.

"Leila. What are you doing?"

I snatched my hand back. "Uh, I . . ."

Maximus's door opened, further startling me, but it wasn't him. A beautiful redheaded woman came out instead.

"I said to meet me at the *third* door, Leila," she said, flashing Shrapnel a brilliant smile. "Not that it isn't easy to get lost in this huge place."

I'd first met her months ago. Vlad counted her as a friend, which was why she'd been one of our wedding guests, but for the life of me, I couldn't remember her name. Still, I gave Shrapnel an apologetic shrug and seized on the excuse, tucking my hand into my skirt pocket. He'd run straight to Vlad if he knew what I'd really been doing.

"Sorry, wrong door." Then to the redhead I said, "Ready?"

She flashed another dazzling smile. "Sure am."

Her Barbie-doll perfect looks jogged my memory. Right, her name was Cat and she was married to Bones, the vampire that had taught me how to block Vlad's mind reading by mentally singing. That's how Cat had known I was about to be busted by Shrapnel. She could read minds, too, and her helping me showed that she could be trusted. Otherwise, she would've let Shrapnel bust me.

Thank you, I sent to her.

She waved an airy hand. "I can't wait to see the communications room," she said, as though continuing a conversation we'd had before. "It's on this floor, isn't it?"

That question was directed to Shrapnel, whose

frown was back. "Yes, but only authorized persons are allowed."

Cat snorted. "Vlad's *wife* isn't considered 'authorized'?"

Shrapnel opened his mouth . . . and nothing came out. Now that I'd married his boss, he couldn't be certain if anything was off-limits to me. Cat took my arm, whistled at the current that shot into her, and then went on with her cheery chatter.

"I bet Vlad's got the most high-tech stuff available to protect his people, so the communications room should give you great ideas for what you want in voice-activated software."

It was all I could do not to kiss her. Where would the traitor have likely left the most incriminating essence trail? In the room that would've been used to locate Maximus's cell phone signal. Cat must've been listening to my thoughts this morning for her to know exactly what I was after.

I controlled my grin with effort. "Great. I'm sick of not being able to use any tech stuff." Then I turned to Shrapnel. "Which way is it again?"

Those generous lips pursed in disapproval, but he said, "Left at the end of this hall, then it's the first door on the second hallway to your right."

"Thanks!"

As soon as Cat and I were out of his sight, I stopped her.

You don't have to go any further, I thought rapidly. *If Vlad finds out you helped me do this, he'll be pissed.*

"That's why Bones is packing now," she said with a little laugh. Then her voice lowered and she leaned in close. "But you don't shelve your best weapon just because using it is risky. Vlad told me that once. He's just too deep in Overprotective Male Mode now to remember it."

"You nailed that one," I said dryly.

An eye roll. "I've had lots of experience with it. One night we'll swap stories over drinks. But be smarter than I was, Leila. Know your limits, and when you reach them, ask for help."

"Believe me, I'm not looking to jump into the grave."

The stare she gave me made me wonder if I'd misjudged her age. It seemed to hold the weight of centuries even though I'd pegged Cat to be recently undead.

"Sometimes the grave finds you whether you're looking for it or not."

I said nothing, once again covering my thoughts with Vanilla Ice's one-hit wonder. Even if it did bring the grave one step closer, I was doing this. Until we found the traitor, no one in this house was safe, least of all me.

The communications room looked like a smaller version of something NASA would have. A dozen manned computer stations were spread out around a large map of the world with multiple pinpoints indicating safe houses for Vlad's people. Another interactive map could be rearranged by grabbing things out of thin air, and a third 3-D image was a digital recreation of this house. Right now, all the lines on it were green. If any of them turned red, it indicated a security breach.

When Cat and I opened the door unannounced, the area for this room went red. Then, much like Shrapnel, Vlad's staff decided they didn't want to be the ones to tell me I needed better clearance than the wedding ring on my finger and it returned to green.

"Check this out, Leila," Cat said, pointing at the screen nearest to her. "The different sections on this security grid indicate that it checks for trespassers on the grounds, in the air, and a hundred feet *below* the ground, too."

"That's right," the monitor tech said with faint surprise.

Brisk nod. "I designed a similar system for my old job."

I leaned in next to Cat, pretending to be fascinated by the security details. In reality, I palmed a pen and stuck it in my skirt pocket. Then we moved to the next station, where I swiped a paper clip. By the time I'd feigned interest in every workstation, my skirt pocket was full of stolen items.

Cat helped by angling her body to shield what I was doing, but I could only hope that if a sharp-eyed employee *had* seen anything, he'd chalk it up to me being a kleptomaniac. Now, to beat a hasty retreat. I'd used up every minute of the half hour I'd arranged for releasing Maximus. With luck, by the time Vlad heard where I had really been, I'd already have psychically sorted through my stash to see if any of the employees on this shift were the traitor.

"This has been great, thanks," I told the group as we left. Once in another hallway, I gave Cat a grateful smile.

"I owe you. Now, get the hell out of here."

She grinned. "You've made Christmas come early for my husband, you know. Vlad once mocked Bones for his overprotectiveness by saying he should've married a docile girl who wouldn't stray too far from the kitchen."

Then she enveloped me in a quick hug before dashing off with a cheeky "Karma's a bitch!" thrown over her shoulder. In the next blink, Cat was gone.

I was still smiling over that when I rounded the next corner—and almost ran right into Vlad. *Ice Ice Baby, too cold!* rang across my mind as I gave him my most guileless look.

"Hi. Cat was just keeping me company until you came back."

He glanced in the direction she'd disappeared to before returning his attention to me.

"Fourteen hundred and thirty-one."

I blinked. "What's that?"

"The year I was born, which is not, as you'll note, *yesterday*."

I stifled a groan. Busted already. "Vlad, I—"

"Not here," he interrupted, grasping my arm. Then he propelled me down the hall and into our bedroom far less romantically than he'd done last night. Once the door shut behind us, I started back in on my defense.

"Look, I was being careful. See? No blood, no problem."

Vlad leaned down until his mouth was near my ear. "Before Maximus walked out of this house, I hadn't paid your bride price yet. You could've picked using your powers to find the traitor instead of his freedom."

"That is *not* fair," I hissed, my voice equally low.

A light kiss preceded his response. "Neither is life."

I pushed him away, sending my next message with my mind because I was too angry to trust keeping my voice down.

You can't expect me to do nothing when my abilities could find the traitor that leaked information to Hannibal AND probably helped the person that blew up the carnival, too.

Vlad crossed his arms over his chest almost casually. "When it could kill you at any moment, I can."

I'm fine! I mentally shouted.

"You were also fine the time before when your powers caused you to hemorrhage to death in my arms."

Spoken in a whiplike tone I'd seen centuries-old

vampires cower under. All it did was add to my growing ire.

Oh, but all's well if I bleed to death in your arms while you're turning me into a vampire?

Not a hint of shame colored his tone when he said, "Yes."

Pride stiffened my spine.

Unless you lock me in this room, you can't stop me from using my powers to find the traitor.

The grin he flashed me said I'd made a critical mistake.

"Don't you dare," I said out loud.

He closed the space between us, that charming wolf's smile never leaving his face. Then his arms went around me. I remained stiff despite things inside me reacting to the feel of his body.

Seriously. You try it and there will be DIRE consequences.

His lips brushed my ear again. "Imprison my new bride in our bedroom? I'd be a walking Dracula caricature."

He wasn't giving up that easily. That's why I didn't relax my rigid posture even when he sensually nibbled on my earlobe.

"But if you use your powers again," he murmured, "I will coat you in enough of my aura to suffocate them for months."

Son of a bitch! For all I knew, he was doing that right now. I shoved him, but he didn't budge this time.

"You're safe for the moment, and you're right—I

can't stop you from doing what you feel you must. But then *I'll* do what I must, and you can't stop me, either."

Using the words I'd once challenged him with against me. *Now* he decided to act like a modern man.

His mouth slid to my jaw, showing the slight curl to his lips. "Be careful what you wish for, isn't that the saying?"

Before I could answer, he kissed me with such raw carnality that I responded despite my frustration. Anger gave an edge to my lust, and I grabbed him hard enough to yank out a few strands of hair when I pulled his head down to kiss him back.

A chuckle vibrated against my mouth before he flung me to the floor and ripped off my skirt with one hard swipe.

"Looks like we're having angry sex after all."

Chapter 32

 Hours later, I got up, wrapping the sheet around me as though it were a huge towel.

An amused snort sounded from the other side of the bed. "It's a little late for modesty."

My bladder urged less talking and more walking to the nearest bathroom. "It's not for you. It's in case one of your staff decides to clean the lounge when I'm crossing through it."

"I take it you didn't notice the new addition to the bathroom this morning."

New addition?

I went into the black marble bathroom, which I hadn't used earlier because I'd showered in my old one out of habit. In the space that used to bridge the enormous tub and glass shower was now a gleaming black toilet. Such an ignoble item, yet its presence was like being surprised with a room full of roses.

"Vlad, it's . . ."

"You're supposed to use it, not compose sonnets about it."

I shut the bathroom door. He could mock all he wanted, but I was touched by the gesture anyway. A few minutes later I returned, hair combed and teeth brushed, too. The toilet hadn't been the only new addition. Half of the marble vanity was now stocked with everything I'd ever need.

"Your people must've been *crazy* busy yesterday," I noted.

"Those weren't put in yesterday."

He said it without opening his eyes. Firelight played across his body, turning his pale skin into a warm amber shade. I got back into bed and traced the groove in his chest before following it down to his hard, flat stomach.

"You had it done when I was comatose?"

His eyes remained closed. "I had everything done the day after you told me you were leaving."

I was speechless, but my mind wasn't. *What? Why? You didn't act like you wanted me back. You avoided me for days and didn't even say good-bye before I left!*

"I thought you would change your mind." Sardonic smile. "My pride wouldn't let me believe you'd actually leave, so I upgraded the bathroom while waiting for you to apologize."

A strangled sound escaped me. Vlad's mouth curled downward.

"Imagine my shock when you boarded that plane.

Then I reasoned that in a week or two, you'd realize how much you missed me and return. And so I waited again, but the only call I received was from Martin telling me about the explosion. Once I realized you hadn't been killed . . . I was through waiting."

I'm coming for you, he'd said the first time we spoke after that. I'd thought it was a dream, and then later figured he was just keeping up his reputation as a formidable protector of his people. Looked like we'd each underestimated the other.

"You've never asked why I offered to make you a vampire."

The statement caught me off guard for more reasons than the abrupt change of subject. Vlad opened his eyes, the rings of emerald encircling his copper irises almost shimmering.

"I'm not changing the subject, in fact."

I swallowed to relieve the lump that rose in my throat. "I thought it was because you're worried my powers will kill me."

"That's a reason. Not the main one."

He traced the scar from my temple down to my fingers before he spoke. "I offered before that, and if your powers killed you now, you've had enough of my blood to be brought back as a ghoul. You'd be no less immortal, so that's not the reason why."

"Then what is?" I asked softly.

"For one, most vampires don't recognize our marriage."

"*What?*"

He smiled slightly at my tone. "Vampires honor

only a blood vow in front of witnesses, and you must be a vampire to make that vow. My people consider you my wife because I say you are, but in vampire society, you aren't."

Now that he mentioned it, Marty had told me the same thing years ago when I first asked him about his species. It also explained Vlad's comment about this being our *first* ceremony.

"You want to change me into a vampire to make an honest woman out of me? How chivalrous," I teased.

"Normally I don't care about others' opinions, but you'd only be granted certain protections in my world as my legal wife. That I care about, yet it's not my primary reason."

Vlad caressed my hand. My currents were muted from all the electricity I'd released making love to him, so only a faint crackle remained. That didn't compare to the jolt I felt at the sudden intensity in his gaze.

"I despise flowery speech since those who use it are usually guilty of the worst betrayals later. That and the type of life I've lived have made me incapable of saying the pretty words you deserve to hear, yet if I made you a vampire, you'd feel my emotions as clearly as I hear your thoughts now."

Then he drew my hand to his chest, placing it over his heart.

"I never turned any of my previous lovers because I didn't want them to feel how little I cared. You I loved, yet you left me because I wouldn't verbalize my emotions. That will probably happen again, but if you could feel what you mean to me, Leila"—his voice deepened—"words wouldn't matter."

His heart was silent beneath my hand. It had been that way for centuries, yet Vlad was more alive than anyone I'd met. He was also the most complex man I knew, so the thought of peeling away his layers through connection to his emotions filled me with voracious longing. I wanted to know his feelings, his secrets, and everything else that made up the man I loved. But as much as I wanted that, it wasn't enough to make me say yes.

I touched my own chest. The steady beats beneath my hand kept me alive, yet they weren't the sum of living. My abilities had taught me that. Instead, heartbeats were only the sum of humanity. Love and hate, passion and pain, strength and stumbling, despair and forgiveness—*that* was living, so the real question was, how did I want to live? As a human who needed to drink vampire blood? Or a vampire who needed to drink human blood? Both came with their share of heartache and bliss, yet when I thought of my future, only one seemed the right path.

I rolled on top of Vlad, brushing his hair back so I could see every nuance of his expression when I gave him my answer.

"This word matters. Yes, Vlad. The answer is yes."

Vlad was gone when I awoke, but it wasn't a surprise this time. Before I fell asleep, he'd said he was meeting with Mencheres this morning to begin tightening the noose around the traitor. Since Vlad already had all calls, texts, and e-mails monitored, plus his staff wasn't allowed to leave, under the pretense of continued wedding celebrations, I couldn't imagine how he'd further clamp things down, but he must have a plan. I'd find out what it was once he was back.

Until then, I had some issues of my own to take care of, like telling my family about my decision. I wasn't going to take the undead plunge *today*, but I also saw no reason to put it off for months or years. Between my abilities plus living with two different vampires, there was little I didn't know about what I was getting into. Hell, compared to how my accident had changed my life, turning into a vampire wouldn't even be the biggest transition I'd ever undergone.

I got out of bed, my foot catching on something soft as I headed toward the bathroom. Vlad's shirt. I caught it after an upward kick and then began to pick up the other clothes strewn around the room. He might be used to having servants clean up after him, but I wasn't. When I got to my turquoise skirt, however, the lumpiness in its pocket made me pause.

My stolen stash was still there. When Vlad ripped this off me, I thought its contents would've scattered. Feeling the items through the material filled me with the same temptation Pandora must've experienced when she stroked that box. Was the traitor's identity locked inside one of these? Or were these items the gateway to me losing my mortality sooner than I'd intended?

The idea of eating the occasional meal of "long pig" as a ghoul wasn't appealing, but how could I shy away from avenging the deaths of everyone at the carnival plus protecting those here? I hadn't suffered any ill effects from using my powers yesterday. Maybe I still had so much of Vlad's blood in me that it countered the damage my powers caused. For now, anyway.

There was another reason I shouldn't wait. Changing into a vampire could wipe out my psychic abilities altogether. At the very least, it could put them out of commission for a long time. This might be the only chance I had to discover who'd betrayed Vlad before anyone else got hurt—or worse.

I can't stop you from doing what you feel you must, Vlad had said, while warning me about what he'd do if he found out. I drew in a long, slow breath before taking off my right glove.

I must.

Then I plunged my bare hand into the pocket. Images overtook me as I touched all the items at once. Through the fast-forward-type reenactment of several staff members, one person stuck out, and it was the last person I expected to see.

What was Sandra doing in there?

Chapter 33

Vlad gave me a look of such suspicion that, had I been anyone else, I'd expect it to be followed by interrogation.

"You want to go shopping?" he repeated.

"Yes," I said, and it was the absolute truth. "Come on, nothing I'm wearing even belongs to me—"

"They do, those clothes are new," he cut me off.

"—and you did everything for our wedding down to picking out your own ring. Even if I didn't want to buy a few things for myself, which I do, I also want to get *you* something. If you go with me, it won't be much of a surprise, will it?"

That earned me another what-are-you-really-up-to look, but my thoughts agreed with my words and my expression wouldn't have been more innocent if I'd borrowed it from an angel.

"Come on, you *own* the town we're going to," I added. "It's not like I want to borrow the jet for a quick jaunt to Paris."

From his expression, he was weighing his misgivings against the time-tested truism that women liked to shop.

"Guards will accompany you," he said at last.

"Of course. I'm bringing Gretchen and Sandra, too."

He waved a hand, humans not concerning him. Inwardly I smiled, but continued to think of nothing aside from clothing, shoes, and sexy lingerie. From the flare to his nostrils, that last one pleased him.

"I'll have your escort ready to leave in twenty minutes."

Then he leaned down, his stubble grazing my cheek as he murmured, "Don't bother getting me anything. You're all I want."

I didn't hold back my smile this time. *And you say you're not good with pretty words.*

"I won't be long," I promised.

Twenty minutes later Sandra, Gretchen, and I piled into the back of the limo. Shrapnel drove, since with Maximus gone, he'd moved into the position of Vlad's right-hand man. Oscar rode shotgun, and four more guards followed us in another vehicle.

"What's with the entourage?" Gretchen asked. I shrugged as if I had no idea.

"As the *voivode*'s wife, guards are expected," Sandra said.

"What's voya-voda mean?" Gretchen asked, sounding it out.

"Prince, basically," I replied. "*Voivode* was Vlad's title back in the day."

My sister slanted a grin at me. "So you're a princess now?"

"No," I said at the same time that Sandra said, "Yes."

"No," I repeated more firmly. "I already get bowed to. If anyone calls me Your Highness, my head might explode."

Sandra laughed, finger-combing her strawberry blonde hair. "If I were a princess, I would insist on it. And on a crown."

Would you? I thought coolly, but smiled as if it were a joke. "Romanians are used to royalty. Americans, not so much."

The limo slanted as we began descending the hill. I glanced out the window in time to see the top of the mansion disappear behind a wall of trees and rock. We wouldn't see much beyond those two things for the next thirty minutes. This was the only road leading to town, and no one but Vlad's people used it.

Gretchen continued to chatter on about how if I was a princess, then that made her famous, too. Like Kate Middleton's sister, Pippa. I didn't bother telling her that no one outside of really old Romanian vampires or Vlad's people considered him a prince. Why spoil her daydreams sooner than I had to?

I waited until we were midway between Vlad's house and the town before I made my move. I hadn't done anything before in case Sandra had been in the communications room because one of

the staff was hungry. If Vlad knew I had the slightest suspicion about her, he'd employ *his* methods
for finding out the truth, and I wouldn't do that to
a friend when I could get the same results without
emotional or physical scars.

So once Vlad was too far away to read my
thoughts and Sandra couldn't escape with Shrapnel
speeding around corners with a vampire's usual disregard for the steep terrain, I smiled at Sandra, took
off my right glove, and laid my hand on her arm.

The shriek she let out at the voltage coursing into
her was lost under the instant swarm of images.

*I'd just fallen asleep when the sound of my
door closing startled me into wakefulness. A dark
shadow contrasted against the cotton candy–
colored pink walls, and when it came closer, moonlight revealed a vampire I recognized at once.*

*"What are you doing here?" My voice was
thicker from drowsiness. "I'm not on the feeding
schedule tonight."*

*He didn't speak, but continued to come toward
me. For some reason, fear threaded through my
emotions. That made no sense. Vlad wouldn't
stand for us to be ill treated and I'd fed this vampire many times before. Yet when he reached the
bed, I shrank back, a bone-deep instinct overrul-
ing my logic.*

Not again! I wanted to shriek, yet I still didn't
know why. *Then terror and guilt rose, the sensations both sickeningly familiar and overwhelming.
Before I could speak, an emerald glow blinded me.*

At once, my concerns vanished. As the vampire whispered his instructions, I found myself nodding. Of course I would relay his message, and I had a message for him, too . . .

Gretchen's scream yanked me back before the last images faded. For a moment, I hung suspended between Sandra's mentality and my own. That's why I didn't react when the vampire in the front seat held up the small device even though I knew what it was. I'd seen one of those before, and while it was no bigger than a cell phone, its presence meant death.

Then the final ties to Sandra's memory dropped. White light suffused my hand as I snapped a current toward the front seat, but it was too late. Shrapnel pushed the button on the detonator the instant before my whip cut through him.

The subsequent *boom!* shook the limo, but we didn't explode. The car behind us did, and the sudden fireball claimed my attention for a few costly seconds. Long enough for Shrapnel to yank the steering wheel to the left, aiming our speeding vehicle right at the guardrail before he bailed out the door.

Gretchen's scream as we hurtled over the cliff was the last thing I heard before everything went black.

Blood.

Its taste flavored my mouth while its coppery scent hung in the air. I swallowed, expecting the pain radiating through me to vanish, yet it didn't. That's when I realized I wasn't swallowing vampire blood for healing. It was my own.

I forced my eyes open even though it felt like razors had replaced my eyelids. Then what I saw made me forget the pain. Gretchen hung above me, her black hair hiding her face, red drips falling onto the smashed glass that surrounded me. Sandra was also suspended by her seat belt, her blood flowing in a thicker trail. Between us was a thick tree branch, of all things, its leaves spattered with crimson.

Why aren't we dead? was my first thought, followed immediately by *Where's Shrapnel?* I sat up, trying not to scream from the pain. A glance at the front of the limo showed the driver's side was empty. The passenger side wasn't. Oscar's pale face had an expression of shock that even his rapidly mummifying skin couldn't erase. He was also suspended upside down by his seat belt in the flipped limo, the hilt of a silver knife buried in his chest.

I lurched toward that knife, sending more fiery arcs through my body. It felt like my ribs, collarbone, and left arm were fractured, plus I had more cuts than I could count from all the broken glass. Still, I was lucky. Without the side and front air bags, I'd be dead. I hadn't been wearing a seat belt since I wanted to grab Sandra in case she tried anything. Little did I know the danger came from the front seat, not the back.

Grunts of agony escaped me as I hoisted myself

over the broken glass into the front of the limo. Once there, I saw through the smashed windshield that a tree had stopped our descent down the cliff. That was the good news. The bad news was the orange flickers licking up the underside of the hood.

I yanked the knife from Oscar's body, intending to cut the seat belts from Gretchen and Sandra, when noise outside made me freeze. Someone was coming, and I wasn't naive enough to think it was rescuers.

I licked the blood-coated knife so fast that I cut my tongue, but before that pain fully registered, it vanished. In the seconds it took me to lick the other side, my whole body hurt less. By the time Shrapnel ripped off the passenger side door, I was crouched in front of Gretchen and Sandra, holding the knife in one hand while electricity crackled from the other. He immediately leapt back several feet, body tensed to dodge anything I aimed at him.

"Why?" I spat.

Half of his shirt and jacket hung in tatters, the red-stained slash showing where my whip had penetrated. Despite the severity of the wound, it hadn't killed him. It had only slowed him until he healed enough to come back and finish the job.

"Because now you know," he said in a hard voice.

"I don't mean this," I said, a jerk of my head indicating the ruined limousine. "Why did you betray Vlad?"

"I didn't intend to."

Now his voice was almost a whisper. Despair skipped across his mocha features, followed by weary resolve.

"None of this was supposed to happen. You think I wanted to kill my friends in that car? I don't even want to kill you, but I have no choice."

I raised my right hand higher. "You so much as twitch and I'll cut you in half for real this time."

He was too far away for me to attempt it now, but if he came closer, he'd be in range. I didn't dare risk charging him due to the steep incline, plus that would leave Gretchen and Sandra helpless. Instead, I waited for him to lunge at me with his inhuman speed, but as the seconds ticked by and Shrapnel didn't move, I grew suspicious. Sure, he knew I wasn't bluffing, but it wouldn't take long for word of the crash to reach Vlad. He had to know that, so why wasn't he at least attempting to—

Then the wind blew a noxious fume my way. Once I smelled it, I understood. Shrapnel didn't have to move to kill me. All he had to do was wait for the fire to reach the leaking gas tank.

Chapter 34

"If you run now, you might make it before Vlad gets here," I said, switching tactics. I couldn't free Gretchen and Sandra *and* fight off Shrapnel before the car blew. We both knew that.

"It's already too late. You didn't die in the crash and it took too long for me to heal before I reached you."

Again he sounded more weary than villain-ish. He even sighed as though burdened beyond what he could bear.

"Now all that's left is to ensure your death."

"What did I ever do to you?" I snapped, hoping someone from the mansion had seen the smoke and help was on the way.

"It's what you will do if you live." His gaze shifted to my right hand. "My death is already certain. Hers is not."

Her. I took a last stab at making him run or charge me.

"You mean the pretty brunette vampire?" I

said, betting it all that it was the same woman I'd glimpsed in my vision. "Hate to break it to you, but she was found out days ago. Vlad's already got people hunting her down. We just didn't know who the traitor was."

"Lies," Shrapnel hissed.

He took a step forward and I held my breath. *Come on, just a little closer!*

"How's this for lies? She's five foot four, curvier than me, thick walnut-colored hair, lilting accent . . . want me to go on?"

I couldn't, but as the scent of gasoline increased, so did my desperation. I debated charging him despite the steep hill and his incredible speed. Then he took another step closer.

"How did you break her spell to reach her?"

"Oh, it was easy," I said, thinking it was a damn good thing Shrapnel wasn't a mind reader because I had no idea what he was talking about. "Where do you think I got all this straight black hair from? I'm one quarter Cherokee and my grandmother was a powerful medicine woman. She taught my mother and me all kinds of mystical tricks, so your little bitch's spell was no match for the magic *I* know."

Except for the one quarter Cherokee part, the rest was all lies. I held my breath, hoping that Shrapnel didn't realize that.

"Don't speak of her that way!" he roared.

He took another step forward and that was my chance. I exploded toward him, snapping all the electricity I could muster into a whip that shone as bright as lightning. He lunged to avoid it, but even his speed wasn't enough. That dazzling cord caught him in the hip and continued all the way through.

His legs dropped like felled tree limbs, pitching the rest of him forward with his momentum. He ended up landing on me, his weight knocking the breath from me. Before I could push him off, he began pummeling me while his fangs tore at anything close enough to bite.

I screamed at the brutal double assault. Being almost cut in half hadn't diminished Shrapnel's ferocity. Instead, he seemed almost demonic in his determination to kill me. A stunning blow caved in my rib cage, cutting off my scream. The savageness of the pain stole all thought, triggering blind survival instinct. I didn't consciously grab him and send a current into him. All I knew was that his weight was suddenly gone and I was transported into a decrepit alley.

The streetlights were broken, but I didn't need them to see as I strode down the narrow path between the buildings.

"You killed the bomb maker, too? When will you stop taking such reckless, stupid risks!"

My bellow drew several glances. I didn't care. Most vampires avoided places where the homeless dwelled. They smelled too much to make eating them palatable.

"It wasn't too risky" was my lover's unruffled

reply. "I took care of it, dearie. He's dead, ending any chance this will be traced back to us."

Fury made me grip the phone before I forcibly relaxed my hand so it wouldn't shatter and end our call.

"If you hadn't used him to kill Leila, he wouldn't have needed taking care of. I wouldn't have told you where she was if I knew what you intended. If Vlad doesn't believe the explosion was an accident, he won't rest until he finds her killers."

"You're overreacting," she said, and the boredom in her tone hit me like a splash of acid. "Even if there are suspicions, they won't lead anywhere. Whatever she might have been worth to him alive, she's less dangerous to us dead."

My laugh was harsh. "One day, you'll tell me the real reason you don't want Vlad to know about us. Until then, the only motive I see for you killing Leila is jealousy."

I'd intended the accusation to sting, but I hadn't anticipated the venom in her response.

"My reasons don't matter. What does matter is you are the one who gave me her location. He'll kill you for that, dearie, and only after years of torturing you. Unless that sounds appealing, you have no choice but to keep this a secret."

I hung up, my sense of despair equal to the knowledge that she was right. Vlad would respond only one way to my part in Leila's death, and he wouldn't stop there. He'd do the same to her, and despite my anger, I couldn't let that happen. I *loved her, and if lying would keep her safe, then I would lie.*

The alley dissolved and I expected to fall back into my own reality, but without even trying to, I linked to Shrapnel's accomplice next. For a split second, I saw her, wearing a skirt suit and reclined on a couch with a martini in her hand. Before I could focus on her face, her features blurred, leaving nothing but a blob surrounded by lustrous walnut-colored hair.

Then a wave of dizziness assailed me, as if someone just whacked me over the head with a two-by-four. I dropped the link, returning to the present where I was curled on my side, coughing between tortured gasps for air. Blood dribbled from my mouth and the pressure in my chest increased until it was excruciating.

This wasn't from the beating Shrapnel had given me. No, I recognized this pain. My abilities had hit the lethal zone, and the only vampire near enough to heal me wanted me dead.

Frustration made me want to howl at the unfairness of it all. I was only supposed to use my abilities on Sandra to see if she was guilty or innocent. I hadn't meant to pull Shrapnel's worst sin, let alone link to the bitch who'd started this whole mess with the carnival bomb. Now those things would kill me.

A groan made me open my eyes. Through a haze of red, I caught a glimpse of Shrapnel. The current I'd blasted into him had thrown him over a dozen feet away. Both his arms were now missing in addition to his legs, and his skin looked like meat someone had put through a grinder. Despite all the damage from the current, he was still alive. Then his head lolled toward me and our eyes met.

A sliver of surprise threaded through my fading consciousness. I hadn't expected any empathy from him, but I was unprepared for the mixture of relief and pride in his expression. Relief made sense; he wanted me dead, and from the crushing pain in my chest, he'd soon get his wish. But why pride? He had nothing to do with my abilities overloading enough to put the final nails in my coffin . . .

Far too late, I figured it out.

How did you break her spell to reach her? Shrapnel had asked. I thought he meant the brunette vampire had cooked up something magical to prevent me from getting a clear look at her face if I linked to her, but it was more than that.

The spell was also meant to kill me.

Chapter 35

"Leila!"

My sister's voice cut through the agony that made me want to stay in the fetal position or die, whichever hurt less. *Gretchen. Sounds afraid* penetrated past my pain, followed by an ominous memory. *The limo's on fire.*

I pushed myself to my knees, a gurgling scream escaping me. Through vision that was starting to blacken, I caught a gleam of orange. The flames had spread farther up the vehicle. They could reach the leaking gas tank any second.

I lunged at the limo, blood spewing from my mouth as I tried to breathe through the almost paralyzing pressure in my chest. My vision was too blurry to find the knife I'd dropped, and the pain made me feel like I was on fire. Maybe I was and didn't realize it. Still, I couldn't stop. I focused on my sister's screams and they were like a shot of adrenaline, giving me the strength to lunge forward again, and again. The side of the car hit me in the face as I staggered into it.

My vision was now totally black and Gretchen's voice was fainter, but my mind still worked. With my left hand, I fumbled until I found the lock for the seat belt. Then I dragged my right hand over my arm until it reached the spot. With the last bit of energy I had, I sent a bolt of electricity through it.

The sudden thump of weight onto my shoulders was the most wonderful thing I'd ever felt.

"Save Sandra," I tried to say, but all that came out was an unintelligible gurgle.

Something shoved me roughly, blasting more pain into me. *Had Shrapnel come back?* I wondered, and then didn't care as a lovely numbness began to creep over me. *Not good*, a shred of rationale warned. *Don't pass out! You won't wake up!*

I tried to force my way past the darkness and the addictive bliss of diminishing pain. It felt like swimming in quicksand—the more I struggled, the deeper I sank. Then consciousness returned at the brutal sensation of being dragged. My ribs felt like twigs someone snapped within me, but I managed a few ragged gulps of air. That and the fresh deluge of pain chased away the ominous lethargy. Then a thunderous noise snapped my eyes open, an orange haze momentarily blinding me.

The fire had reached the gas tank at last.

Through the tiny slits that remained of my vision, I saw I was now behind some trees, their trunks taking the brunt of the exploding debris. Sandra was unconscious nearby, and Gretchen . . .

I had to be hallucinating. If I wasn't, then my sister was about twenty feet away, crouched on top of Shrapnel. She had the knife he'd killed Oscar with sticking out of his chest, and though her expression showed she was terrified, both her hands were firmly wrapped around the hilt.

"Don't even think of trying anything," she gasped.

Shrapnel's eyes were fixed on her while the stick-like things growing from his shoulders and hips twitched. Soon his arms and legs would be fully regenerated and the damage to his insides healed. I was about to warn Gretchen that he *would* try something when three forms dropped next to them with the abruptness of crashing meteors. The fourth landed next to me, green eyes ablaze and dark hair whipping wildly as he tore his wrist open before shoving it against my mouth.

Vlad. Someone must've spotted the smoke after all.

As I began to drink from the deep slash, Vlad's guards hauled Shrapnel up, one of them removing the knife before he could spare himself by taking his own life. Then my vision went completely dark. I swallowed again, but the pain wracking my body didn't lessen. Instead, it grew until it felt like razors were being shoved into my skull while the tightness in my chest spread to engulf the rest of my body. I couldn't swallow anymore. I couldn't even summon the strength to take another breath. When coldness swept over me, replacing the pain with its icy caress, I knew he'd arrived too late.

"No!"

Vlad's shout held me down, but only for a moment. Then inner chains I'd never felt before broke and I burst forth like a bullet being fired through a gun. I wasn't broken on the ground anymore. I was soaring, and it was more exhilarating than any of the dreams I'd had where I could fly. My vision was no longer an ugly haze of crimson and darkness. Instead, everything was bathed in brightest light while the comforting scent of rainwater and freesia enveloped me. I'd smelled that before, so long ago I'd forgotten it, but now I knew at once who it belonged to. And then I saw her.

The streaks of silver in her black hair looked radiant. So did the tiny lines on her face when she smiled. All at once, the guilt I'd carried fell away. She didn't say anything. She didn't need to. I *felt* that she'd never blamed me for her death and that she'd forgiven me all my other wrongs. I rushed toward her, but with that lovely smile, she held out a hand to ward me off.

Not yet, baby, whispered across my mind.

Then something yanked me down with brutal force. Her sweet scent vanished, as did the crystalline sunshine I'd been flying in. I began to fall with terrifying speed, every attempt to catch myself countered with another relentless tug. The ground was fast approaching, yet I could do nothing to fight the invisible grip that pitilessly continued to wrench me downward.

When I landed on that unyielding surface, the impact broke me apart. I waited for the soothing cold caress of death to come, but it didn't.

Instead, all I felt was fire.

Chapter 36

Blood.

My mouth was wet with it while its scent perfumed the air, no longer coppery and sharp, but heady and intoxicating. I swallowed and inhaled simultaneously, trying to fill myself in every way with the blissful liquid that made the pain go away. For a few moments, I was lost in satiation so complete it was like coming and cresting an incredible high at the same time.

Then, like every high I'd relived through my abilities, the crash left me shivering, hurting, and desperate for another hit.

Someone snarled, "More," in a tone I'd expect from a rabid animal if it could talk. The response was a wet, chilly cloth to my face. It took away the blood I'd been licking, and my eyes snapped open in outrage. Once they did, everything was so bright and vivid that for a second, I couldn't focus.

"I said more!"

Two things registered at the same time. That savage voice came from me, and I hadn't breathed in between speaking. Feeling tiny daggers jab me in the lip was almost redundant.

You've really done it this time, my inner voice mocked.

My teeth ground, driving what I knew were fangs deeper into my lower lip. Seemed that dying and being brought back as a vampire *still* hadn't killed my hated internal voice.

Then the kaleidoscope of colors became distinct shapes and Vlad came into focus. His black pants and indigo shirt reeked of smoke and burnt rubber, but under that, I caught the rich aroma of blood, and everything else vanished.

I leapt on him, seeking those luscious traces with an urgency that had me tearing into his skin and clothes with my new fangs. He murmured something I didn't comprehend in my search for the source of that scent. Part of me was appalled at my savageness, yet the rest only cared for one thing.

Blood. Need it. NOW.

Vlad shoved me away, one hand holding my snapping mouth at bay while the other reached behind him. That inner burning had returned, ravaging me with pain so intense I couldn't think past the need to make it stop. Then ambrosia slid down my throat, dousing my anguish so thoroughly that grateful tears slid down my cheeks. I swallowed as though I was trying to drown, my eyes closing with relief so profound I thought I might pass out.

Then something else edged through my relief.

Anger, followed by a tidal wave of the rawest, most unbridled emotion I'd ever felt. Calling it love was likening a spring shower to a hurricane, and when I realized it didn't come from me, but the vampire still holding my jaw in an iron grip, I was shocked.

"I can feel you."

The whisper made his gaze gleam brighter than I'd seen before, yet now, it didn't hurt to hold his stare.

"Because your shopping deception cost you your humanity."

The harshness in his tone would've made me flinch except for the fresh surge across my emotions. More anger, yes, but born from fear of losing me. I hadn't thought Vlad was capable of being afraid, yet it threaded through my subconscious along with another wave of love's seething, unhinged second cousin. I thought his controlling behavior stemmed from arrogance, but it came from a pathological need to protect me. If I wasn't still fixated on thoughts of blood, I'd be amazed at all he'd acquiesced to while that compulsion raged in him.

Then another crippling pain hit me, erasing the rest under a hunger so severe it was like starving to death a thousand times in the space of seconds. I would've collapsed if not for Vlad's grip, and before I could scream from that awful inner burning, a new mouthful of ambrosia took the agony away.

I swallowed as greedily as before, this time returning to my senses before he pried the sodden shreds of plastic out of my hands. *Plasma bags*, I noted while licking my hands clean with an impulse I couldn't control. How modern of him. If memory served, I'd be a blood-crazed maniac for days until I garnered enough strength not to murder the first living person who crossed my path. The thought was depressing.

Then another realization belatedly struck.

"How am I a vampire instead of a ghoul? I remember dying . . ."

And seeing my mother. That stunned me into momentarily forgetting my question. She hadn't been a dream or an illusion; I knew that as surely as I knew my own name. That meant there *was* something after death. I'd never believed it because I hadn't seen it from the other deaths I'd relived, but maybe glimpsing what lay beyond had to be personally experienced.

Vlad's grip loosened until he stroked my throat instead of restrained my jaw. "My blood wasn't enough to heal you this time. It did, however, start the transformation process."

"How?"

His teeth flashed in a humorless smile. "In normal transformations, I'd drain you to the point of death before having you drink my blood. You drained yourself to the point of death with your injuries, and you had enough of my blood in you that the additional amount I gave you tipped you over the edge."

Then his hand dropped, rage-infused anguish scraping across my emotions before he went on.

"Of course I didn't know that until after you died, when suddenly, you began tearing at my throat."

I didn't remember that, nor did I have any recollection of being brought here. The last thing I remembered was seeing Shrapnel hauled up by guards and Vlad kneeling beside me.

"Gretchen. She's okay, isn't she?"

"Minor injuries only."

This time the relief I felt wasn't fueled by ingesting a bellyful of blood. "And Sandra?"

"More serious injuries, but she'll recover."

I didn't want to ask, but I had to know. "Shrapnel?"

His mouth tightened. "Where he belongs."

That meant the dungeon, no doubt. Maybe that's where we were, too. This room looked like a fancier version of one of Vlad's prison cells since the walls, ceiling, and floor were solid rock with no apparent exit, but there were two stacked mattresses in the corner covered by several thick blankets. That hadn't been standard in the dungeon accommodations I'd seen, though the absence of lights was—

And I could still see perfectly. I blinked as if expecting that to change, which of course it didn't. No light illuminated the tight quarters, yet I saw every inch down to the red smears streaking the walls that smelled so good I wanted to lick them. When twin pinpricks of pain jabbed me in the lip, I knew my new fangs had sprung out again.

I closed my eyes, feeling overwhelmed. I hadn't wanted this so soon and I didn't know if I could handle it. But ready or not, I was now a vampire. My hand slid down my chest to my heart. Twenty-five years of beating, and yet forevermore it would be as silent as a drum that someone had abandoned.

When I opened my eyes, Vlad was staring at me. He said nothing, yet an odd mixture of empathy and ruthlessness strafed my subconscious. *You brought this on yourself*, his emotions seemed to relay, *but you will not face it alone.*

I stared back, noticing a tiny scar by his nose that I hadn't seen before. That wasn't the only thing. His skin no longer seemed pale; it looked faintly luminescent, as though covering a light he carried within. His hair wasn't merely dark brown, but a rich collage of black, umber, and chestnut. The air around him crackled with energy, and when he stroked my throat again, his hand tingled as if he were the one suffused with inner electricity.

"You're different now, too," I said in wonder.

His mouth curled; half mocking, half amused.

"You're a vampire. You see details humans are blind to, sense powers they don't understand, and feel emotions more strongly than they can even imagine."

Then he grasped my hair, using it to pull my head back before lowering his mouth.

"Now feel this," he muttered.

The rough caress of his stubble and sensual suppleness of his lips paled next to emotions blasting across my subconscious. Lust tore through me like a flash fire, almost dropping me to my knees. It burned my nerve endings as thoroughly as the hunger had, but not with pain. Instead, I was over-whelmed with a need to dominate by pleasure until rapturous screams rang in my ears, and to do it right now.

My mouth opened, tongue tangling with his while I grasped his shirt. It fell apart in my hands as easily as wet paper, and then his heat made me gasp when he yanked me to him. He'd always been warm, but now he felt like flame encased in flesh. He ripped off my dress, bra, and panties just as ruthlessly as I'd destroyed his shirt before flinging me onto the nearby mattress.

I moaned when his body covered mine, shocked at how different this also was. Every brush of his skin heightened sensations that had me arch-ing against him with primal demand. Each caress seemed to penetrate into hidden parts of me that were starved for his touch. Everything before faded to a colorless memory like the psychic glimpses I caught of the past. It was as though this was the first time we were making love, and when he pushed my thighs apart and his mouth descended between them, a flare of ecstasy made me scream.

I don't know how long I writhed against him, pleasure rending me asunder with every sear-ing flick of his tongue. When he rose up and tore the front of his pants open, I was still shuddering from orgasm, but seeing that thick length of flesh swelled need in me all over again. I slid down, pulling him on top of me. Then my head fell back from the force of his kiss as his mouth claimed mine.

His taste was sharper, saltier, and so explicitly carnal it made me ache where I was wet. His body was an inferno, and anticipation cut my emotions in a visceral swath when he reached down between us. I broke our kiss and bit his shoulder without thinking, shocked at how natural it felt. Pleasure rippled through me as I sank my fangs deeper. Whether it was mine or his, I didn't know, and when he yanked my hips up to meet his thrust, I didn't care.

I stopped biting him to scream when his scorching flesh pushed inside me. Had it felt like this before? No, it couldn't. I wouldn't have been able to stand the exquisite clenching of my inner muscles when he ground against my clitoris after he could go no deeper. Or the bliss when his mouth closed over my throat and he bit down where my pulse would have been. Then he thrust forward, my throat still captured in his fangs, and the sense of being utterly dominated and yet never more powerful ripped away my inhibitions.

I tore his mouth away, barely noticing the sting from his fangs as my skin tore. Then I wrapped my arms around him and bit him in the same spot. Pleasure overloaded my nerve endings from the connection to his feelings, driving me to a frenzy. He moved faster, deeper, his grip turning bruising, and I gloried in it, sinking my fangs into his neck to match every hard thrust. My nails ripped across his back, drawing a slickness that wasn't sweat. Ecstasy grew along with an inner ache that demanded more without caring if it was too much. He was too hot, too big, too rough—and I'd die if he stopped.

I tore my mouth away from his neck, gasping, "I love you so much," right before another orgasm left me shaking from its intensity. Through half-slitted eyes I saw Vlad's head was thrown back, streaks of crimson marring the sleek line of his throat. Then his head lowered and he stared at me while his searing hands stroked my face.

"And I love you, my wife."

I didn't have a chance to respond. He slid down, his mouth descending between my legs with passionate ferocity. I arched against him with a moan that was half rapture, half frustration. This felt incredible, but I wanted him inside me again—

All thought cleared my mind when his fangs replaced his tongue, piercing my clitoris instead of licking it. White-hot pleasure blasted through me, making electricity shoot from my right hand. Smoke curled from the hole it drilled into the bed, but all I could do was clutch the sheets as he began to suck with long, deep pulls.

His name left my throat in a strangled sob. Another strong suction had me shouting it, and then I couldn't think enough to do that. All I could do was clutch him while wordless cries tore from me, and when he flipped me over after a final, mind-shattering suction, I couldn't even move.

He pulled my hips up, a deep thrust drawing another choked cry from me. My flesh throbbed and tingled, tightening around him convulsively as he withdrew. He lifted me, drawing me into his lap. Another arch of his hips cleaved him into me again. I gripped his thighs as I rocked back against him, feeling his burning lips on my neck when he drew my hair aside to kiss me there. Then there was nothing except the fierce rhythm that brought me to climax the instant before he reached his, and the shudders that shook us within and without.

Chapter 37

 When Vlad let me go, I fell back against the mattress, not panting only because I didn't need to breathe. I'd never smoked before, but if this cell had a cigarette, I would've lit up in salutary commemoration.

Then my stomach clenched. My satiation vanished, replaced by hunger so intense that I began to shake.

Vlad jerked me up, pushing me against the wall with one hand while the other punched numbers on a keypad I hadn't noticed before. A drawer slid out of the stone surface, and one glance at what it contained made my mind go blank with need.

The next few minutes were a whirling carousel of pain and relief. When my sanity returned, I was still against the wall, sucking at the remains of a plastic bag while Vlad watched.

He held out his hand and I forced myself to relinquish the bag even though it had some luscious crimson streaks remaining. Still, I would *not* act like an animal a moment longer than necessary.

He took it and the other cellophane remains at my feet, depositing them in the same slot the bags had come from.

"How did you know?" I managed to ask calmly.

A shrug. "It's the same with all new vampires. Sex, anger, and violence will trigger your hunger. Until you can control it, you need to learn to anticipate it."

I glanced down. Blood splashed my front from how madly I'd torn at the plasma bags, making me look like an actress from a pornographic horror movie. I had several more days of mindless feeding frenzies ahead, but some things couldn't wait for me to master my new hunger.

I went over to the bed and wrapped the sheet around me. What I had to say was too serious to talk about while naked.

"So you figured out Shrapnel was the traitor," I began.

A snort cut me off. "I didn't think you cut him into pieces because he *accidentally* drove you off a cliff."

I held his gaze. "He was the only traitor in your house, but he wasn't the only accomplice."

Vlad's gaze turned bright green. "Explain."

"Sandra was passing messages—"

I didn't get to say anything else before Vlad whirled, pressing a part of the wall that looked no different from the rest, yet a door suddenly appeared.

"Waters," he barked into the open space. "Secure Sandra immediately."

Don't, I mentally yelled. *It's not her fault!*

He didn't reply. Right, he couldn't hear my thoughts anymore. I'd put that and spectacular sex in the plus column of being a vampire.

"She didn't know," I said out loud. "Shrapnel mesmerized her into doing it. I saw it when I touched her."

He turned, his expression no less foreboding, but he did add, "Secure her *gently*, Waters," before closing it by pressing another indistinguishable panel.

"What else did you see?"

I couldn't tell if his displeasure curling into my emotions was due to Shrapnel's actions or mine.

"First promise me you're not going hurt Sandra."

He folded his arms across his chest. With his muscular build and the blood spattered on him from my rabid feedings, he couldn't have looked more menacing, but I refused to back down.

"Promise me," I repeated.

"I do have other ways to find out," he said silkily.

I let out a grim snort. "Why do you think I went behind your back? I'm well aware of your 'ways' for getting information. That's why I wasn't going to subject my friend to them if she'd done nothing wrong."

His mouth tightened while echoes of his anger slashed my emotions, yet that wasn't all. As poignant as a bittersweet memory, regret floated into my subconscious. Losing my mortality was my fault, but I realized Vlad blamed himself, too.

Then he pressed the wall and that hidden door appeared again.

"Well, go on," he said with a sweep of his hand.

I looked at the open entry suspiciously. "Aren't I supposed to be in lockdown because I'm a blood-thirsty menace right now?"

"Yes, but you're coming with me to see for your-self that Sandra won't be harmed, as long as she didn't knowingly betray me. Unless, of course"—a sharklike grin—"you end up ripping her throat out yourself."

I hadn't expected to return to the dungeon so soon, yet after showering, getting dressed, going into another feeding frenzy, showering and redressing again, here I was. When we entered the first cham-ber of the dungeon, the stench made me recoil. It smelled like someone had mixed together kerosene, rotten fruit, stale blood, urine, and dog shit, then blown it up. How had I not noticed this before? I wasn't even breathing, but the rancid odor found its way into my nose anyway.

"This place *stinks*."

"Did the guards forget to spray Febreze?" Vlad asked in mock indignation. Then he gave me a jaded look. "It's a dungeon, Leila. They're sup-posed to smell."

Mission accomplished. The stench might have actually killed my new appetite. If Hell could fart, it would smell like this.

"Leila!"

I turned toward Sandra's voice. She wasn't restrained to the large stone monolith, to my relief. Instead, she was huddled on the floor, her expression so stricken it was clear she thought she'd never leave this place. As soon as she saw me, she lunged toward me.

"Please, tell them there has been a mistake!"

One of the guards appeared out of nowhere, catching her before she reached me. Good thing, too. She'd also showered and changed clothes since the accident, but I could smell dried blood from her scratches, scabs, and the stitched wound in her head even above the horrid stink. Fangs pressed against my gums.

You just ate, I reminded myself, *and Sandra is NOT dessert.*

"It's okay," I told her. "Vlad just needs to peel back your memories on a few things."

We were doing that here because he wanted Shrapnel to witness the exposure of his betrayal and there was only one place *he* was staying. Despite the challenge to my control, I wasn't leaving until Vlad was finished probing Sandra's mind. I was the only ally she had, and the dungeon was terrifying enough without having a friend at your side. Vlad might taunt me about ripping out Sandra's throat, but he'd never let me do it.

Besides, I also wanted to hear more about the brunette vampire Shrapnel had been getting it on with. Like why she'd been so determined to kill me, for starters.

Of course, being down here meant coming face-to-face with Vlad's dark side, and he wasted no time in letting it out.

"Take him down," he said, pointing at Shrapnel.

Three vampires again appeared like ninjas, but as they removed the many manacles binding Shrapnel to the stone wall, their movements no longer appeared blurringly fast. Before the last silver chain fell, Vlad picked up a lengthy wooden pole and rammed it the long way through Shrapnel's midsection.

Sandra gasped. I tried not to notice how her heart rate sped up as if trying to catch my attention. Surreptitiously, I squeezed the plasma bag I'd tucked into my jacket. If I felt a hunger stab, I'd rip into that instead, giving the guards more time to protect Sandra. How was that for anticipating?

Vlad carried Shrapnel over to one of the holes in the stone, dropping the end of the pole in as casually as putting a flower in a vase. Through it all, Shrapnel let out several harsh grunts, but that was it. His fortitude was impressive, but the stronger he was, the more he'd endure while Vlad sought to discover who he'd betrayed him to and why. Shrapnel had tried to kill me twice, yet I still couldn't help but pity him.

A sniffle directed my attention back to Sandra. Her head hung low, long reddish-gold hair shielding her expression.

"I did something awful, didn't I?" she whispered.

"I don't remember it, but when you touched me in the car, I *felt* it."

I wanted to pat her consolingly but her pulse was already starting to sound like a dinner bell, so I didn't trust myself to get any closer.

"Vlad's not angry at you," I said in my most reassuring voice. "In fact, you're going to help us find the other person who forced you to betray him, and then we're going to stop her."

Vlad's brow arched.

"Her?"

"Her," I repeated, glancing up at Shrapnel. "And apparently, she's a spell caster."

Chapter 38

Shrapnel stared at me and his obsidian gaze became sprinkled with green.

"You lied to me. You *don't* know who she is."

He sounded more surprised than angry, not that he'd have any reason to point fingers on the subject of dishonesty.

"We don't know yet, but we're about to," I replied coolly.

With Shrapnel now getting a bird's-eye view, Vlad strode over to Sandra.

"If you were aware of none of your actions because they altered your memory, I will hold you blameless."

Conditional words of comfort, but they worked. Sandra knelt on one knee and bowed her head.

"You took me from the streets after my parents abandoned me. Gave me a home, an education, and the promise of a better future. I would never knowingly betray you."

Vlad's mouth curled sardonically as he cast a

look up at Shrapnel. "Then you would be more faithful than two of my closest friends turned out to be."

At those words, a stinging mixture of anger and pain threaded into my emotions. I winced, reminded that Shrapnel's actions were more than a vampire going against his sire. A knife in the back hurt so much worse when it came from a friend.

Sandra rose and brushed her hair aside. "*Lasă-mă să-ţi dovedesc, prinţul meu!*"

Vlad grasped her neck and lowered his mouth. As he bit her, something rose in me I didn't expect. Not hunger, though the fresh scent of blood made my own fangs spring out. Not concern for Sandra losing more blood since she was already in rough shape. Instead, I had an overwhelming urge to rip her out of Vlad's arms and then lash her with a sizzling electrical whip until nothing remained but ragged pieces.

I was jealous. How *absurd*. He was a vampire, she was a human who'd had her mind altered, and the best way to get around that was to take her blood before mesmerizing her. I knew that, but it didn't stop the surge of emotions that made sparks fall from my hand.

His mouth on her. Her head falling back in a way that didn't denote pain. The line of his throat as he swallowed . . .

A bolt torpedoed into the rock floor beneath my hand. Turning into a vampire hadn't dulled my inner electricity a bit. At once, I covered the crack with my foot, as if that would stop anyone from noticing.

Vlad lifted his head, his gaze going unerringly to the spot before he looked at me. I expected an eye roll for my display of irrational jealousy, but instead, he looked thoughtful.

Then he released Sandra, dabbing the puncture wounds in her neck with his thumb after he pierced it with a fang. I tried to rein in my emotions—and the currents that kept my hand sparking—while mentally singing Sting's "Every Breath You Take." *Life-and-death stakes going on, Leila. Get your priorities straight.*

"He came into her room to mesmerize her," I said, in case that detail helped.

Vlad's eyes turned green as he stared at Sandra like she was the only person in the room.

"Shrapnel came into your room," he repeated, his voice resonant. "He wanted you to pass along a message. What was it?"

"I don't know," she whispered.

"Yes you do."

The air crackled, causing the hairs on my arms to stand on end. An invisible wave seemed to roll off Vlad, filling the room with enough energy to make my skin crawl. What was he *doing*?

"You can see him in your room," Vlad continued in that same vibrating tone. "Hear his voice even now. What is he saying?"

"He says"—her face tightened as if straining to hear a far-off whisper—"tell her that her powers are back. She almost died using them, but Vlad revived her and now he won't leave her side. I will attempt tainting her food if she wakes up."

I swung an accusing look Shrapnel's way. While I was in a coma, he was planning to poison me?

Rage brushed my emotions but Vlad said nothing and he didn't glance away from Sandra.

"That wasn't his only message. What else?"

In the monotone I'd come to associate with people under a vampire's influence, Sandra recounted Shrapnel telling his accomplice all the details of my abilities, my location at the carnival, and my location at the hotel with Maximus. He even stated that Maximus would need to be neutralized by extreme measures. The liquid silver bullets flashed across my mind. It didn't get much more extreme than that.

When Vlad ordered Sandra to repeat the woman's messages, they started off as benign inquiries about me that seemed more curious than threatening. That changed after the carnival bombing. Once her real intentions were exposed, it wasn't a surprise that subsequent messages consisted of variations of *Kill Leila. Kill her now.* While my anger grew, most of this we already knew, and I didn't need to feel Vlad's emotions to know he was frustrated by that, too.

"Where do you meet her to relay these messages?" he asked.

Sandra frowned. "I've never met her, but every two days, I go into town to the bookstore. I write the messages down and put them in *The Odyssey* by Homer. If *The Odyssey* has a new message waiting from her, I memorize it, throw it away, and then repeat it to Shrapnel, but *only* if he asks me to. Otherwise, I never mention it. I don't even remember the messages."

Sandra said the last part like she was repeating a set of instructions. No doubt she was, and they'd been given to her under the same mind-controlling circumstances she was in now.

"Get to the bookstore," Vlad said without looking away from Sandra. One of his guards bowed smartly and then left.

"You've never met her, but did he tell you her name?"

More of that hair-raising energy rolled out of Vlad, until I was rubbing my arms to chase the tingling sensations away. Was this what Marty meant when he told me vampires could measure each others' strength by feeling their auras? If so, then Vlad's had *Badass: Do Not Engage* written all over it.

"I don't think I'm supposed to know it." Sandra sounded bemused. "But once, Shrapnel called her Cynthiana."

Vlad's features hardened as though his face had been transformed into stone. Clearly he recognized the name. It sounded familiar to me, too, but I couldn't place where I'd heard it. Shrapnel closed his eyes, his expression showing more pain than when Vlad rammed a long wooden pole through his torso. Despite everything, Shrapnel still loved her, and his worst fear was now realized because she'd just landed herself at the top of Vlad's most wanted list.

My gaze swung back to Vlad as memory clicked. "Cynthiana. Isn't that the name of the woman you dated before me?"

"It is," Vlad said, still staring at Shrapnel.

I wracked my brain to recall what else Maximus had said. She'd been with Vlad for a ridiculously long time—*that* I remembered—and when he dumped her, she did something. What was it? Right, she dated one of his friends trying to make him jealous. Oldest trick in the book, but it hadn't worked . . .

And that friend had been Shrapnel. I goggled at him.

"Did Cynthiana think if I were dead, she'd have another chance at Vlad? If so, *why* would you go along with that? You love her; I felt it when I linked to you."

Shrapnel said nothing. His silence was further proof of his feelings, but if she wasn't motivated by jealousy, why would Cynthiana risk her own life by repeatedly trying to end mine?

Whatever her reasons, she'd murdered a bunch of innocent people before her linking booby trap had finally killed me—temporarily. Dawn's face flashed in my mind. She hadn't deserved to die before she could find her way in life. Neither had anyone else at the carnival, and Vlad's guards hadn't deserved getting blown up because Shrapnel was making a last-ditch effort to cover his tracks. Finally, *I* hadn't deserved any of the crap I'd endured because of Cynthiana's murderous intentions.

"You can go, Sandra," Vlad said, his eyes darkening back to their normal copper color. "Your part in this is forgiven."

Released from his gaze, she blinked, then said something very fast in Romanian.

"Of course this is still your home," Vlad replied impatiently. Then he waved a dismissive hand. "Go."

A bearded guard escorted Sandra out. I was glad to see her leave. She'd done nothing to warrant being here, unlike the vampire suspended on the tall wooden pole.

Vlad stared at Shrapnel. For an instant, a tornado of rage, frustration, and regret assaulted my emotions. Then it was as if a wall slammed down, cutting off everything except my own angry feelings. Even the swirling energy coming from Vlad dissipated.

"You know what happens now," he said, sounding utterly dispassionate.

I did, too. *Bring it on!* a vengeful part of me snarled.

Then I remembered the grisly machines in the next cavern. Vlad would show no pity in order to discover where Cynthiana was, but if I could link to the brunette vampire, I could spare Shrapnel some of that. He deserved to die for what he'd done, yet if my powers had hung on through my transformation, I could make it a quicker, less painful death. If I didn't at least try, wasn't I as heartless as the bitch who'd cold-bloodedly murdered several people in her attempts to kill me?

"Let's try something else first."

Only Vlad's eyes moved as he glanced at me. "He's come too far to be cajoled into giving her up now."

Shrapnel bared his teeth. Not a smile. One predator's warning to another. Then he said something in a language that sounded like Romanian, but more guttural. Vlad grunted.

"I have no doubt you'll make me work for it, my friend." Then to me he said simply, "Leave. You won't want to see this."

That, I had no doubt, but I wasn't finished.

"He's tough as nails, so you can do your worst for weeks . . . or let me do my best in minutes."

Vlad glanced at my hands with a hard little smile.

"It's very likely your abilities won't work so soon after your transformation, if they return at all."

"I'm still filled with voltage. The rest has to be there, too."

So saying, I bent and touched the ground with my right hand. Nothing. After a few seconds, a sound escaped Shrapnel; half sigh, half laugh. Even though he knew it meant his torture, he was glad.

My mouth thinned as I touched the ground again. Still nothing but cold, uneven stone. I did it a third time, yet despite how essence-soaked these rocks must be, I saw nothing.

"Leila." Vlad sounded almost weary. "You can't stop this."

He didn't realize it, but those words only fueled my determination. All my life, I'd been told, "You can't." First it was "You can't compete at an Olympic level," yet I won a shot at making the gymnastics team. Then after all the nerve damage from the accident, it was "You can't walk again," but not only did I walk, I joined the circus as an acrobat. Then it was "You can't touch anyone," but I met Marty, a vampire who became my work partner and best friend. Then later, it was "You can't ask me to love you," but now I was *Mrs.* Vlad Dracul, thank you very much.

I glared at the gray stone floor. No way would a hunk of rock defeat me after everything I'd been through.

I didn't touch it again—I raked my hand over it so hard that I cut it on the tiny edges in the stone. Then I concentrated until I didn't hear Vlad's continued admonitions to stop or Shrapnel's mocking laugh.

There. No louder than a whisper, far more fleeting than a glimpse, but something was *there*, dammit! I concentrated until all my being was focused on the stone beneath my hand, and then I saw it. Gloriously gruesome images of a charbroiled vampire thudding to the floor where I touched, his mouth open in a final, silent scream.

I rose, only now noticing that Vlad knelt next to me, giving me a look of exasperation as he drew my hand away.

"Leila, enough—"

Whatever he saw on my face made him stop speaking. Very slowly, he let me go. Then he rose while the oddest mixture of pride and irritation peppered my emotions.

"Good news is, you get out of torture," I told Shrapnel. "Bad news is, I'm going after your girlfriend, and now her spell doesn't matter because I'm already dead."

Chapter 39

I wanted to start trying to link to Cynthiana immediately, but Vlad said dawn was almost here. I took his word for it since I had no idea what time it was. Besides, Cynthiana didn't know the tables had turned.. Now she was the one who'd be relentlessly stalked, and once the sun set tonight, the hunt was on.

We left the lower level and headed for the secured room on the fourth floor. I'd been right that most new vampires were housed underground near the dungeon, but Vlad had the equivalent of a presidential suite for vampires he wanted to show special favor to. Yet as soon as we were back on the main level of the house, a plethora of noises assaulted me.

The clamor of footsteps above and below. Numerous metallic clangs in the kitchen as pots and pans were used to make breakfast. Voices from people or electronic devices, and underneath it all, the rhythmic throb of multiple heartbeats.

My stomach clenched and little daggers poked

me in the lip. *Almost there*, I thought in relief as we passed the indoor garden and headed toward the grand staircase. All I had to do was keep from going blood berserk for a few more minutes.

"Leila, thank God!"

My sister's voice made me groan out loud. Gretchen ran down the stairs, looking both relieved and mad.

"His goons said you were too injured for us to see you, which is a lie since you look fine—"

Another sound escaped my throat that made her stop in mid-sentence. "Did you just *growl* at me?" she asked in disbelief.

Vlad glanced at me and then his hands closed around my arms. "Stay back," he told Gretchen sternly.

Too late. Pain ripped through me, flipping a switch in my brain that made me incapable of seeing the little sister I loved. Instead, I only saw the cure for my agony inside a flesh package that was easy to tear.

The next few moments were a blur of struggling followed by relief as that impossibly delicious nectar slid down my throat, extinguishing the burn that made fire seem blissful by comparison. After I swallowed every drop, I became aware of a scream consisting of the same panicked question.

"What is wrong with her, what is wrong with her, WHAT IS WRONG WITH HER?"

"Nothing."

Vlad's voice. Hearing it cleared away the lingering insanity, as did feeling his calmness through the fractured layers of my emotions. He was behind me, his arms unbreakable bands that kept me from hurting her or anyone else. I sagged in relief against him, the mindless haze finally leaving my vision.

Gretchen stood as if frozen on the bottom step of the staircase, eyes wide and expression so stricken I worried that she might faint.

"It's okay," I said. My voice was hoarser, but at least it wasn't that animalistic growl anymore.

"It's okay?" she repeated. "How is it okay when you just tried to *kill* me?"

I had no response to that. Gretchen sat down suddenly, as if she'd been yanked, and then she buried her head in her hands.

"I get it now. He had to change you because you were too far gone to heal. That's why they wouldn't let us see you."

Unlike her previous screech, her voice was now almost a whisper. Pangs of a different kind made my insides twist. I hadn't even gotten the chance to tell her this was something I intended to do in the future. Now she found out when I tried to eat her.

"I understand if . . . if you can't deal with this," I began.

Her head snapped up, blue gaze bright.

"You don't get it. You saved me, but I couldn't save you." Her voice broke and tears spilled from her eyes. "I'm so sorry."

Tears welled in my own gaze. She'd soldiered on

through our mother's death, my nightmarish abilities, my suicide attempt, and my leaving when I thought cutting ties with my family was the kindest thing I could do. She had her own flaws, but I should've known not even this would prove too much for her.

"Don't. Without you dragging me away from the car before it exploded, I *really* would've died."

At that, Vlad let me go. "You pulled Leila out of the vehicle?"

Gretchen tensed at his curt tune. "After she cut my seat belt off, yeah. She was in bad shape and I was afraid moving her would make it worse, but it was gonna blow."

"You did great," I told her, thinking, *Ease up!* before remembering he could no longer hear it.

"Hold her," Vlad stated, nodding at me.

"What?" I gasped.

That was all I got out before two guards I hadn't noticed seized me, giving me faintly apologetic looks as they held me immobile between them.

"It's for your sister's protection," Vlad stated, striding over to Gretchen. She looked like she wanted to run but she didn't move when he loomed above her.

"Hold out your hand," he told her in that same crisp tone.

Haltingly, she did. Vlad grasped it and then pulled out a knife, his grip tightening when she tried to yank away.

"Vlad," I said, drawing his name out in warning.

He didn't glance at me. Instead, he drew that blade across his hand, coating my sister's palm with his blood.

"Drink," he told her, "and be known as one of my people."

Gretchen gave the blood on her hand a distasteful look. Then she glanced back up at Vlad.

"Aren't I already as your sister-in-law?"

His smile was coldly pleasant. "Not in the vampire world."

She looked at me next. "What's the catch?"

I remembered when I'd asked Vlad a similar question before an equally irrevocable situation.

"If you do this and then betray him in the future, he'll kill you," I summarized bluntly.

Instead of being intimidated, she snorted. "Like he wouldn't do that *now* if I betrayed him. On the upside, if I do this and then someone messes with me, he'll have to answer to Vlad, right?"

Emerald glinted in his gaze. "That's exactly right."

She looked at her hand and then clapped it over her mouth as if thinking about it longer would make her lose her nerve.

"Yuck," she said as she licked the red smears clean.

I closed my eyes. Gretchen wasn't a child and she'd made this decision of her own free will. That didn't stop me from worrying that she'd taken one more step away from the human world. *Not to mention Dad is going to lose it when he finds out.*

"Wow, that's like liquid speed," she muttered. Then she stared in amazement as her scrapes, scabs, and bruises began to disappear as though wiped away by an invisible eraser.

"What is going *on* here?"

My father's furious tone cut the air like a machete. I cringed at how I must look, blood soaked and restrained by two burly guards, and that surge of emotion made my fangs pop out.

Which, of course, was the wrong reaction.

"No," my father whispered as he stared at me, horror pinching his features. Then he began to descend the stairs as fast as his permanently stiff leg would allow.

"What have you done to her?" he thundered at Vlad.

Vlad shot my father a scalding look as he came over and then swept me into his arms, the guards bowing as they backed away.

"If you say any more of the thoughts in your head, I'll take away your ability to speak for a week."

My father's jaw dropped. I squirmed in Vlad's arms. This was *not* how I'd imagined breaking the news to my dad, either.

"Put me down, I'm not feeling bitey anymore."

"It's dawn," he replied, still glaring at my father.

"Okay, so I'll be tired, but that doesn't mean—"

My mouth stopped working. Then so did every muscle in my body. Before my father's next heartbeat, I was completely unconscious.

Chapter 40

 I came awake so suddenly that it startled me. One second, I was dead to the world, the next, I was on my feet and hungry as hell, my gaze darting around in search of food.

"There," Vlad said, pointing to the open slot in the wall.

I fell on the bag it contained, tearing into it like the shark from *Jaws*. When I was done, blood dripped from my face, hands, and chest. I only became aware that I'd started licking myself when Vlad's low laugh broke my hunger-induced trance.

"I must admit, this gives me ideas."

Embarrassment rose, giving me the strength to stop cleaning my hands like some deranged cat. Vlad sat on the mattress, back braced against the wall and legs casually splayed. He'd changed since I last saw him, and though his deep purple shirt was spotless, as were his ebony pants, with one whiff, I knew where he'd been before coming here.

"You went back to the dungeon."

His smile held more than a hint of grimness. "Perhaps I'll have it sprayed with Febreze after all."

I ran my hand through my hair after one final lick. "We agreed I'd look for Cynthiana the *other* way."

"With you asleep, I had some time to kill."

His voice was light, but an undercurrent of tempered irritation brushed my emotions. I sighed.

"I know you're not used to explaining yourself, but that's marriage. *I'm* not used to waking up with an uncontrollable hunger, so we're both going through an adjustment phase."

Now a different kind of smile curled his lips. "Yours will only last a week. Mine, a lifetime."

I laughed dryly. "If you wanted a wife who never questioned your actions, you shouldn't have married me."

Something else teased my emotions, sliding through them like swaths of sensual fire. A richer, warmer scent filled the room, reminding me of simmering spices and wood smoke.

"Agreed. But I wanted you more than subservience."

His voice was throatier, tightening things low within me. I swallowed, hunger of a different sort making my fangs lengthen. He looked so polished in his tailored clothes, so relaxed leaning against the wall, yet his emotions told a different story. I might be the one bloody and disheveled, but I wasn't the real feral creature in the room.

And I wouldn't have him any other way.

Then I shook my head to clear the explicit thoughts starting to crowd it. I had a murderous vampire to hunt plus a traumatized father to calm down. My dance card didn't have room for hours of sex and Vlad didn't do quickies.

"I need to shower," I said, and it sounded breathless even though I didn't breathe anymore.

His smile turned dangerously carnal. "Afterward."

"Vlad, really, there's so much we need to do—"

"Remember when you said you wouldn't accept ranking a constant second to others?" he interrupted in a silky voice. "Neither will I."

He was beside me in a blink, pressing an inner button in that retractable drawer. Another blood bag popped out as if it were a vending machine. Before I could speak, Vlad crushed it against his chest, covering himself in crimson rivulets.

Need rose with such ferocity that it annihilated my conscience. I wasn't embarrassed by how I flung myself at him. Didn't care that he tore my clothes off as savagely as I ripped away his in my quest for every last drop, and I *really* didn't mind when he backed me into the wall and yanked my legs around his waist. Then there was nothing except the taste of blood on his skin and the exquisite roughness of his body plunging into mine, over and over, until the ecstasy searing through me made me forget about my hunger.

It was a quarter after ten when I emerged fully clothed from the bathroom. Vlad was already redressed and waiting since I'd made him shower elsewhere. Otherwise, it would have been even later, which he had no qualms about. Shrapnel wasn't going anywhere, Cynthiana didn't yet know she'd been discovered, and our honeymoon had been ruined enough, he'd stated.

"Before I get started with Shrapnel, I need to see my dad," I told Vlad. "He's pretty freaked out. Can you stay close in case I get slammed with the bloodthirsties again?"

Vlad had been drinking wine, but at that, he set it down.

"Many humans who know about vampires have difficulty accepting a loved one's transformation. It can cause feelings of fear, alienation, and helplessness. For someone used to being in control, like your father, those feelings are often magnified."

His carefully worded statements made me uneasy. Normally, Vlad was blunt to the point of brusqueness. Something was up. "No sugarcoating. What happened?"

"He doesn't want to see you right now and he's insisting on leaving with Gretchen," he replied with his usual directness. "I do have other houses where they'd be safe, but I refused to let him go unless you agreed to it."

I now had superhuman strength, but I sat as though my knees had turned to jelly.

"Gretchen doesn't want to see me, either?" Maybe I'd misread her demeanor before . . .

"No, your sister was vehement about staying

here, which only made your father more determined to take her with him."

Then Vlad gave me a jaded look. "He doesn't
realize it, but he's trying to regain control where
there is none. He still loves you. If he didn't, his
reaction to you becoming a vampire wouldn't be
so emotional."

I said nothing, thinking how strange life was.
When I was a child, my father's job moved us from
place to place without regard for how upsetting
those upheavals were. Now it was my circumstances that kept uprooting him from the life he'd
built. *Karma's a bitch*, Cat had said, yet I didn't
want my dad to receive any comeuppance. I wanted
him to be happy, and be safe.

"Let him go, but wait until tomorrow morning.
I want a chance to talk to Gretchen first."

My voice was soft yet steady. I knew what it was
like to need to leave, if only to prove to yourself
that you could. As for Gretchen, it was better that
she go with him. With my ravenous new hunger,
I couldn't trust myself to be around her. Besides,
things were about to get more dangerous around
here, not less.

Then I rose, giving Vlad a crooked smile.

"Now, let's see if I can find that crazy bitch you
used to date."

I thought we'd go back to the dungeon and I'd pick
up Cynthiana's essence trail from touching Shrapnel, but Vlad led me to the Weapons Room instead.

There, he handed me a silver dagger with a Celtic design in its filigreed hilt.

"Hers," he stated.

It took me a second to remember why it looked familiar. Then I let out a short laugh.

"It sure was. I touched this when I was going through your other weapons. Shortly after glimpsing the woman connected to it, I started hemorrhaging to death."

Just as Cynthiana's linking spell intended, though she hadn't counted on Vlad being there to revive me. Or on Maximus doing the same the other time linking to her caused lethal damage. Now my own inhuman state was all I needed to protect me.

Karma's a bitch sounded just fine for these circumstances.

I pulled my right glove off and touched the pretty weapon. To my surprise, my first instinct was to jerk away. The metal made my skin itch in a way that reminded me of when I'd fallen into a poison ivy patch as a child.

"That feels . . . wrong. Is that from the silver?"

His amusement curled through my emotions. "You'll get used to it. All vampires do."

I tried to ignore how irritated the metal made my skin feel and focused on the essence it contained. After a few minutes of concentrating, colorless images took over.

We reached my door, but when Vlad started to leave after bidding me good night, I caught his sleeve.

"Wait." Then I drew the knife from the folds of my coat and extended it to him hilt first.

"For you," I murmured.

He took it, his mouth curling into a half smile. "What's this? An early Christmas present?"

"Do I need occasion to give you a gift?" I asked lightly.

He flipped the blade before catching it. "Perfectly balanced. Thank you, Cynthiana. It's lovely."

Then he leaned over, his warm lips brushing mine. When he started to pull away, I held on.

"Don't go," I whispered against his mouth.

He drew back with a frown. "One of my people is missing. I won't wait until morning to search for him."

"I'm sorry, of course not, dearie," I said, knowing better than to point out that he could send someone else.

He put the knife away in his coat. "Good night, Cynthiana."

"Good night, Vlad."

I watched him go, masking my frustration with a smile in case he glanced back. He didn't. He never did, and his visits had become more infrequent. I hadn't lived three hundred years without knowing what that meant. He was growing tired of me.

My smile turned brittle. I'd been too long without the protection I deserved and I wasn't about to lose my place by the side of such a powerful vampire. Risky or not, it was time to employ more *persuasive means to keep Vlad with me. If I was careful, he'd never know the cause for his new-found affection.*

My link to the memory dissolved and I returned to reality to find I clutched the knife so hard, it had cut my hand. Then I stared at Vlad, a suspicion growing.

"Did Cynthiana move in with you shortly after she gave you this?"

His brow arched. "I believe so, why?"

"Just wondering. Did you know she was into magic?"

A shrug. "I knew she dabbled, but magic is against vampire law so a more serious pursuit wasn't worth the risk to her."

"Or she was more involved than she let on."

What if it wasn't coincidence that Cynthiana moved in with him shortly after she decided to use more "persuasive" means to keep him from dumping her? If so, then we weren't dealing with an amateur who dabbled in the occasional spell, but a full-blown witch who might be more dangerous than either Vlad or I realized.

Chapter 41

 I looked at the knife with more wariness than before. As a vampire, another heart attack or spontaneous hemorrhaging would hurt, but they wouldn't be fatal. Still, if she was a powerful witch in disguise, there was the chance that Cynthiana had rigged her spell to do something lethal to vampires, too.

"Keep an eye on what I do with the knife, okay?"

When I looked up, Vlad's eyes had narrowed. He inhaled and then smiled so pleasantly I should've taken it as a warning.

"Why?"

"If your ex turns out to be more Wicked Witch of the West than we realized, there's a chance that her spell might make me try to stab myself, heh heh, in the heart."

My little laugh to indicate how remote I thought this possibility was didn't work. His whole face began to darken, though that charming smile never slipped.

"You might be the cruelest person I've ever met," he said in a conversational tone.

"What?" I gasped.

"My first wife killed herself. Took me centuries to get over it and love again, yet you weren't going to mention that you might be compelled to slay yourself *in front of me*."

His casual tone vanished, replaced by one of pure rage. That was nothing compared to the fury that flooded my emotions, abrupt as a dam bursting and so forceful I took a step backward.

"Vlad, I—"

"Don't. Speak."

Fire erupted from his hands, climbing up his arms to his shoulders before haloing his whole body with an orange glow. I would've thought he was trying to intimidate me, except from the maelstrom of his emotions, he couldn't stop it.

"I've tried to let you do what you feel you must because I respect your bravery, but you push me too far." Another flare of fire. "Attempt one more time to willfully endanger your life, and I swear I will imprison you."

Before I could voice my outrage at that ultimatum, he vanished, leaving nothing behind except the smell of smoke.

"Hey, kid."

I glanced up to see Marty in the doorway of the stone cell. I hadn't even noticed it opening. I'd shut myself in here because I didn't want to hurt anyone if another hunger attack struck, plus it had the plasma bag delivery system. Drowning my frustrations with blood sounded disgusting in theory. In practice, it was as effective as liquor and ice cream combined.

"Maximus was right when he warned me about Vlad," I said glumly. "Did you overhear him threaten to imprison me?"

A pitying look crossed Marty's face, which was my answer.

"I don't know what I'm going to do," I went on, patting the spot next to me in invitation. "I love Vlad, but sometimes he is *so archaic*. Can you imagine how he'd react if I told him he wasn't allowed to risk his life for his people anymore?"

"He wouldn't listen," Marty said, sitting by me on the bed.

"Right. So how is that different from me assuming some risk in order to hunt down the bitch that nearly killed me three times and succeeded on the fourth attempt?"

"He's a chauvinist?" Marty offered.

"Exactly." Then I glanced over, seeing the wryness stamped on his features. "What?"

"You're the only one surprised by this, kid. You married a borderline psychotic who conquered the brutal circumstances he grew up in by being even more brutal. Add turning into a vampire and centuries of undead power struggles, and you have the crazy cruel bastard you fell in love with."

He patted my knee in a companionable way. "Did you really think someone like that would let

his wife fight his enemies for him? They call him
Vlad the Impaler, not Vlad the Emasculated."

I let out a scoff. "I'm not trying to fight his enemies for him."

"In his eyes you are, and worse, you're ready to
die to do it." Another pat. "Like you already did
once, baby vamp."

I leaned against him, angling my head so it
rested on his shoulder. "What am I supposed to
do? Let him dictate my every move because he's
the medieval version of old-fashioned? I didn't sign
on for that."

He chuckled dryly. "No, you signed on for
something harder. Marriage."

"Smartass," I said, but my voice lacked rancor.

Deep down, I knew he was right. Marrying a
dragon meant dealing with the times he breathed
fire, but I wasn't giving up. I was in this for the
long haul, so it was time to quit brooding over how
rough the road was and brace for the bumps while
keeping my foot on the gas.

I kissed Marty on the cheek. "Thanks."

He grunted. "For what? I told you not to get
involved with him and I haven't changed my mind
that it was a bad idea."

"Thanks for being a good friend."

Then I stood, filled with renewed determination. Vlad might be a crazy cruel bastard, but he
was *my* crazy cruel bastard and we were going to
work this out.

"Since you were eavesdropping, did you catch where he went? Oh, wait, never mind. I already know."

I descended the narrow staircase, wrinkling my nose as the smell got more pungent. Piss off a modern guy and he'd likely go to a local bar. Piss off a vampire with an impalement habit and an in-house dungeon, and it was a no-brainer where *he'd* go.

"Hi," I said to the guard who eyed me cautiously as I approached. "Please tell Vlad I'd like to speak with him."

The guard bowed, looking relieved that I didn't try to barge past him, I guessed. Then he pinched something in his collar and spoke into it in Romanian. Ah, the wonders of technology. I'd need a full-body rubber suit to wear a wire without frying it.

My new super senses meant I heard the reply the guard got, but as it was also in Romanian, I didn't understand it.

"Please wait here," he finally said in accented English.

I said nothing, wondering if that meant Vlad was coming, or I was waiting to be escorted out by someone else.

About ten minutes later, Vlad appeared. A fine layer of ash darkened his clothes, skin, and hair, which was cause for comment since it was impossible for him to catch fire. The added swarthiness to his appearance made him look even more dangerous, as if his expression wasn't already foreboding enough.

"What?"

One word meant to send me on my way with its curtness, and he'd done that lockdown thing where I couldn't feel any of his emotions. I straightened my shoulders and planted my feet. If he really didn't want to see me, he wouldn't have come.

"I have a solution that will work for both of us," I said.

A brow arched. I glanced pointedly at the guard.

"You want to do this here?"

Vlad's mouth tightened, but he swept past me and started up the stairs. I followed him to the enclosed hallway that was the main corridor for the basement. There, he stopped and faced me.

"What?"

Still abrupt, but his tone was less curt. I closed the distance between us and started brushing the ash off his clothes. He tensed, yet made no attempt to stop me.

"From your mood, you haven't gotten Cynthiana's location from Shrapnel yet," I noted casually. "He's tough, plus she may have bewitched him so he *can't* tell you where she is."

His gaze followed every move I made, yet he held himself completely still. "That also occurred to me."

"Of course it did." I ran my fingers through his hair to brush the residue from it. "You've been doing this a lot longer than me."

His smile was so cold it could've turned steam into dry ice. "If flattery is your solution, don't bother. You're not using her knife to link to her. I've already disposed of it."

I continued dusting the gray film from him. "That's fine."

His gaze narrowed at my easy compliance. "You're not touching Shrapnel to link to her, either."

"Don't want to," I said breezily. "I can do without psychically reliving your interrogation techniques, thanks."

At that, he grabbed my hands and pulled me closer. "Stop lying, Leila. You haven't given up and we both know it."

His face was mere inches away, stubble darker from ash and lips thinned into a hard line. I stared up at him, unbowed by the fierceness in his gaze.

"All Shrapnel has to do is hold out a few days until Cynthiana realizes he's been caught and she bolts. He knows it and you know it. But she lived here, so her old room must be filled with essence-laced objects I can't possibly kill myself with. If you really want to go overboard ensuring I stay safe, chain me up before I try using one of those to link to her."

At that, both his brows rose. "Chain you?"

I flashed him an impish smile. "Come on, I'm sure you've fantasized about it."

"More and more each day."

Muttered in a sinister tone, but the wall around him cracked and I felt a flash of his emotions. He was still angry, yes. Frustrated, too. Yet under that was a hint of appreciation. If anyone could understand my single-minded determination to take down an enemy, it was Vlad.

Then he let out a harsh sigh. "That occurred to me as well, but in her room, you might see things I don't want you to see."

Blind rage shot through me at the thought of psychically experiencing Vlad making love to another woman. I'd never known I was the jealous type, but clearly I had some issues. Then I forced those feelings back, replacing them with the coldest, darkest part of me.

"If so, I'll have to get over it by watching you kill her later."

He stared at me in a penetrating way that measured my words against pieces of me only he could see. I stared back. If he thought I didn't mean what I said, he was wrong.

At last, he inclined his head, the barest smile ghosting across his lips. "As it happens, I do have some chain."

Chapter 42

I looked around Cynthiana's old bedroom with cynical curiosity. So this was where the witch used to stay.

Like all of the rooms in Vlad's house, it was opulent. It also had an obvious feminine theme with the lilac and cream decor, lace draperies, dainty crystal fixtures, and a balcony that overlooked the exterior garden. Dried flowers shot through with web-thin gold strands adorned the fireplace mantel, scenting the room with a pleasant, natural fragrance. I was beyond glad I didn't smell Vlad's scent, bless his diligent cleaning staff.

"How long ago did you two break up?"

My voice was casual, belying the inner battle within me. Spiteful Leila was gleeful that Vlad kept Cynthiana two full floors below him on the same wing that all his guests stayed at. Practical Leila was deciding which fixture to touch for a sufficient essence impression.

"A few years ago."

I gave him a jaded look. "Pretending she doesn't matter enough to remember? Then why did you keep her bedroom exactly the way she had it when she lived here?"

He folded his arms, the silver chains he'd draped over his shoulder rattling with the motion.

"If she still mattered to me, I wouldn't have married you. This room remained unused because you were my next lover and you slept with me."

I glanced away, my gaze drawn to the bed. Gossamer material wrapped around the bedposts before pooling at the floor in elegant heaps. What would I see if I touched that bed? Cynthiana had over three hundred years of experience on me. Maybe I'd see Vlad looking happier with her than he did with me.

"Leila."

I glanced back almost guiltily. That's when I became aware that my fangs had come out and I'd been grinding my teeth so hard, I'd ripped open my bottom lip.

"Sorry. I don't know what's wrong with me," I muttered, sucking my lip so I didn't drip blood on the thick white carpet.

"Don't apologize."

No censure colored his expression, and the emotions that slid over mine had the soothing caress of satin. "All vampires are overly possessive when it comes to what's ours."

I could blame my seething jealousy on vampirism? Done!

Then Vlad began to bind my wrists with multiple lengths of chain. With how strong he was, I doubted this was necessary even if Cynthiana *had* managed to add a vampiric form of hara-kiri to her linking booby trap, but if it made him feel better . . .

"Going to save some of that for later?" I joked.

The look he gave me made me forget how unpleasant the silver felt against my wrists.

"When I tie you up, I'll use silk, and I'll leave your hands free because I love to feel them on my skin."

Not if. When. Despite the erotic promise, being chained up while in his ex's bedroom should've cooled my response. Instead, I felt all the desire Vlad usually elicited in me along with a visceral urge to assert my claim on him in the very place that someone else had dared touch him.

Overly possessive? Yeah, I had it bad.

"If you leave my hands free," I asked in a throaty voice, "what's the point of tying me up?"

His wicked smile affected me as much as the heat that swept over my emotions, lashing me with thousands of invisible, sensual whips. Then he leaned in, the soft sandpaper of his jaw grazing my cheek.

"Why tell you when I can show you?"

I closed my eyes, taking in a breath to smell the rich spiciness of his scent. Now I knew how I wanted to spend the rest of the evening, but first things first.

He drew back, continuing to drape chains around me until they went all the way up to my elbows. If I still had circulation, my hands would have been numb. Then he threaded more silver through them to secure my bound arms to my body with more loops of chain. Now all I could do from the waist up was wiggle my fingers and bite.

Satisfied, he dropped the remaining chains onto the floor and went over to the bed. I tensed, but all he retrieved was a lamp from the night table.

"Gently," he warned as he held it out to me.

Did he think I'd never touched something fancy before? I grasped the smooth crystal base with my right fingers—and it shattered like I'd smashed it with a crowbar.

"What the hell?" I exclaimed.

He gave me a sardonic glance as he brushed the shards from my hand. "You're not used to your new strength. Until you are, treat everything as though it's more fragile than eggshells, and whatever you do, don't touch a human."

I looked at the glittering shards with a wince. Now I had another reason for not giving my sister a hug good-bye later.

"Were those dried flowers on the mantel hers?" I asked, seeking something that wouldn't cost a lot if I broke it.

"She picked them, yes," Vlad replied, pulling a chunk out of the arrangement without care for how that spoiled it.

I told myself it wasn't petty to enjoy seeing

something of Cynthiana's ruined. She'd killed me, after all.

I stroked the flowers when Vlad held them out. Most of them disintegrated on contact, telling me I was still using too much strength, but something flared in the remaining batch.

There you are, I thought with dark satisfaction, and then everything around me changed.

I walked through the meadow, adding flowers to the growing pile in my basket. Vlad's staff would be happy to add to the garden outside my room, but I was careful not to have all the spell's ingredients in one place. Just in case someone recognized the significance of these particular flowers.

The beautiful spring day did nothing to improve my foul mood. It had only been six months since the last spell, yet Vlad was already acting distant again. I yanked out a handful of lilacs, damaging them in my frustration. Any other man would be madly, irrevocably in love with me, but after seven spells, I could barely keep Vlad from leaving me.

The problem, of course, was the same reason why he was such a valuable protector. His power. It was why I'd worked so hard to gain his attention in the first place, and also why he was practically immune to my spells. I didn't dare use stronger magic on him. He might dismiss all the flowers as feminine fancy, but he'd notice ingredients for darker magic. What the Law Guardians would do to me would be nothing compared to his wrath if he found out I'd been using spells on him.

I grabbed another handful of lilacs, refusing to dwell on the repercussions of being caught. That wouldn't happen as long as I was careful, and besides, I had no choice. Most vampires had Masters to protect them. Others had enough strength to protect themselves. The rest of us—Masterless with only average power—were left to fend for ourselves. After my sire was murdered, lovers gave me the protection other vampires took for granted. When that wasn't enough, magic made up the difference. The day I became a vampire, I swore no matter the cost, I'd never be helpless again. I had my fill of that as a Scottish peasant living under English rule. I brushed off those memories to give a critical look at my basket's contents. Perhaps more mallow would make the spell last longer . . .

When I morphed back into my own mindset, I stared at the crumbled bits of dried flowers in my hand, torn between rage and incredulousness.

"Do you know what these are?"

He shrugged. "Lilacs, poppies, amaranth—"

"Ingredients for a spell," I cut him off. "Lilacs to prompt love, red poppy for true love, mallow for being overwhelmed with love, blue poppy for the unattainable made possible, amaranth for undying love . . . see where she was going with this?"

"I *never* loved her."

His voice vibrated with forcefulness. I smiled grimly.

"Yes, and it ticked her off that you were too strong for her spell to fully work. Still, you stayed with her for the better part of three decades so her efforts weren't a total bust." Vlad opened his mouth and . . . nothing. I'd never seen him speechless before, but finding out your free will had been messed with would be upsetting for anyone. Finding it out when you had his level of arrogance would be stunning.

"See if you can find her" was what he bit out. I wouldn't want to be Cynthiana for all the money in the world right now.

I stroked the dried flowers again. The memory of her picking them was fainter now, allowing me to push past it to focus on her essence trail.

There. Like a fishing line with her swimming at the end of it. I concentrated, but every time I pulled on that line, I came back with nothing. I kept trying, an internal clock pitilessly noting the passage of time as I continued to fail to reach the other side. Ten minutes. Twenty. Thirty. Forty.

"Leila, stop."

Vlad brushed the floral bits out of my hands. Frustrated, I watched as they scattered to the ground.

"I don't know why I can't see her. I used to glimpse her before my health went haywire. Now, I don't even get that."

"You've been a vampire exactly one day," Vlad said as he began to unwind my chains. "Every cell in your body has been drastically altered. It's remarkable you're able to use any of your abilities this soon."

"Remarkable. That and four quarters will get me a dollar."

I had reason for my glumness. Even if Vlad's people didn't breathe a word about Shrapnel to outsiders, any day now, Cynthiana would figure out something was wrong and go into hiding. When she did, it could be years before she resurfaced again. Sure, Shrapnel would eventually break, if Cynthiana hadn't bewitched him into never revealing her location, but she'd be long gone by then. I might have all the time in the world to hunt her now, but my family didn't. I couldn't expect them to stay in hiding for years until we caught her, yet if they didn't, they were walking targets.

It might already be too late. Cynthiana would be expecting new word from Shrapnel already . . .

"I know how we can get her," I said, struck by inspiration. "Send Sandra into town to leave another message, this one telling Cynthiana where and when Shrapnel wants to meet her."

Vlad unwound the final chain from me. "She's not foolish enough to fall for such a trick."

"Foolish? Maybe not. Arrogant? You betcha," I countered. "This woman cast spells on you under your own roof, knowing all the while that you'd kill her if you found out. That's so arrogant it's like she had two boulders in a sack for balls."

His lips thinned at the reminder of how she'd

manipulated his willpower. I continued on as if I hadn't noticed.

"No wonder she hates my guts. You said vampires were psycho possessive. In a few months, you offered me more than you offered her after three decades under her magical influence, yet I left because it wasn't good enough. She probably had Adrian making that bomb even before Shrapnel gave her my location."

More whitening of his mouth, and then suddenly, he smiled.

"I know why you're goading me, but you will not get me to act rashly out of injured pride."

"You wouldn't," I said, holding his gaze. "But she would. Since news of our marriage must've reached her by now, I bet she's hit a whole new red zone of woman-scorned rage."

Vlad stared at me. "Perhaps," he said at last.

I couldn't help but glance at the bed again. In fairness, I shouldn't point fingers at Cynthiana for crossing into insane jealousy territory. The thought of the hours, days—hell, years!—Vlad had spent entwined with her in that bed upset me far past normal "vampire possessiveness." In fact, my urge to manifest an electrical whip and start lashing the bed into pieces was so strong, my hand began to spark.

Vlad glanced at my hand and then at my face. Before I could say anything, the bed burst into flames.

My mouth opened in disbelief. In the few moments I took to close it, the wooden frame had buckled from the extreme heat and nothing was left of the blankets, pillows, and mattress except a smoldering black heap. Instead of that delicate floral fragrance, the room now stank of burnt foam and smoke.

The violently tender emotions sweeping mine told me why he'd done it, and it had nothing to do with his anger toward Cynthiana. He simply wanted to destroy something that hurt me.

I said nothing. Neither did he. Words were unnecessary now.

Chapter 43

 I woke with the same suddenness as on the past five days, going from unconscious to on my feet in less time than it took to say, "Good evening." The only difference was that tonight, my first thoughts weren't of hunger.

"Did she buy it?" I asked at once.

Vlad had been standing by the open slot in the wall. In response, he held out the blood bag I hadn't leapt upon.

I ignored it despite my fangs popping out and my stomach clenching as though it were a fist opening and closing. Four days ago, Sandra left a message for Cynthiana telling her where Shrapnel wanted to meet. The next day, the bookstore owner, also mesmerized into betraying Vlad, drove seventy miles away to make a call that wouldn't be routed through the cell tower Vlad owned. Today, while I was asleep, Sandra went back to the bookstore to see if *The Odyssey* contained Cynthiana's RSVP.

"Did she?" I repeated.

"Yes and no."

He stroked his jaw in a seemingly absent way, yet he only did that when he was in deep contemplation.

"She agreed to meet him tomorrow at seven, but changed the location to the Bucharest Metro."

I'd never taken the main Romanian subway for obvious reasons, but it wasn't hard to figure out the problem.

"She picked rush hour in a busy public place."

We'd chosen a warehouse in a sparsely populated town. Easy to surround, fewer bystanders to worry about. Cynthiana must've figured that out, too. Looked like Vlad and I were both right about her. She might be arrogant enough to come, but she wasn't stupid enough to do it without adding protections. "It presents several difficulties, starting with being impossible to secure." He gave me a brief, sardonic smile. "Many members of the Romanian government are in my line, yet I can't order the entire Metro shut down. Even Mencheres couldn't freeze tens of thousands of commuters and dozens of trains to catch her."

"And if the Metro is suddenly filled with vampires, she'll get suspicious and bolt." I sighed. "Is tracing the bookstore owner's call the next move?"

Vlad continued to stroke his jaw. "Already done. It went to a burner phone that led to nowhere. That leaves the Metro."

"Did she even say which station?"

He snorted. "No, but it's obvious."

I let that alone. "Vlad, if she catches sight of you, she'll run. In fact, after living with you for three decades, I bet she knows most of the vampires in your line *and* your allies, so a glimpse of one of them would make her a rabbit, too."

He didn't dispute any of the above. "After tomorrow, she'll realize Shrapnel has been compromised. I'll put a large bounty out on her, but catching her will take time. Difficult or not, the Metro is still my best chance."

"Yes," I said steadily, "it is, but you're forgetting something important."

A brow arched. "And that is?"

"Me."

"Not this again," he muttered.

"I'm the obvious choice. She doesn't know what I look *or* smell like, so I could be standing right next to her and she wouldn't feel the slightest bit threatened."

"Why should she? She's three hundred years older than you."

His tone was scathing, but I wasn't going to let him sidetrack me taking it personally.

"When we met, you insisted that I learn how to use my electrical abilities to fight, and you were right. They ended up saving my life when I took down vampires a *lot* older than me. But more than that, you keep saying 'I' when this isn't only about you. Cynthiana killed my friends at the carnival. She had me kidnapped. Then it was her spell that stole my mortality from me before I was ready to give it up. If I was the type of person who'd let all of that slide, you wouldn't love me because that sure as hell isn't who you are."

His stare could've bent a laser from its intensity.

"You expect me to forgo my vengeance in favor of yours?"

"No," I said, adding with an inward smile, "they call you Vlad the Impaler, not Vlad the Emasculated. All I want is to go into the Metro and find her. Then I'll either flush her out or tail her and give you her location. Either way, you'll be the one to bag and tag her, but she'll know—and so will I—that I helped take her down."

He was silent for a long while. Then he said, "You've never even seen her face."

Not a *Hell, no!* I began to feel a tingle of anticipation.

"Don't worry. I've seen enough to spot her."

I couldn't remember the last time I'd been surrounded by so many people. Maybe it was American snootiness that made me assume a Romanian subway wouldn't be much busier than some of the larger carnivals I'd worked; maybe it was being underground that made everything feel more crowded. Whatever the reason, as I crossed the fourteen platforms of the Gara de Nord, I actually had to fight back a sense of claustrophobia.

At least I didn't have to worry about electrocuting any of the commuters that brushed past me on their way to or from one of the Metro's many trains. Underneath my business casual pants and blazer was a full body wetsuit, the rubber thicker because it was normally used for icy water dives. A silk scarf hid where the suit rose to the base of my neck, while theater-thick makeup covered my scar.

Aside from the annoying squeaking noises it made when I walked, the wetsuit could be a new wardrobe staple. I hadn't been able to pass through a crowd without worrying about electrocuting people since I was fourteen. If it wouldn't have attracted undue attention, I might have hugged a stranger just because I could.

Of course, there was another issue that being so close to thousands of people brought up. My hunger. Everywhere around me, countless veins bulged with the tantalizing nectar I now craved like a drug. Under normal circumstances, I'd be slowly introduced into limited-contact settings with humans to make sure I had enough control to handle it. Going into an underground Metro at rush hour was akin to jumping in the deep end to sink or swim. More than once, my fangs popped out and I had to hastily put a drink to my face to hide it. Good thing Vlad had suggested getting a cup of coffee as a prop.

The unpleasant smell of my surroundings helped curb my hunger, actually. With the bustle of people and the different sections of tunnels came all types of odors. Certain parts of the Metro were only a few shades more aromatic than Vlad's dungeon. My first trip by a public bathroom almost made me throw up.

A screeching noise preceded a train on the M1 line coming to a halt. I sipped my coffee and watched the throngs of people load and unload, paying special attention to the women. No thick walnut-colored hair or telltale skin a shade too creamy, plus the only vibes I felt came from the electricity running through the tracks. I glanced at my watch. Six fifty-nine p.m. Time to check the next set of tracks at the Basarab stop.

Yes, Vlad had a Metro station named after him. No wonder he said it was obvious where Cynthiana would expect to meet Shrapnel. The M1 side of the tracks was done in bland shades of white and gray, but the M4 side had orange walls, black granite floors, and yellow neon lights. Somehow, I thought the bolder-colored section was where I'd find Cynthiana. If its vividness reminded me of Vlad, it would probably remind her, too.

We had an appreciation for him in common, after all.

Another ear-splitting screech announced a train coming into the M4 station. I leaned against one of the wide columns, my hair falling over part of my face as I studied the commuters. Could that brunette be her? Nope, she had a fresh pimple, something no vampire could get. Maybe the woman in the ball cap . . . no, not with that deliciously throbbing vein in her neck from how she hurried off the track.

I muttered a curse as my fangs sprang out again. Now I knew how teenage boys with unwanted erections felt. I pretended to take a long sip from my coffee as I silently willed them back into my gums, and then I felt it—an aura of power, invisible yet potent, like a cloud of perfume, and coming right toward me.

I kept the coffee cup in front of my face as I sought the source. Not there, not there . . . *there*. Oh yes, I'd know that thick, walnut-colored hair anywhere, not to mention her gliding grace made her stand out like a ballerina amidst a stampede of bulls.

With my gloved hand, I pinched the wire my scarf concealed and whispered two words into the microphone.

"She's here."

Then I stared, finally getting a full look at the woman who'd wreaked so much havoc in my life. Taken piece by piece, her face was full of flaws. Her mouth was too wide, nose a trace too long, and cheekbones so high they looked artificially enhanced. Put together, though, she was beautiful in a way you'd find hard to forget because it wasn't "pretty" beauty, but the bold, striking kind that made it difficult to look away.

And that's why I recognized her even though our previous meeting had only lasted seconds. No wonder Cynthiana had used a spell that not only made it impossible to get a fix on her location, but also blocked me from seeing her face. That spell hadn't just prevented us from hiring a sketch artist to discover her identity sooner. Unintentionally, it had also kept me from recognizing her as the same vampire who'd watched Dawn and Marty's last performance the night of the carnival explosion.

Then dark topaz eyes met mine as Cynthiana looked up and stared straight at me.

Chapter 44

 As casually as possible, I glanced away, pretending to smile at someone farther down the walkway. *Just another vampire meeting a friend, nothing to see here.* When I could still feel her gaze on me, I headed in the direction I'd been looking, hoping the skin-scouring version of a deodorizing treatment I'd undergone had removed all traces of Vlad's scent from me. Then I picked a person at random, coming toward her while saying, "Hello!" in Romanian as if we were old friends.

Something punched me in the back, a hard double tap that made me spin around so fast, I splashed coffee on the person closest to me. As that man began to sputter out a curse, another hard double punch hit me square in the chest.

I looked down. Silvery liquid oozed out of two holes onto my blazer, but before my mind even registered that I'd been shot, instinct took over. I leapt up, clearing the crowd and hitting the roof of the tunnel in less than a second. A piece of concrete exploded near my head and I spun away as fast as

I could. Then gravity brought me back down into the crowd. I landed on a few people, inadvertently knocking them over. As soon as I hit the ground, the screaming started.

I couldn't see anything through the sea of legs surrounding me, which meant the shooter couldn't see me, either. Still, I wasn't about to use them for cover. Liquid silver bullets might be as dangerous to me as regular ones were to humans, yet thanks to Vlad's insistence, I wore a bulletproof vest underneath my clothes. The people around me didn't have such protection. I began to crawl away from the crowd, throwing my coffee cup aside after noticing with disbelief that I'd held on to it this entire time. As I crawled, I pinched the wire underneath my scarf. I hadn't seen her do it, but it didn't take psychic powers to guess who'd shot me.

"The jig is up," I said shortly. "And she's firing liquid silver bullets."

I reached the end of the crowd and stood up. As if my gaze was drawn, I saw Cynthiana amidst the terrified commuters, almost casually tucking her gun back into her jacket. She must've thought the silver bullets had done their job and I was dead beneath the stampeding crowd.

Vlad's voice barked through the receiver. "Don't engage her. Go to the Crangasi station. We'll be there soon."

Cynthiana whirled, either sensing my presence or hearing Vlad's voice over the noise from the commuters.

She stared at me for what only took a second, yet felt like an eternity. I don't know what possessed me to rake my coffee-coated hand over the side of my face, but I did, using the liquid and the material from my glove to wipe away the thick makeup that hid my scar. When she saw it, her dark topaz gaze turned bright green and she bared her teeth in a snarl.

"*You.*"

I expected her to go for the gun again. Or to charge me; she looked as furious as I felt. Both would've been fine. I'd lead her away from the people if she charged, and if she shot at me, at least she wouldn't be shooting at any innocent bystanders. But Cynthiana didn't do either of those things. Instead, she raised her hands and shouted something in a language I didn't recognize.

As if yanked by invisible strings, every commuter who'd started to flee stopped in their tracks. Then they turned around and headed straight toward me, their hands outstretched like claws and their expressions murderous. Over the horde, I saw Cynthiana's snarl change into a smirk. Then she ran down the subway tunnel in the opposite direction from the Gara de Nord.

I muttered a curse as I began to plow through the crowd, trying not to hurt them as I shoved them away. I wasn't shown the same consideration. My hair was yanked, multiple fists punched me, and I was even bitten when a woman latched on to my leg and wouldn't let go despite my dragging her as I ran. My first attempt to use vampire mind control to get them off me didn't work. I was either doing it wrong or Cynthiana's spell was too strong. I managed to get free only after losing my jacket, scarf, and several pieces of my pants courtesy of the biting woman. Then I dashed away before the rest of the mob joined in the melee.

As I ran toward the Crangasi station, I squeezed the wire near my neck. "She went down the M1 tunnel," I shouted, then let out a groan as I saw the frazzled end of the wire sticking out of the Kevlar vest. Someone had torn it in two. Without hesitation, I turned around and began to run in the same direction Cynthiana had. With no way to tell Vlad where she was going, if I didn't track her, she might get away before his people converged on the Metro.

A shrill sound and blinding light signaled a train headed right for me. I jumped off the tracks and onto the concrete lip of the tunnel, hugging the wall as I continued as fast as I could along the narrow ledge. When the subway passed me, the wind from its velocity tried to suck me into its path, yet my new muscles held me to the wall as if I'd been glued. Once it was gone, I jumped down and dashed along the tracks, my gaze lighting up the darkness with green.

If not for my enhanced vision, I would've missed the slot in the tunnel across the tracks that marked the entrance to another passageway. No light shone from within and the walls were wet from what looked like a recurring leak, leaving a shallow, dirty puddle in front of the entrance. Must be one of the many unused passages that made up the underground labyrinth of the Metro. I paused, glancing between that and the rest of the tunnel. If I were Cynthiana, which way would I go?

Seeing a muddy footprint leading into the passageway made up my mind. I ran over the tracks and into the narrow entrance, grimacing at the smell that suggested indigents used this as a shelter. Now there was no point trying to track Cynthiana by scent, though over the stink, I caught an odd, earthy odor. Was that her? If so, she needed to change her perfume.

I ran faster when I heard sounds ahead, almost like a mad scrabbling. Had Vlad's people entered the passageway from the other side and caught her? The narrow tunnel forked ahead so I couldn't see. Just in case Cynthiana was waiting with a gun aimed for my head, I hunched so I'd be a few feet shorter than expected, and then peered around the corner.

What looked like hundreds of glowing eyes stared back at me. That scrabbling noise increased. So did harsh chirping sounds as a mass of gray fur and fangs charged right at me.

"You bitch!" I yelled down the passageway.

Cynthiana wasn't done with her tricks. Now it seemed she'd bewitched every rat in these tunnels to attack me.

Despite my revulsion, I began to run toward them. *Vampires can't get rabies*, I mentally chanted as dozens of the rodents flung themselves onto me as though I were covered in meat. I crushed several of them as I plowed onward, but just as many held on with razorlike teeth and claws. Pain exploded in almost every part of me except what was covered by the Kevlar vest. Some fell off as they chewed through the rubber wetsuit and bit into my current-filled skin, but more of them took their place.

I wanted to dance around madly while shaking them off, yet I continued on while only clearing the disgusting rodents I could reach as I ran. If Cynthiana thought she'd empty a clip of liquid silver bullets into me while I was distracted by the results of her latest filthy little spell, she'd thought wrong.

My refusal to look away from what lay ahead is why I saw them. Large forms hugging the wall of the next corner, covered in so much grime they almost blended into the dank concrete. I caught a whiff of that strange earthy scent even over the stench from the rats and the smell of my own blood, and when I stopped running, they must have guessed that I spotted them because they came out of their hiding place. All dozen of them.

They looked human, but their eyes gleamed with an inner light no normal person had. It wasn't vampire green and they didn't have fangs, yet they moved with a quickness that only came from supernatural ability. When their mouths opened obscenely wide as they charged at me, I knew what they were.

Ghouls, I realized with a sinking feeling. And ghouls ate people, including vampires.

Chapter 45

With rats still chewing on me, I tore off my right glove. A thin line of white pulsed from my hand, growing until it reached the ground. The ghouls looked at it without the slightest bit of fear, which wasn't necessarily a good thing. If they were tunnel dwellers attacking me because I looked tasty, they'd cease once I proved not to be easy prey. If Cynthiana had managed to spell them into doing this, then like the rats, they'd continue to come at me until all of them were dead.

Or I was.

I didn't have time to ask what their motivation was. Three of them covered the distance between us with cheetah-like speed. I cracked the whip and spun in a circle, sending more currents into it as I felt it meet the resistance of bodies. Multiple thumps sounded and the surge of voltage through my body made the rats briefly abandon ship. Then they leapt back onto me just in time for me to see that I'd decapitated two out of the three ghouls. The third lay on the ground, trying to pull his lower body back onto the gaping stump that remained of his upper one.

With a roar, the rest of the pack charged. I spun the whip around me as if it were a large, deadly lasso, the current slicing through anything that dared come into contact with it. Two more ghouls fell lifeless to the ground, joining a growing pile of rats as the voltage in me surged to levels I'd never manifested before. I snapped the whip at another ghoul who got close and he fell in two pieces. The pack circled me more warily now, but from the empty look in their eyes, they weren't in control of their will. They would keep trying to kill me no matter the consequences. If I wasn't in a life-and-death fight, I would've marveled at the extent of Cynthiana's powers. "Dabbled" in magic, my ass!

Another two ghouls dropped in pieces when their lunges were met by the crack of white across their necks. Only four more to go, and thanks to my new vampire strength, my arm wasn't even feeling tired. More rats began to fall off me as the rubber suit became torn in so many places, electricity leaked out like water through a colander. The rodents' bodies crunched under my feet as I took the offensive, charging at the ghouls instead of falling back, my whip ruthlessly slashing through them and the rats that still came at me from every direction.

Now only one ghoul remained on his feet. When I got him in range, I snapped my whip in victory, but it fizzled where it struck. Instead of cutting through the ghoul, it seemed to bounce off him. He looked down as if confirming that he was still in one piece and then his lips pulled back impossibly far, revealing a smile like the open maw of a snake.

Oh shit. I shook my right hand as if to force more juice into it, but the strand dangling from it only flickered the way flashlights did when they were running out of battery. Then I whirled, ready to run for it, but at the opposite end of the tunnel, new snarls echoed, followed by another wave of musty, earthy air.

My path to escape was blocked.

The ghoul I'd failed to kill started toward me. Panicked and out of all other options, I began throwing rats at him. They bounced off his hulking frame, as ineffectual at stopping him as they had been at stopping me. As if to punctuate this, he caught one, biting its head off and spitting it at me. Behind him, two of the fallen ghouls stirred, one hopping toward me on one leg, the other crawling through a carpet of rat bodies because everything below his waist was gone.

One ghoul I'd have a chance against. Not several of them. Fear made me immune to the spikes of pain as the rats that hadn't been electrocuted continued to chew their way across my body. Soon it would be more than rodents feasting on me. Despite never being more powerful, I was still helpless to stop my own death.

Then I squared my shoulders, kicking the rats

from my feet. I'd make them earn their meal. Before they ate me, they'd have to catch me.

Right as I began to take that first step, the tunnel lit up with an orange glow that was both ominous and the most welcome sight I'd ever seen.

Then Vlad's voice thundered out. "Leila, get down!"

I dropped to the ground, putting me nose to nose with countless living and dead rats. In the next moment, an inferno roared down the tunnel, blanketing everything that was more than three feet off the ground. As fire rushed over me in searing waves, I covered my head with my arms and pushed my face deeper into the disgusting mass of bodies. Better to be closer to them than the fire shooting out with the force of a hundred geysers.

Seconds later, hands closed over my arms. I tried to jerk away, thinking the crawling ghoul had reached me, but then I realized the hands were hot as a stove. When they pulled my arms away from my head, I didn't resist, and when a booted foot kicked at the swarm of rats around me, I didn't hesitate to sit up despite the continued roar of flames.

Vlad bent over me. Except for a two-foot perimeter surrounding us, fire filled the tunnel from ceiling to floor, burning so fiercely I couldn't hear anything over the crackle of flames. Then he lifted me into his arms and began to walk through that blistering wall of orange and red.

It parted before him like drapes held back by

invisible hands. As he walked, I swiped at the rats still chewing on me, knocking them off into the flames. By the time he reached the end of the tunnel where there was a closed door, there were only a few left that I couldn't reach.

Vlad opened the door, carrying me into a far narrower tunnel that could've been an abandoned service hallway. Instead of being filled with flames, this space was filled with Vlad's people. Well, all except one.

Cynthiana had four vampires restraining her, which might not have been enough considering her real strength lay in magic. Yet with one glance, I saw why Vlad wasn't worried about her working any spells on his men. She couldn't utter a word. Her mouth was filled with so much silver that shards of it protruded from her cheeks.

"Where'd you get that gag?" I asked.

He set me down, knocking away the rats that clung to my back before crushing them underfoot.

"I melted silver knives together and then shoved them into her mouth."

Some days, I really loved his dark side.

"Why didn't you wait in the Crangasi station?" he demanded, grasping my shoulders now that the last of the rats were gone.

"She spelled the commuters into attacking me and one of them ripped my wire. I couldn't tell you which way she went so I followed her."

"Why?" he asked with even more emphasis.

I blinked. "Because she was getting away."

His grip tightened while a wave of frustration and another, far stronger emotion washed over me.

"When I heard the ghouls coming for you, all I cared about was reaching you in time. How often must I tell you that you mean more to me than vengeance? I can live without defeating my enemies, but I cannot live without you."

Before I could respond, he crushed me to him, his mouth covering mine in a blistering kiss. I forgot that I was covered in blood, dirt, and rat hair. Didn't care that a roomful of people were watching, or about anything else. I kissed him back with all the relief I felt at being alive to do so. Now that the fight was over, all the fear I'd held back came rushing forth, reminding me how close I'd come to losing everything. Vlad was right. Enemies would come and go and battles would be won or lost, but nothing mattered more than what we had. Everything else was replaceable.

When he finally drew away, slow tears were running down my cheeks. "I love you," I whispered.

He brushed them away, a sardonic smile twisting his mouth. "And I love you, which is why I intend to lock you inside the house as soon as we're home."

I let out a watery chuckle. "You won't need to. I'll gladly stay put."

Then I fingered my Kevlar vest, the only thing on me that hadn't been chewed or ripped to shreds.

"This was a good idea. I must suck at being a covert operative. Cynthiana took one look at me and started shooting."

The smile he flashed me reminded me of the fire that was so much a part of him—alluring yet deadly, consuming and yet quicksilver.

"It was her determination to kill you that doomed her. When she bewitched the tunnel-dwelling ghouls into a mindless murdering state, she cut off her exit behind her, leaving her nowhere to run except straight to me."

I turned and stared at Cynthiana with a surge of coldness I hadn't known I was capable of. "Time to take her home, and I hope you have a pole with her name on it."

Chapter 46

A few of Vlad's men stayed behind to make sure any ghouls who survived the fire didn't make their way to the Metro stations and try to eat the innocent commuters. The rest of us returned to his house via helicopters. As soon as we landed, I followed him and Cynthiana's guard entourage into the dungeon. After being covered in enough rats to give me screaming nightmares, I might long for a shower more intensely than Midas had coveted gold, but I was seeing this through.

Vlad ordered Cynthiana chained onto the large stone monolith. Then he had Shrapnel brought in from the other side of the dungeon to be restrained next to her. He'd done his best to kill me, and yet I couldn't help but feel a twinge of pity at the grief in his expression when he saw her. Cynthiana, on the other hand, didn't seem to be at all upset over her lover's predicament. In fact, her gaze passed over him in a manner that could only be described as annoyed.

"He really was just a pawn to you, wasn't he?" I asked in repugnance.

She didn't answer, of course. Despite being captured, gagged with silver, and facing a truly horrible future, Cynthiana wasn't cowed. Her gaze flicked over me in the way women perfected when they wanted to raze your self-esteem without saying a word, yet all I did was smile wide enough to show my new fangs. I might be covered in filth, blood, and rat hair, but a centuries-old vampire had nothing on the belittling looks I'd received while attending high school with a zigzagging scar, a limp, and the growing ability to shock anyone who touched me.

"Did I mention it was nice to see you again?" I almost purred. "Though you don't remember the first time we met, do you?"

The look Vlad shot me was almost as surprised as hers. Then he went over to Cynthiana, ripping the silver from her mouth.

"If you utter one word of magic, I'll fill you with enough silver to drive you mad before dawn."

Cynthiana stared at Vlad for a long, silent moment before she looked my way dismissively.

"I don't know what you're talking about, dearie. I've never seen you before tonight."

"I don't blame you for forgetting. You were busy staring at a young girl named Dawn who was performing under my stage name. You thought she was me, and that's why you detonated the bomb right after she went into our trailer."

Now her gaze raked over me with calculated

intensity. "You used your hair and a hat to cover your scar," she said at last.

"Habit. Now, let's see what your worst sin is."

With luck, it would lead us to whoever else she was working with. I came toward her and she recoiled as much as her restraints allowed.

"Don't touch me."

I didn't reply, but grabbed her arm with my right hand. Only a faint current of electricity slid into her. I'd used most of it up on the ghouls she'd sent to kill me.

Then the dungeon disappeared, morphing into a room that didn't look much different because it consisted entirely of stone walls. It seemed familiar, yet what I experienced next made me forget about that. By the time those surroundings faded and I was mentally back at the stone monolith, I snatched my hand away.

"You sick bitch," I breathed.

"What?" Vlad asked instantly.

I stared at Cynthiana with loathing. "She needed a fireproofing spell, but she wasn't strong enough to do it without crossing into the darkest kind of magic. So she did."

And that magic had required the highest price: lifeblood of a newborn. I'd seen many terrible things through my abilities, but I'd never seen something as brutal as that.

"A fireproofing spell?" Vlad repeated. "Did you think that was the only defense you needed against me?"

She said nothing to that.

Then Vlad sighed. "I know you, Cynthiana. You would never cross me without a protector, so tell me who he is. Refuse, and I'll find out after you've experienced more agony than you can imagine."

She glanced away. "I have no protector."

He laughed in that scary, humorless way.

"Yes you do, although you betrayed him because he wanted Leila alive."

Why would Vlad think that? Every message Cynthiana sent Shrapnel after the bombing had been demands for him to kill me.

Then I remembered what Hannibal said after he'd kidnapped me. *You're worth three times as much alive.* Dead was the only way Cynthiana wanted me, so Vlad was right. Someone else had been pulling her strings at least part of the time.

She glanced at me. The pure loathing in her gaze I expected; the fear, I didn't. After Vlad's threat, why would she be afraid of *me?* I'd already done all I could, though finding out her worst sin had revealed only revolting information, not useful—

"Vlad, wait," I said, something about that stone room nagging at my memory.

"Shrapnel told you everything he knew about my abilities," I said slowly, the idea still forming in my mind, "but you know more, don't you? Like, for instance, my ability to feel other people's essences in someone else's skin."

Her gaze widened while her scent changed to a putridly sweet aroma. I knew what that was. I'd smelled it all over this dungeon. It was the scent of fear.

Vlad caught it, too. His expression changed, chiseled features switching from chilling friendliness to sculpted granite.

"Who is he?"

Three soft words that managed to be filled with all the menace of a thousand shouted threats.

I stared at Cynthiana, measuring the spikes of hatred and fear in her gaze as I approached.

"Do you know what I overheard the first time I linked to you? You told Shrapnel, *Whatever she might have been worth to him alive, she's less dangerous to us dead*."

I let out a short laugh. "At the time, Shrapnel thought the 'him' was Vlad, but you really meant your new protector, didn't you? He was interested in me and you already had the inside track."

Then I glanced at Shrapnel. "Cynthiana came back into your life right around the time I came into Vlad's, didn't she?"

Pain creased his features, but Shrapnel said nothing. Maybe he was still trying to protect her. More likely, he was under the effects of a spell. Maybe he hadn't betrayed Vlad or tried to kill me of his own free will.

A searing hand slid along my arm as Vlad drew near, yet he didn't look at me. His gaze was fixed on Cynthiana.

"Your protector must be powerful or you wouldn't bother with him. He's also an enemy of mine or he wouldn't dare risk my wrath by using one of my ex-lovers to kidnap another. That leaves a small list. Smaller still if he was interested in Leila before Shrapnel told you about her abilities."

A very small list, indeed. In fact, I could only think of one name, and though it didn't seem possible, it fit with the facts, right down to Hannibal's capture-or-kill order. That hadn't been the first time a vampire had been given those instructions regarding me, and while Cynthiana's preference had been dead over alive, her protector disagreed.

Funny thing was, everyone except Maximus and Vlad thought my psychic abilities were gone when Hannibal kidnapped me. Cynthiana's protector was either gambling that they'd come back . . . or he knew another reason why I'd be a valuable hostage.

Only one other vampire had guessed how Vlad really felt about me even before he'd admitted it to himself. The same vampire had attempted to use my abilities against Vlad before I even met him. It had been the reason we were first thrown together, but Mihaly Szilagyi had died in an inferno months ago.

Hadn't he?

I took another step closer. Cynthiana thrashed in her restraints, eyes flashing emerald and fanged mouth snapping while she spat out threats as vicious as they were futile.

"Shut her up and hold her still," I said quietly.

Vlad had her jaw in an unbreakable grip before the last word left my mouth. His other arm slammed across her waist so hard that I heard several ribs snap. Unlike the time Shrapnel pulverized my rib cage, her pain would last mere seconds until she healed. Unless she kept struggling, that was.

I closed my eyes when I touched her, glad my abilities let me relive a person's worst sins only once. Then I let my right hand drift, seeking out other essences on her skin.

There, on her upper arm. A fresh one embedded with rage that I recognized instantly as belonging to Vlad. My hand roamed further, finding another one on the back of her neck. I didn't recognize the imprint so I moved on, stroking her face while ignoring the furious noises she made in her throat.

Someone who loved her had left an imprint on her forehead, and with a pang, I recognized Shrapnel's essence.

I continued on, not finding anything else on her upper body. I'd reached her left wrist when I felt it. A thread with a very familiar essence, made from someone touching her with enough threat to leave a permanent imprint in her skin.

I dropped my hand and opened my eyes.

"It's him," I said simply when I met Vlad's gaze.

His eyes seemed to burst into green flame and a lava flow of rage poured over my emotions.

"What must I do to kill that man?" he muttered.

Then he released Cynthiana. By the time he strolled to the front of the pole, his thunderous expression had changed to a charming smile and that lava flow of rage to a glacier of determination.

"Tell me about how you conspired with Mihaly Szilagyi, and you can start with how the hell he managed to survive that explosion."

"I think I know the answer," I said, staring at Cynthiana without pity. "Burn something on her."

Both her legs went up in flames. She screamed, thrashing in her restraints. Shrapnel began to yell, too, pleading with Vlad to stop. He didn't until everything from her thighs down was covered in charred, blackened flesh.

As I watched Cynthiana start to heal with only the regular abilities that all vampires had, the final piece of the puzzle fell into place.

"You didn't work that fireproofing spell for yourself. You did it for Mihaly Szilagyi, the only vampire who was both as strong as Vlad and as committed to hurting him as you were."

My gaze swung back to Vlad. "*That's* why he didn't hesitate to set off that explosion when you had him trapped on the mountain. He knew if you found him there, the only way he'd get out alive was if you thought he was dead. Just like he did centuries ago."

"The greatest trick the Devil ever pulled was convincing the world he didn't exist," Vlad murmured, sounding like he was quoting from memory.

Then he smiled at Cynthiana. "Now, dearie," he said in his most genial tone. "You're going to tell me where he is."

The much anticipated next Night
Huntress novel is here!

Keep reading for a sneak peek
and see what
Cat and Bones have been up to . . .

UP FROM THE GRAVE

by Jeaniene Frost
Available soon from Avon Books

Ignoring a ghost is a lot more difficult than you'd think. For starters, walls don't hinder their kind, so although I shut the door in the face of the specter loitering outside my house, he followed me inside as if invited. My jaw clenched in irritation, but I began unloading my groceries as though I hadn't noticed. Too soon, I was done. Being a vampire married to another vampire meant that my shopping list was pretty short.

"This is ridiculous. You can't keep shunning me forever, Cat," the ghost muttered.

Yeah, ghosts can talk, too. That made them even harder to ignore. Of course, it didn't help that this ghost was also my uncle. Alive, dead, undead . . . family had a way of getting under your skin whether you wanted them to or not.

Case in point: Despite my vow not to talk to him, I couldn't keep from replying.

"Actually, since neither of us is getting any older, I *can* do this forever," I noted coolly. "Or until you ante up on everything you know about the a-hole running our old team."

"That's what I came here to talk to you about," he said.

Surprise and suspicion made my eyes narrow. For almost three months, my uncle Don had refused to divulge anything about my new nemesis, Jason Madigan. Don had a history with Madigan, a former CIA operative who'd taken over the secret government unit I used to work for, but he'd kept mum on the details even when his silence meant that Madigan had nearly gotten me, my husband, and other innocent people killed. *Now* he was ready to spill? Something else had to be going on. Don was so pathologically secretive that I hadn't found out we were related until four years after I started working for him.

"What happened?" I asked without preamble.

He tugged on a gray eyebrow, a habit he couldn't break even after losing his physical body. He also wore his usual suit and tie despite dying in a hospital gown. I'd think it was my memories dictating how Don appeared to me except for the hundreds of other ghosts I'd met. There might not be shopping malls in the afterlife, but residual self-image was strong enough to make others see ghosts the way they saw themselves. Don had been the picture of a perfectly groomed, sixty-something bureaucrat in life, so that's what he looked like in death.

He also hadn't lost any of the tenacity behind

those gunmetal-colored eyes, the only physical trait we had in common. My crimson hair and pale skin came from my father.

"I'm worried about Tate, Juan, Dave, and Cooper," Don stated. "They haven't been home in weeks, and as you know, I can't get into the compound to check if they're there."

I didn't point out that it was Don's fault Madigan knew how to ghost-proof a building. Heavy combinations of weed, garlic, and burning sage would keep all but the strongest spooks away. After a ghost had almost killed Madigan last year, he'd outfitted our old base with a liberal supply of all three.

"How long exactly since you've seen them?"

"Three weeks and four days," he replied. Faults he may have, but Don was meticulous. "If only one of them was away that long, I'd assume he was on an undercover job, but all of them?"

Yes, that was strange even for members of a covert Homeland Security branch that dealt with misbehaving members of undead society. When I was a member of the team, the longest undercover job I'd been on was eleven days. Rogue vampires and ghouls tended to frequent the same spots if they were dumb enough to act out so much that they caught the U.S. government's attention.

Still, I wasn't about to assume the worst yet. Phone calls were beyond Don's capabilities as a ghost, but I had no such hindrances.

I pulled a cell phone out of my kitchen drawer,

dialing Tate's number. When I got his machine, I hung up. If something had happened and Madigan was responsible, he'd be checking Tate's messages. No need to clue him in that I was sniffing around.

"No answer," I told Don. Then I set that phone aside and took another cell out of the drawer, dialing Juan next. After a few rings, a melodic Spanish voice instructed me to leave a message. I didn't, hanging up and reaching for another phone from the drawer.

"How many of those do you have?" Don muttered, floating over my shoulder.

"Enough to give Madigan a migraine," I said with satisfaction. "If he's tracing calls to their phones, he won't find my location in any of these, much as he'd love to know where I am."

Don didn't accuse me of being paranoid. As soon as he'd taken over my uncle's old job, Madigan had made it clear that he had it in for me. I didn't know why. I'd been retired from the team by then, and as far as Madigan knew, there was no longer anything special about me. He didn't know that turning from a half vampire into a full one had come with unexpected side effects.

Dave's phone went straight to voice mail as well. So did Cooper's. I considered trying them at their offices, but those were inside the compound. Madigan might have enough taps on those lines to locate me no matter how I'd arranged for the cell phone signals to be rerouted.

"Okay, now I'm worried, too," I said at last. "When Bones gets home, we'll figure out a way to get a closer look at the compound."

Don regarded me soberly. "If Madigan *has* done something to them, he'll expect you to show up."

Once again, my jaw clenched. Damn right I'd show up. Tate, Dave, Juan, and Cooper weren't just soldiers I'd fought alongside for years when I was part of the team. They were also my friends. If Madigan was responsible for something bad happening to them, he'd soon be sorry.

"Yeah, well, Bones and I had a couple months of relative quiet. Guess it's time to liven things up again."

My cat Helsing jumped down from my lap the same time that the air became charged with tiny invisible currents. Emotions rolled over my subconscious. Not my own, but almost as familiar to me. Moments later, I heard the crunch of tires on snow. By the time the car door shut, Helsing was at the door, his long black tail twitching with anticipation.

I stayed where I was. One cat waiting at the door was enough, thanks. With a whoosh of frigid air, my husband came inside. Snow coated Bones, making him look like he'd been dusted with powdered sugar. He stamped his feet to dislodge the flakes from his boots, causing Helsing to jump away with a hiss.

"Clearly he thinks you should pet him first and deal with the snow later," I said.

Eyes so dark they were nearly black met mine. Once they did, my amusement turned into primal female appreciation. Bones's cheeks were flushed, and the color accented his flawless skin, chiseled features, and sensually full mouth. Then he took his coat off, revealing an indigo shirt that clung to his muscles as if reveling in them. Black jeans were snug in all the right places, highlighting a taut stomach, strong thighs, and an ass that could double as a work of art. By the time I drew my gaze back up to his face, his slight smile had turned into a knowing grin. More emotions enveloped my subconscious while his scent—a rich mixture of spices, musk, and burnt sugar—filled the room.

"Missed me already, Kitten?"

I didn't know how he managed to make the question sound indecent, yet he did. I would've said the English accent helped, but his best friends were English and their voices never turned my insides to jelly.

"Yes," I replied, rising and coming over to him.

He watched me, not moving when I slowly slid my hands up to lace them behind his neck. I had to stand on tiptoe to do it, but that was okay. It brought us closer, and the hard feel of his body was almost as intoxicating as the swirls of desire that curled around my emotions. I loved that I could sense his emotions as though they were my own. If I'd realized that was one of the perks of him changing me into a full vampire, I might have upgraded my half-breed status years ago. Then his head lowered, but before his lips brushed mine, I turned away.

"Not until you say you missed me, too," I teased.

In reply, he picked me up, his grip all too easily subduing my mock struggles. Smooth leather met my back as he set me onto the couch, his body a barricade I didn't want to dislodge. His hands settled around my face, holding me with possessiveness as green filled up his irises and fangs slid out of his teeth.

My own fangs lengthened in response, pressing against lips that I parted in anticipation. His head bent, but he only brushed his mouth over mine with a fleeting caress before chuckling.

"Two can play at teasing, luv."

I began to struggle in earnest, which only made his laughter deepen. My high kill count had earned me the nickname of the Red Reaper in the undead world, but even before Bones's startling new powers, I hadn't been able to best him. All my thrashing did was to rub him against me in the most erotic way—which was why I kept doing it.

The zipper on my hoodie went all the way down without his hands moving from my head. My clothes accounted for most of his practice with his fledgling telekinesis. Then the front clasp on my bra opened, baring the majority of my breasts. His laughter changed to a growl that sent delicious tingles through me, hardening my nipples. But when the buttons popped open on his indigo shirt, its color reminded me of Tate's eyes—and the news I needed to tell him.

"Something's up," I said in a gasp.

White teeth flashed before Bones lowered his mouth to my chest. "How cliché, but true nonetheless."

The baser part of me whispered that I could postpone this talk for an hour or so, but concern for my friends slapped that down. I gave myself a mental shake and grabbed a handful of Bones's dark brown curls, pulling his head up.

"I'm serious. Don came by and relayed some potentially disturbing information."

It seemed to take a second for the words to penetrate, but then his brows rose. "After all this time, he finally told you what he's been hiding about Madigan?"

"No, he didn't," I said, shaking my head for real this time. "He wanted to let me know that Tate and the others haven't been home in over three weeks. I tried their cells and only got voice mails. Actually, that distracted me from pushing Don about his past with Madigan."

Bones snorted, the brief puff of air landing in the sensitive valley between my breasts. "Clever sod knew it would. I doubt it was an accident that he gave you this information while I was out."

Now that concern for my friends wasn't foremost in my mind, I doubted it was accident, too. Don had been by my house enough to know that Bones left for a couple hours every few days to feed. I didn't go with him since my nutritional needs lay elsewhere. Inwardly I cursed. Finding out if my friends were okay was still of paramount importance, but so was discovering what Don knew about Madigan. It must be monumental for my uncle to keep it under wraps even when we didn't speak for months as a result. After all, I wasn't just the only family Don had left—as a vampire, I was also one of the few people who could *see* him in his new ghostly state.

"We'll deal with my uncle later," I said, pushing Bones away with a sigh of regret. "Right now, we need to find a way into my old compound that doesn't involve both of us ending up in a vampire jail cell."

NEW YORK TIMES AND USA TODAY BESTSELLING AUTHOR

Jeaniene Frost

First Drop of Crimson

978-0-06-158322-3

The night is not safe for mortals. Denise MacGregor knows all too well what lurks in the shadows and now a demon shapeshifter has marked her as prey. Her survival depends on Spade, an immortal who lusts for a taste of her, but is duty-bound to protect her—even if it means destroying his own kind.

Eternal Kiss of Darkness

978-0-06-178316-6

Chicago private investigator Kira Graceling finds herself in a world she's only imagined in her worst nightmares. At the center is Mencheres, a breathtaking Master vampire who Kira braved death to rescue. With danger closing in, Mencheres must choose either the woman he craves or embracing the darkest magic to defeat an enemy bent on his eternal destruction.

One Grave at a Time

978-0-06-178319-7

Cat Crawfield wants nothing more than a little downtime with her vampire husband, Bones. Unfortunately, they must risk all to battle a villainous spirit and send him back to the other side of eternity.

JFR1 0312

*G*ive in to your Impulses!

These unforgettable stories only take a second to buy and give you hours of reading pleasure!

Go to ***www.AvonImpulse.com*** and see what we have to offer.

Available wherever e-books are sold.

AVONIMPULSE

IMP 0811